Streiker's Bride

ROBIN HARDY

NAVPRESS
BRINGING TRUTH TO LIFE

The Navigators is an international Christian organiza-
tion. Jesus Christ gave His followers the Great Commission to go and make disciples (Matthew 28:19). The aim
of The Navigators is to help fulfill that commission by
multiplying laborers for Christ in every nation.

NavPress is the publishing ministry of The Navigators.
NavPress publications are tools to help Christians grow.
Although publications alone cannot make disciples or
change lives, they can help believers learn biblical disci-
pleship, and apply what they learn to their lives and
ministries.

Library of Congress Catalog Card Number:
        93-16793
ISBN 08910-97317

Third printing, 1993

Cover illustration: Bill Farnsworth

The stories and characters in this book are fictitious. Any
resemblance to people living or dead is coincidental.

Hardy, Robin, 1955-
        Streiker's bride / Robin Hardy.
                p.   cm.
        ISBN 0-89109-731-7
        I. Title.
    PS3558.A62387S83   1993
    813'.54--dc20   93-16793
                                                        CIP

Printed in the United States of America

FOR A FREE CATALOG OF
NAVPRESS BOOKS & BIBLE STUDIES,
CALL 1-800-366-7788 (USA)
or 1-416-499-4615 (CANADA)

In appreciation to my readers
for your prayers and encouragement

1

Adair had to get into the building without being noticed. She climbed out of the car, brushed dog hairs from her suit, and nonchalantly strode into the bank lobby at forty minutes past eight.

It was a lost cause. Adair could hardly go anywhere without being noticed for her tall, slender frame, electric blue eyes, and especially the grace that a twenty-year devotion to ballet had brought her.

"Adair! Look at the clock! You're *forty minutes* late!" She winced at the reprimand and humbly turned to her boss.

"I'm sorry, Duane; I really was going to be on time today, but there was this dog that ran into the street and got hit by a car right as I was driving by. You can understand that I had to stop and take him to the vet's, can't you?" she implored.

"Sure, if it weren't the third time this month you've been late. And this is only the second week!" he fumed, adjusting his glasses like a schoolmaster who had caught a student cheating.

Duane was Adair's age, twenty-four, but his freckles and tousled hair made him look younger. Unlike her, he was degreed, ambitious, and focused on banking as his career of choice.

"Now get to the drive-through!" he barked.

"Sure, Duane," Adair said appeasingly, slipping her purse under the counter. She never could bring herself to call him "Mr. Minshew." With Duane hovering behind her, Adair sat at the window and smiled.

"Good morning," she greeted the waiting customer as she took his check and deposit slip through the mechanical drawer. When her boss finally turned his attention elsewhere, Adair let down with a sigh. "I hate this job."

"If you keep coming in late, you won't have to worry about it anymore," a voice at her side teased a little too loudly.

Adair glanced around for Duane, then grinned guiltily at her friend Courtney. "The part about the dog was true, but I didn't tell him it only took ten minutes," Adair whispered. "I overslept 'cause I was up late studying my accounting."

"Oh? How's the class going?" Courtney asked, sliding onto a nearby stool. The cuff of her silk blouse caught on a drawer edge. "Drat!" she exclaimed, examining it for snags.

Adair anxiously glanced around again. Courtney, with her long auburn hair and perfect skin, embodied Adair's idea of true beauty, but she was so loud. "Terrible. It's so hard, and we cover the material so quickly. I don't know if I'm going to pass," Adair muttered.

"Why bother?" asked Courtney. "What about your ballet?"

"Madame Prochaska lets me practice with her pointe class several nights a week for free now, but—that won't last forever," Adair replied. "At least an accounting degree will help me earn enough to pay tuition—*if* I get it."

"I know what you mean," Courtney sympathized. "I gave up on drafting and got this great home-study course on interior decorating. I'm going to start on it this weekend." She tapped her long red fingernails on the counter, then studied them for chips.

"Drafting? What happened to the art class?" Adair asked,

making a point to smile at the customer as she cashed his check. He smiled back.

Courtney pouted, "All the men in it were either poor or gay. It was a total waste of time."

"Courtney!" Adair breathed, exasperated. "Why don't you work toward a degree that will pay you?"

"I am! I'm going to marry rich," Courtney explained. "That's why I like working here; you know who has the biggest bank accounts. Let *them* work their tails off for money. You make them happy by letting them give it to you."

Adair shook her head. "With an attitude like that, you're going to start getting hate mail from NOW." Sending a receipt to the last customer at the window, Adair added, "Thank you. Have a nice day." Charlotte, the head teller, was looking toward her, so she turned her back to shuffle paper.

"So?" said Courtney, glancing at Charlotte and turning her back as well. "I don't want to sacrifice my personal life to make money. Do you? Do you want to be like Sergeant Charlotte?"

"She makes a lot more than I do," Adair whispered.

"She hasn't had a date in *three years*," Courtney whispered loudly. A coworker looked at them and over at Charlotte.

"I won't look for anyone to buy my dreams for me," Adair said stubbornly.

"Then you'll *never* be a dancer!" Courtney hissed.

Adair's eyes began watering as the next customer drove up and Charlotte marched toward her two loitering tellers. Courtney passed her, explaining earnestly, "Excuse me; I've got a pile of checks to process."

"Good morning. How are you today?" Adair smiled at the blurry customer as she extended the drawer.

Monday mornings were always busy enough that Adair did not have to create work. The cars paraded past her window: mothers with their kids fighting over the seats of the minivans; society ladies in their Cadillacs en route to the country club; businessmen in their status cars.

One man rode up to her window on a motorcycle and placed in the drawer a draft for $25,000 made out to Fletcher Streiker and endorsed by the same.

Adair knew the name. He was the Dallas-based billionaire philanthropist no one had ever seen. He owned The Rivers Bank, which had branches in Plano, Carrollton, Mesquite, and here in Richardson. And just the mention of his name never failed to raise her hackles. Deep down, she couldn't understand why some people had so much while others (such as herself) could barely scrape by.

She glanced out at the courier. "A deposit, sir?"

"Yes." His voice was muffled by his motorcycle helmet. He wore a black leather jacket and faded jeans.

She turned to her computer, suppressing her irritation at people who would not use deposit slips. "Personal or corporate?"

"What?" he said, leaning toward the window.

"Do you wish to deposit this in the personal or corporate account?" she asked slowly through the intercom.

"Corporate," he said.

"Okay," she said, watching her screen. "The Streiker Corporation has checking, Money Market, CDs—"

"In the checking account," the courier said.

As Adair made the deposit, a lady in a large car drove up behind the motorcyclist. "Here's your receipt. Have a nice day."

"I will," he said, taking the receipt from the drawer. As he started to fold it, the wind caught it out of his hand. "Oops," he said calmly. "How about another receipt?"

"Sure." Adair made out a duplicate receipt while the lady behind him edged up to the motorcycle's rear tire. "Here you go."

"Thanks." He took the second receipt and started to stuff it in his jacket pocket. Adair watched incredulously as somehow it too fluttered away. "Oh, no. Can you get me one more?" he asked without expression in his voice.

Adair stared at the courier, but could not see his face behind the tinted shield of his helmet. "Only if you promise to hold on to it," she attempted to laugh. The lady behind him honked.

Adair quickly filled out another duplicate receipt, but when she placed it in the drawer this time, she included as a paperweight a polished rock with a goofy expression painted on it. "You wanna use that, please?"

He took out the receipt with the rock and laughed. "Yeah, thanks." The woman behind him honked again.

"You're welcome," Adair said warmly. She suddenly liked him. He looked at her from behind his visor as he leisurely put the rock and the receipt in his jacket. Then he commented, "I saw you pick up the dog from the street. What did you do with it?"

Adair was startled momentarily, then replied, "I took him to the vet across the street from the Atrium."

"How's he doing?" he asked.

"I don't know yet. The vet's supposed to call me after he's had a chance to look at him," she replied.

The lady leaned her head out the window to yell, but the motor-cyclist ignored her.

"Is that right?" he said, turning the dark visor back toward her. "Well, I just wondered if you were as nice to people as you are to dogs. See you later, Adair." He started his motorcycle and roared away, leaving her dumbfounded.

The woman finally got to the window. "The nerve of some people, taking so long when others are in a hurry!" she exclaimed.

"Yes, some people are not very nice," Adair quietly agreed, extending the drawer.

———◆———

The rest of the morning was routine, with Adair trying to be equally courteous to an uneven stream of customers: a few pleasant, most preoccupied, a few surly. Around eleven o'clock Pat tapped her on the shoulder: "Telephone, Adair."

She took it at Pat's desk: "Adair Weiss."

"Ms. Weiss, this is Dr. Hogan's office. I'm calling about the

Border collie you brought in this morning. He's going to be fine. Dr. Hogan set his leg and stitched up the gash on his rump, but he doesn't seem to have any internal injuries. You may pick him up tonight, if you like."

"Oh, that's great. Thank you so much. I can't keep him at my apartment, so I'll have to find a home for him," Adair thought out loud.

"That's fine, but we do have a boarding fee of five dollars per day," the receptionist said.

"I see. Umm, how much do I owe you to pick him up tonight?" Adair asked.

"His bill comes to one hundred twenty dollars."

One hundred twenty dollars! I don't even have that much in my checking account! Adair silently exclaimed. Slowly, she said, "Okay. Let me make arrangements. . . . I'll get back with you." She hung up, her head spinning over the cost of her altruism.

She went back to counting twenties in a drawer, and the temptation crossed her mind just to grab a handful. Shoving aside that thought caused her to lose count, so she started over.

Duane suddenly came up behind her. "Have you put in for a promotion, Adair?"

She lowered the fistful of cash, as he had made her lose count again. "Not recently."

"Then you're in trouble," he sang. "Mr. Whinnet is in my office, waiting to see you."

"Mr. *Whinnet?*" she gasped. Why should the president of The Rivers Bank care that she was forty minutes late today?

"The same," Duane smirked. Sauntering away, he beckoned her with a forefinger.

Adair took a deep breath and smoothed the skirt of her suit, trying to assume a professional air as she followed Duane. He opened the door of his small office as if it led to the gas chamber.

A fiftyish gentleman rose from the edge of Duane's desk. Although she had never seen Charles Whinnet in person before, she pegged him at once as a tennis player. He had silver-gray hair that he combed straight back and a healthy complexion—a really handsome man. "You must be Adair Weiss," he said intently.

"Yes. I'm pleased to meet you, Mr. Whinnet." She wanted to add, *Do you have a dog that you love?*

"Ms. Weiss." As he shook her hand, he reached over to shut the door with Duane standing outside.

"I really don't have time now for formalities or explanations," he began, settling back on the edge of the desk and crossing his arms. "This afternoon when you get off work, I would like you to come by my office downtown and chat with me."

"Certainly," Adair said hesitantly. "Is there . . . anything I need to bring to this meeting?"

"No," said Whinnet, glancing at his watch.

"Could you tell me what it's about?" she asked nervously.

"It's of a personal nature," he replied. Adair began agonizing over a graceful way to discourage any advances from The Rivers' president, whom she knew to be married.

He smiled perceptively. "Lest you get the wrong impression, Ms. Weiss, this does not personally concern me. I am acting only as an intermediary."

"An intermediary . . . ?" Adair repeated.

Whinnet opened the door. "I'll be expecting you shortly after five," he concluded.

Duane caught him outside. "Mr. Whinnet, I have the statement of holdings ready—"

"Give it to Bob. Good day." He glanced back at Adair as he left.

Duane edged up to her. "What did he want?"

"I'm not sure," she mumbled, making a quick exit before he could ask any more questions.

Adair went back to her window and Courtney came up to give her something. Adair took it and turned distractedly to her computer. *Well, at least Mr. Whinnet isn't going to fire me for tardiness,* she reassured herself. But the fact that it was personal implied he knew something about her—probably something she'd rather he didn't know. What had she done that would embarrass her the most? Thinking about this caused her to freeze over the computer keyboard until she looked down and wondered what she had been typing in. "Who is he an intermediary *for?*" she asked the keyboard.

"What?" Courtney asked. "Adair, don't you have that account's history yet? Where is your head today, girl?"

"I'm sorry. It's coming," Adair promised. Courtney watched her curiously as Adair finished entering the request.

Partly as penance for being late to work and partly to avoid Courtney's inquisitiveness, Adair worked through lunch that day. She also resolved not to look at the clock, except when it jumped in front of her face. At her two o'clock break, she realized that she would never make it through the day without eating something, so she stole half a ham sandwich she found in the lounge refrigerator, vowing to replace it tomorrow.

As the clock wound down toward five, Adair felt her insides coiling tighter. At 4:47 she was rapidly totaling receipts.

At 4:52 Duane said, "I want you to work drive-through tonight, Adair."

"I can't, Duane. Mr. Whinnet asked me to come directly downtown after work."

"What for?" he asked.

"I don't know." She carelessly furrowed her brow.

At 4:56 an angry customer came in and thrust a letter at Adair. "You people bounced three checks and assessed me a service charge when you recorded my deposit as a withdrawal!"

"I'm so sorry," Adair purred, glancing at the clock. She steered him toward Duane's office. "I'll take you straight to our branch manager Duane Minshew to get it cleared up." Rapping quickly on Duane's door, she nudged the customer inside. "Mr. Minshew, this gentleman is having a problem with his checking account." Then she closed the door on them before Duane had a chance to open his mouth.

At 5:00, she sprang out the bank's doors and sprinted to her little car, a Mazda RX-7. She peeled out of the parking lot onto the access road to the freeway, stopping for nothing so mundane as traffic on her way to this meeting.

Less than thirty minutes later, Adair was pulling into the parking garage of the Streiker Building. The Rivers Bank was one of the Streiker Corporation's holdings, and its offices were located in this sleek thirty-three-story building, which served as corporate head-quarters. Adair parked and boarded the elevator for the thirty-second floor. No one else was going up at this time, so the elevator quietly whisked her up all alone.

When the *ding* sounded and the doors slid open, Adair stared out apprehensively at dark paneling and lighted art, then trod delicately across an Oriental carpet to a mahogany receptionist's desk. No one was there.

"Here, Ms. Weiss." Whinnet stood in the doorway of a nearby office. Adair stepped inside and he closed the door. "Have a seat." He gestured to a leather chair opposite a huge desk. Adair crossed the office, sat down, and waited.

Whinnet went around the desk and stretched wearily. "Excuse me. It's been a long day." He was in his shirt sleeves, and she noticed perspiration stains forming under his arms. So he was mortal after all.

"For both of us, Mr. Whinnet. I can't imagine what you wanted to see me about," she said carefully.

He glanced at her before drawing his chair up to the desk. "I suppose that's true." Then he leisurely donned reading glasses and took up a file folder that had been lying open on his desk. It suddenly seemed to Adair that he was reluctant about this whole matter, whatever it was.

"Are you familiar with the name Fletcher Streiker?" he asked.

"Yes, he's the rich philanthropist who owns this building," she answered.

"Among other things," he said drily. "He asked me to give this to you." He laid the file folder in front of her.

She opened her mouth in astonishment, then slowly began to leaf through the folder. It was full of newspaper clippings, brochures, letters, and scraps. "I don't understand."

"He would like you to know more about him," Whinnet answered. "The folder contains information that he has personally selected about himself and his priorities. That is, a lot of what you may read or hear about Mr. Streiker is preposterous, but all this here is accurate. Not complete, of course, but true."

Adair closed the folder in her hands. "I . . . still don't understand. Does he know me? Why does he want me to know about him?"

"Yes, he knows a good deal about you. And he wants you to know as much about him, in the event that . . . you may want to meet him someday."

"Well," she laughed, "I will be happy to meet him without reading his life history!" *I've heard everything now,* she thought. *How vain.*

"That's not the way *he* wants to do it," Whinnet said quietly. "Mr. Streiker is particular about keeping his privacy intact. If after reading this material you do want a meeting with him, there will be certain stipulations attached."

"Yes? What?" asked Adair.

Whinnet paused. "For you to meet him face-to-face, knowing who he is, will necessitate—er, an assurance of your loyalty and confidentiality."

"What are you talking about?" asked Adair.

"You have to marry him."

Adair was stunned. "That is the most absurd thing I've ever heard. How can I decide to marry someone based on reading something about him? And how could he know he wants to marry me? Hey—wait a minute. Just how much does he know about me?"

"As I said, a good deal," Whinnet replied.

"Like what?" Adair asked angrily.

"Besides the superficial, he knows your background, your attitudes, and the fact that you're not doing too well in accounting right now," Whinnet added with a glimmer of humor.

"Has he been spying on me?" Adair asked, now frightened.

"No. That's hardly necessary. It's all public information, or what you yourself have made public."

"Oh." Adair still didn't like it, but she calmed down. She dubiously opened the folder again. "What if I decide I don't want to meet him?"

"Then you don't, and nothing further is said about it," he answered.

She looked up. "Is all this confidential?"

"All what? The information in the folder? No. But if anyone else asks me to verify this proposal, I'll deny it. You can imagine how it would look in print," he commented, and that seemed to be the source of his discomfort.

"Why are you doing this?" she asked.

"Fletcher is my friend. I've know him for fifteen years, and I would do whatever was in my power that he asked me to do." His manner added his unspoken opinion, *Even if I don't like it.* He stroked his chin, feeling his five o'clock shadow, and pulled an electric razor from his desk drawer.

"You wouldn't do something—illegal for him, would you?" she asked brazenly.

He let the razor down momentarily with an irritated look. "I'll let that question pass. Fletcher lives by a personal moral code that would leave most people in the dust. If you're asking me how many wives he has gotten this way, I'm free to tell you he's never been married."

"How old is he?"

Whinnet hesitated as he checked his reflection in a small mirror, then reapplied the razor to a missed spot. "If the folder doesn't say, I'll ask him what he wants me to tell you."

"Don't you know?" she laughed.

"Yes. But anything I tell you about him needs to be cleared first."

"So . . ." she mused skeptically, "I look through all this, and then . . . I tell you if I'm willing to marry him."

"Basically, that's it, though there's a little more involved. For now, read it, and call me if you have any questions. My office number and home phone number are in there."

"How long do I have to decide?" she asked.

"Take as long as you like; there is no deadline. Though, of course, Mr. Streiker will not consider himself bound to an offer you never respond to."

"I'll have to think this over," she said, standing.

"I would assume so," he replied, standing as well.

On her way out, he said, "Oh—Ms. Weiss." She turned. "Try to be on time to work tomorrow."

"Yes, Mr. Whinnet," she murmured.

<hr />

Driving home, Adair kept glancing at the plain manila folder on the seat beside her. She did not know what to think of the faceless Mr. Streiker and his strange proposition. Her thoughts kept circling back to Charles Whinnet. His part in this seemed incredible. She knew him by reputation as a conservative, respected banker. He had headed a few charity events. He was involved in activities at his church. He had been married to the same woman for some twenty-odd years. It seemed inconsistent for a man like that to play matchmaker.

"People are not always what they seem," she reminded herself as she pulled into her parking space. She checked her mail, flipping through bills as she trudged up the steps to her apartment. "A hundred and forty-three dollars for electricity!" she groaned. "How in the world . . . ?" She unlocked the dead bolt and threw her purse and the file on the kitchen table.

For dinner, she took out of the refrigerator a doggie bag from a restaurant date and tossed it in the microwave oven. As it warmed up, Adair kicked off her high heels, hung up her jacket, and removed her earrings—all the while supremely conscious of the file folder on the table. She stood over the folder, drumming her fingers, then decided, "Whew! It's warm in here." And it was, considering that it was October in Texas. So she had to go turn on the air conditioner and adjust the thermostat.

After pulling steak and lobster leftovers from the microwave, she sat with the file folder in front of her.

The first item was a newspaper clipping about the recent opening of the Fletcher Streiker Arboretum. Adair knew about that; she had remembered seeing the article. The man had built this fabulous arboretum in the middle of north Dallas and had opened it free to the public. So Adair bypassed that article for the next one.

Now she was reviewing a magazine article about a clinic built and equipped by an anonymous donor for use by the Dallas County Health Department. Adair scanned the article, but it did not even mention Streiker's name. She paused to get some ketchup for her steak.

The next thing was a brochure about a ski program, complete with lessons and equipment, specifically for handicapped children. Was Streiker handicapped, then? Again, there was no mention of him at all.

Adair skimmed the rest of the items, which included an article about a privately funded program to evaluate and launch new products; an envelope containing photographs of scenery (no people); an article about the rescue of an American diplomat from a Chilean prison; and a letter addressed to "Mr. Streiker, Streiker building, Dallas, Texas." Adair stopped to read this letter, written in pencil:

Dear Mr. Streiker,
Thank you for sending the helicopter to pick me up and take me to Disneyland. It was great !!! The nice pilot was funny he made me laugh. I have to go back to the hospital tomorow. Mom says I can take Airshow Bear with me.
Love, your frend,
Jeremy Knox

A note in ink at the bottom of the letter read: "Jeremy died 6/27."

Adair held this letter a moment, then put it aside to flip through the remainder of the file—all disjointed bits of this and that, seemingly unrelated to each other or to Mr. Streiker.

There was not one picture of him nor one bit of real personal information about him. Adair shut the folder in extreme dissatisfaction. Where did he live? What did he look like? What were his bad habits? This file read more like a publicity portfolio for some company!

Adair finished her cold dinner in rising anger, sure that this was nothing more than a joke at her expense. She stood to drop the file into the trash can.

Then she had a better idea. Mr. Whinnet had invited her to call with questions. Well, suppose she did just that? It wouldn't take long to poke this little scam full of holes.

She called Whinnet's home number from the file and asked for him politely when a woman (presumably his wife) answered. In a few seconds the man himself was on the line: "Yes, Ms. Weiss?"

Adair began contritely enough, "I'm sorry to disturb you at home, Mr. Whinnet, but this file is actually the biggest pile of nonsense I've ever seen. It tells me nothing about Streiker."

"I don't believe you've had time to read it very thoroughly. As I told you, all of these things have intimately involved Mr. Streiker," he said patiently.

"Okay," she said, flipping open the file at random. "Then this article about the ski program must mean he's handicapped."

"No; he helped design the equipment, and he sponsors four-day vacations each year for a hundred applicants and their families. It's all there in the brochure," he said.

"His name is not in the brochure," she pointed out.

"Perhaps I should mention that when an article says, 'an anonymous donor,' that means him."

"Then, this article about the rescue of the American diplomat—" began Adair.

"He did that," Whinnet reiterated.

"Well, at least this letter from Jeremy is clear enough," she conceded.

"Yes, but I wonder if you have completely understood it. Fletcher himself piloted the boy and his mother from their home in Fresno to Disneyland and spent the day with them there," he clarified.

"How could I tell that just from this letter?" she asked.

"I told you," he said in a tone that suggested his patience was being stretched, "everything there is something that has *intimately* involved Fletcher. Not something he just threw money at, but something he was personally involved in, sometimes at risk to himself."

This was enlightening, but Adair still protested, "It seems such a roundabout way of giving information. There's nothing *specific* about him."

"What do you want to know?" he asked.

"Well, something more personal and tangible . . . what does he look like? How old is he?"

"I'll relay the questions," he replied.

"Where does he live?" she asked.

"He travels extensively, but I suppose he considers the Streiker Corporation his home base."

"And what is he worth?" The question was out before Adair could think twice about it.

There was a brief silence on the other end of the line. "His public and private holdings are so diverse, I doubt Fletcher himself knows that. He is not only chairman of the board of The Rivers National Bank, but the sole owner. He owns real estate, oil leases, a restaurant chain, a software company, and stock in a hundred other ventures. His total assets amount to somewhere in the neighborhood of three billion dollars."

Adair was silent for so long that Whinnet said, "Ms. Weiss? Are you there?"

"Yes," she coughed. "That's very—interesting. I just wish I had something more personal about him," she finished meekly.

"I'll relay the request."

"Thank you, Mr. Whinnet. Good evening." She hung up and sat staring at the folder. Then she opened it up again and read for three solid hours.

2

When Adair woke up the following morning, she wrenched around to look at the alarm clock. "Dang!" she cried, flinging bed covers aside. She skipped her shower, splashed water on her face, and leaped into a clean dress. Still, by the time she pulled into The Rivers Bank branch on squealing tires, it was 8:30.

There was no hope of sliding to the drive-through window to escape Duane. He met her in the lobby and quietly ordered her into his office. Then he safely shut the door before he exploded: "You're thirty-two minutes late, Adair! Again! After that stunt you pulled with that customer yesterday afternoon—! What kind of a wimp do you take me for? Do you think you can get away with this stuff? Well, I've got news for you: You're fired!"

"Duane, I'm sorry—"

"*Sorry* won't cut it! You're history here!"

"All right, Duane; but when you call Mr. Whinnet, please tell him I overslept because I was up late reading." She sat to wait, knowing that Duane had to call Whinnet to approve the termination.

"Yeah, right," Duane said sarcastically, picking up the telephone and punching numbers. "Duane Minshew calling for Charles Whinnet," he said importantly. "Mr. Whinnet? Minshew here. Adair Weiss was thirty minutes late to work today—again—so I fired her on the spot . . . yes," his face flushed slightly. "Yes, she is." He held out the receiver. "He wants to fire you himself."

"Hello, Mr. Whinnet," Adair said meekly.

"Didn't I ask you to be on time today?" he demanded lightly.

"Yes, sir, you did. I'm afraid I was up late reading."

"Were you? Good. I passed along your questions, and this is what I got: He says he has no pictures of himself. He is in his mid-thirties and in good health. As to your other request, he'll see what he can do," Whinnet said.

"I see. Well, thank you." She could not remember what her other request was. "Oh—am I fired, Mr. Whinnet?"

"Fired? I doubt the chairman of the board would allow it. Put me back on to Duane."

"Thank you, sir." As she handed the receiver back to Duane, she could not resist remaining nearby while he mumbled, "Yes, Mr. Whinnet. Ah, no. No. Sure. Right. Goodbye." After he hung up, he sniffed, "He said if you're late one more time, you're history."

"Okay, Duane," she said, trying not to sound cocky.

"What do you have on Whinnet, anyway? What does he care if you stay or go?" Duane suddenly asked.

"I was doing some research he gave me," she replied on her way out of his office.

Adair did not have the major concentration problems that had plagued her yesterday, but her mind was hardly on her work. Suddenly she remembered the dog she had dropped off at the vet's yesterday. She picked up the phone apprehensively, still unsure of how she would pay for his treatment.

She called the vet's office and said, "This is Adair Weiss. I . . . wasn't able to come by last night to pick up the Border collie, but I'm working on making arrangements for—"

"The Border collie that got hit by a car?" the receptionist asked.

"He was picked up and his bill paid last night."

"He was?" Adair asked, astonished. "By whom?"

"I don't know—I wasn't here then. Let me check his records." She put Adair on hold, then came back and said, "It doesn't say who picked him up, and his bill was paid in cash. Was this your dog?"

"Well, no, not exactly," Adair admitted. "I'm just glad it's all been taken care of . . . thanks," she said, and hung up. *Now who would have done that . . . ?*

She shook off the mystery, then went to her post at the window to go through the motions. She absently repeated "good morning" and "have a nice day" while thinking, *All right, what did I learn about Streiker last night? Jeremy's letter told me he likes children, and he's not afraid to get personally involved in a painful situation. The episode with the prison escape tells me he can handle danger, and again, that he's not afraid to take personal risks. That's how—*

"Adair?"

"What?" Startled, Adair looked up at Sharon Betschelet, who worked in the checking department.

"Adair, did you handle this deposit? I think there's been a mistake," Sharon said timidly, pulling a limp strand of hair behind her ear. "The guy deposited a check for $142.90. You credited his account for $1,142.90."

"Oh, dear!" Adair seized the deposit and corrected it, then entered the correction on her computer. "Thank you for catching that! And thank you for bringing it to me before Duane saw it. He's about ready to fire me."

"That's okay." Sharon smiled shyly and went back to her desk.

Adair took a deep breath and resolved to keep her mind on her work, but her rebellious stream of thought took up where it had left off: *That's how an entrepreneur succeeds—by taking risks. The venture assistance program tells me he believes in entrepreneurship and wants to help others succeed. The ski program for handicapped children? He loves kids, doesn't he? He wants them to see that anything's possible for them. . . .*

Through these ruminations, the faceless Streiker was at least developing a personality. But it wasn't nearly enough to convince her to marry him. Nor was it enough to excite her imagination, or make her fall in love—

She looked up with interest as a motorcycle entered the drive-through. It was the courier from yesterday—she recognized him from his helmet and jacket. He pulled up to the window and said, "Hi, Adair."

"How do you know my name?" she asked smilingly as she extended the drawer.

"From your picture in the bank brochure," he said, leaning forward to put a check in the drawer. Yes, her first name and picture were in that advertisement. She had forgotten about that.

She took out the check, this time with a deposit slip. "That's not fair," she pouted. "You know my name, but I don't know yours."

"Well," he said, leaning back on the bike, "my sister calls me Panny. Kind of a pet name. So that's what I've been calling the dog."

"The dog . . . ? *You!* You're the one who picked up the dog from the vet's!" she exclaimed.

"Yup," he said, crossing his arms. "I left him with a friend. Maybe you can come see him sometime."

He had a very nice voice. And the inflection he used was so interesting. She tried to be careful entering his deposit on the computer, but kept hitting the wrong keys.

"Is there a problem?" he asked.

Yeah, you're messing me up, she whispered under her breath. "No," she said through the intercom as she sent his receipt out through the drawer. "Yes, I'd like to come see Panny—the dog," she said casually. "Did he make it through the night okay?"

"Just fine," he said, taking the receipt from the drawer.

"Don't lose that," she said sternly.

He looked up under his helmet. "No problem. Still got the paperweight." He pulled the goofy rock from his pocket and wrapped the receipt around it before stuffing both back in his jacket.

Adair laughed. There was no one behind him, so he lingered at the window, tinkering with something on his bike. All she could see of him was his tanned hands. "Take off your helmet," she requested.

He looked toward her. "Can't ride without it."

"Just for a second," she urged.

"Why?" he asked.

"So I can tell when you're looking at me," she said.

"I'm looking at you all the time, and I'm smiling," he said.

Adair glanced over her shoulder to make sure no one else was nearby, then leaned closer to the intercom and said in a low voice, "I want to see your eyes."

"Please," he said with sudden fervency. "Please do." Then a car pulled up behind him. He glanced back as he started his bike and drove away. Adair watched him until he was out of sight, then took the next customer's deposit with a distinct air of distraction.

In a little while the ever-chipper Courtney bounced over. "Ready to go to lunch, Adair? Yeech, you look awful. Didn't you even mousse your hair this morning?"

"My hair?" Adair was suddenly self-conscious. "Oh dear, how bad do I look?" she asked, putting a hand to her head. "Well, it doesn't make any difference now ... uh, sure, Courtney. Where did you want to go?" she asked cautiously.

"Poco's, of course," Courtney said.

Adair protested, "I can't afford Poco's, Courtney; you know that. I'll just get a hot dog today."

"Suit yourself," Courtney shrugged. "But if you ask me, I think you need to find yourself a rich boyfriend." She swung out.

It's not that simple, Adair thought. Streiker was rich, all right, but he wanted to be her husband. And she just couldn't see tying herself down to some wealthy recluse when there were so many other interesting men in the world. Sighing, she went out to find the hot dog vendor roaming the complex. Then she sat on a stone bench under a tree and consoled herself with a loaded Coney.

When Adair arrived home after work that evening, she showered, ate the first thing she found in the refrigerator, and sat down with her accounting book. As she opened it up, her eye landed on Streiker's file still sitting on the table. She contemplatively fingered the file. Face it, a rich man could do a lot for her. She'd never have to worry about the cost of pursuing a dancing career, and that was all she really cared about. But then there was the sticky little question of what *he* might expect from their relationship.

"No," she decided. "Not if you were the richest man on earth. I'd rather be poor and free." She got up to toss the file in the trash can, then sat down to wrestle with the mystery of numbers.

The telephone in the bedroom rang. When she answered it, she heard, "Ms. Weiss, Charles Whinnet here. My wife and I would like to have you over for dinner tonight, if you are free."

"Thank you, Mr. Whinnet, but it's not necessary. I've decided not to pursue Mr. Streiker's offer," she replied.

"As you wish. But we've already made arrangements—we're having *coq au vin* catered by Deux Frères," he mentioned.

"Sounds like a special occasion. Will he be there?" she asked.

"Oh no. You recall those were not the terms," he said. Adair paused, trying to remember what exactly she had eaten out of the refrigerator. Now, she would do almost anything for a free meal, but—should she accept this invitation after she had already ruled out the proposal?

"May we expect you at eight?" he asked.

"Sure, why not?" she caved in, so Whinnet gave her their address on Papillon Court. Adair thanked him and hung up to get ready.

At five minutes till eight, she was ringing the doorbell at the sprawling Whinnet home. A maid answered the door and showed her through the marble foyer to a stunning white dining room. Across the foyer was a companion drawing room, also in white. An attractive, petite woman in her late forties entered, extending her hand: "You must be Adair. I'm Alicia Whinnet." She had animated blue eyes set in a pixie face, pale blonde hair swept back in a French twist, and a tennis player's grip.

"I appreciate the dinner invitation, Mrs. Whinnet, but I should tell you that I've decided not to take Mr. Streiker's offer. I assume that's what this is all about," Adair said, glancing at the glittering table set for three.

"Call me Alicia," she said, and there was something knowing in her smile. "And this was my idea. I just wanted to meet the woman who turned Fletcher's head so. Jackie," she turned to the maid, "please see if Charles is ready, and then bring the appetizers."

"Right." The maid nodded and left as if Mrs. Whinnet had just confirmed her own plans.

Adair couldn't help being a little flattered and intrigued by Alicia's statement, so she ventured, "I don't understand why Mr. Streiker would choose me. A billionaire could have anyone he wanted."

"Obviously, he saw something he liked," Alicia smiled again. "Forgive me, Adair. I overheard him talking about you to Charles, but I'm not free to repeat the conversation. It's terribly rude, but I'm afraid you'll have to take my word for it that it was all complimentary."

"I can't imagine what he would have to talk about, since I've never even spoken to him," Adair murmured. She heard a dog barking in another room, and Alicia took the appetizers from Jackie to ask her quietly to go do something about it.

Whinnet came in as Jackie left. "Glad you could make it, Ms. Weiss." He looked relaxed in a knit shirt and khaki pants.

"People who invite me to dinner get to call me Adair," she smiled sheepishly. His careful courtesy embarrassed her, for some reason.

"An admirable policy. Have a seat, Adair," he said, pulling her chair back. After he seated her, he pulled out his wife's chair.

"It's especially kind of you," Adair said, taking a breath, "considering that I'm not interested in marrying Mr. Streiker. And I really don't understand why I can't just meet him."

As the maid reentered with their plates, Whinnet replied, "Let me put it this way: Fletch is extremely dependent on his anonymity to be able to do the things he does. If he became known by sight as a wealthy good Samaritan, then he would have the press all over him wherever he went. He wouldn't be able to go to the bathroom by himself. As it is, he was able to walk into Santiago right under the noses of the Western press, and no one even knew he was an American. And if he were to start dating women like he *should* be, why, soon there wouldn't be any place on earth he could hide." He paused to uncork the wine and fill their glasses.

Adair let his explanation sink in as she took a bite of tender chicken. "Well, that may be," she said. "But it sure puts a crimp in trying to get to know him. How could I marry someone I know so little about?"

Whinnet looked at her over the centerpiece. "If you knew more about him, would you reconsider?"

Adair shrugged noncommittally. "Possibly. Can you at least tell me something about . . . how you met him?"

"Yes," he said, relaxing. "Fletch came to Landmark—that was the name of the bank before he acquired it—for a business loan when I was a loan officer there. He had already been denied at three other banks because he had virtually no collateral, no background, not even a permanent home address. All he had was an ingenious idea for preserving live plant specimens. It was so simple." Whinnet glanced up as the telephone in the other room rang, then shook his head slightly at the maid.

He continued, "I gave him the loan, and almost lost my job over it. But he used the money to finance tests validating his method, then sold it lock, stock, and barrel to a food industry giant. That's how he made his first million—and, by the way, paid back the loan within three months. Of course, after that he could have gotten an unsecured note from any bank for almost any amount, but that's when he decided to keep the risks and profits to himself, and use his own money. He remembered me, though. He's done me many a good turn."

Surveying the elegance of his home, Adair didn't doubt it. She wondered what kind of accommodations Streiker preferred for himself.

"He gave our daughter a Ferrari when she graduated from

Hockaday," Alicia noted.

"Then your daughter has met him?" Adair asked.

"No, though she tried to for a long time," Alicia chuckled. "She had a severe crush on him."

"Due to the mystery surrounding him, I'm sure. Fletch used to joke that if she ever did meet him, she'd call off their affair," Whinnet added. They heard the dog barking and whining again. Alicia shot a quick look at her husband and turned to ask Jackie again to *please* do something about that animal.

"Has he always been so reclusive?" Adair asked.

"Basically, yes. And that intensified shortly before his first windfall. A novice reporter developed an interest in him and started following him around. She ruined a project of his when she wrote it up for the newspaper," Whinnet told her.

"What was the project?" Adair wondered.

"Ah, I'd better let him tell you about it. But you've seen the kinds of endeavors he takes on." Whinnet leaned over his plate to finish off his meal. "More wine?"

"No—thank you." Adair put her hand over her still-full wineglass. Alcohol made her nauseated, and she did not wish to end the evening by getting sick at Alicia's beautiful table. She looked up with interest as *pave au chocolat* came around for dessert. The conversation shifted to less interesting matters—specifically, work at the bank—and when Adair glanced down at her watch, it was 9:45.

"Oh—please excuse me. I hate to eat and run, but I *must* be on time to work tomorrow, and I still have to study my accounting." She rose, as did the Whinnets. "Thank you so much for the lovely dinner."

"I'm sure we'll see you again," Alicia smiled.

"Goodnight, Adair," Charles nodded.

———◆———

When Adair arrived at her apartment, she wearily undressed, glanced at the impenetrable accounting book, and fell into bed.

The next morning, Wednesday, Adair startled awake and

grabbed the alarm clock. "Oh, it's only 6:30," she mumbled, sinking back down on the bed. "So I'd better get up *now*," she said, forcing her feet to the floor.

It was nice to have time to dress properly and eat breakfast for a change, even if it was just cold cereal. As she put her bowl in the sink, she congratulated herself on leaving early for work this morning.

Her doorbell rang. Adair glanced at her watch again to make sure it really said 7:30. When she opened the door, a courier stood outside. "Adair Weiss?"

"Yes," she said cautiously.

"Special delivery. Sign here, please." She signed and he handed her a letter. The envelope carried only her name and address in typescript.

"Oh dear," she muttered, closing the door. Special mail always meant bad news, and that's why she immediately thought this must be from her mother and stepfather.

Adair felt a stab of guilt. She had left home in rebellion over a bad situation that was much of her making. Having shown early promise in dance, she had begun taking lessons at the age of four. Her natural father's import-export business amply provided for tuition through her growing years. Even after he was divorced from her mother when Adair was fourteen, he continued to pay for dance.

The following spring Adair had won a partial scholarship to the prestigious Fort Worth School of Ballet. It would pay $400 a month beginning in the fall, but that still left $450 a month to be paid in tuition and expenses. When Adair's mother remarried that summer, her natural father disappeared and his checks stopped coming. Her stepfather, a man of more modest means, insisted there was no way the new family budget could meet dance expenses.

Adair was forced to drop out. She expressed her disappointment and frustration with angry defiance, and when her half-brother was born the following year, Adair's mother gave up on her rebellious daughter altogether.

So the day of her high school graduation, Adair packed her belongings, took what money she had from summer jobs and graduation gifts, and set out for the big city to the east. She would never have made it if it hadn't been for Lance, but . . . to this day she had not seen nor spoken to anyone in her family.

As she gazed at the letter, the old feelings of grief and bitterness welled up in her once more. "Well, I can't let it make me late for work. I'll read it at lunch." She stuffed the letter in her purse, wiped her eyes, and went to work.

She sauntered into the bank at ten minutes till eight, but Duane was in his office and did not see. "Good morning, Charlotte," Adair waved at the head teller, who merely nodded at her over her glasses. Adair placed her purse under the counter and took a deep breath at the sight of stacks of checks in front of her.

Then it hit her that the letter might just as well be good news, like an inheritance or something. She still had a few minutes before the day officially began, so she retrieved the letter from her purse, opened it, and read the following, neatly typed:

Dear Miss Weiss:

Chuck Whinnet said that you needed more personal contact with me before you could decide on my offer. I hope this helps to fill in the gap. Alicia also said you asked why I had chosen you. All I can say is that something about you told me you might respond. You'll be the one to say whether I was right or not.

Is this really such a strange way to approach you? Other people hide behind masks of what they think the other person is looking for when they meet. They talk and date and marry without ever really seeing what is behind the mask. I am showing you the real me, without any kind of a mask at all. At the same time, I am trying to shield you from a lot of unwanted attention. So, until such a time that we fully commit to each other (if you choose), it's best that whatever develops between us not be widely known.

If you wish to respond, you may write me at the Streiker Corporation, or give your reply to Chuck. (I'd prefer the latter; I'd get it sooner.) I also want it understood that if at any time you ask me to leave you alone, I will.

Sincerely yours,

Fletcher Streiker

Adair grappled with the letter, reading it over and over, until Duane's sarcastic voice shocked her back to the immediate present: "Well, if it isn't Miss Industry!" Everyone was working around her while she stood at the counter reading the letter. She shoved it into her purse and turned to the mountain of checks waiting to be photocopied.

She began running them through with shaking hands. This guy was serious. Was she? Could she be? She shook her head, thoroughly confused.

She looked up in time to see a black motorcycle pull up to the drive-through window. Abandoning the checks, she hurried to the window and nudged Courtney aside. "I'll take over for you now," Adair said, watching the courier turn off his bike.

"Fine," Courtney said, glancing out. She moved away, but only a little bit.

"Good morning," Adair said, extending the drawer.

The courier looked up at her. "I don't have anything today," he commented.

"You don't! What're you here for?" Adair exclaimed.

He shrugged. "Just wanted to see you."

"That's not fair. I can't see you," Adair complained.

"Poor baby," he sympathized drily.

Adair put a hand on her hip and puckered her lips. "What if I come out there and rip that helmet off your head?"

"Come try it," he invited.

Adair stood at the window, then suddenly turned and marched out of the bank around to the drive-through lane. As she approached the motorcycle, she failed to notice that he had started the engine. She walked right up to him and put her hands on his helmet.

But then he pulled her onto the seat in front of him with one arm and used the other to throttle up. As the bike lurched forward, she grabbed him to keep her balance. He drove with her around the parking lot to the rear of the bank and cut the engine. Taking her hand, he got off and opened a door in the building.

It was dark inside, especially after coming in from the bright sunshine. Adair did not even know what room this was. But he reached up and took off his helmet. As hard as she strained, she could not see anything more than a dim outline.

With his helmet in one hand, he put his arms around her and drew her close to him. When she felt his lips touch hers, she responded intensely, reaching up to his head. His hair was thick, damp with sweat, and hung over the collar of his jacket. His face was clean-shaven. His arms were strong and his chest was solid.

When he pulled away Adair was breathless—but her eyes were adjusting to the dark. "Be seeing you, Adair," he whispered, then suddenly he had put his helmet back on and stepped out into the sunshine. She stood at the doorway in mute disappointment as he started the motorcycle, glanced back, and drove away.

Adair turned around to see where she was. Now she knew— it was a little-used conference room. And this door was always supposed to be locked. Shaking her head, she went out into the hall and back to her work area. As she stood over the checks once more to resume processing, she glanced at Courtney leaning to look as far out of the drive-through window as she could.

"Whatcha looking at?" Adair asked.

Courtney spun around. "There you are! What happened? Where did he take you?" she demanded.

"Just around the building, for a laugh," Adair said casually.

Courtney came up closer. "Who is he?"

"His name's Panny. He's a courier," Adair said.

"*Panny*? Right," Courtney snorted skeptically.

"That's what he told me. It's a pet name," Adair shrugged.

Courtney started to say something else, but Charlotte was staring down at them, so she moved back to the window.

Adair glanced down at her purse with the letter inside. It was such a nice letter that the only decent thing to do was reply. What could she say? *Dear Mr. Streiker: I can't marry you because I kiss strange men on motorcycles.* It was scary and funny at the same time—some man she'd never met wanted to marry her while she was falling in love with a man on a motorcycle whose face she couldn't see.

At her lunch hour, Adair found the hot dog vendor and then sat on her usual bench to draft a reply to Streiker's letter. Suddenly she wondered, "Why won't Panny let me see his face? Could *he* be . . . ?" The notion transfixed her. Then she decided, "Nah. He's probably just got bad skin."

She took a bite of hot dog. "Dear Mr. Streiker," she began on a legal pad borrowed from the bank. No, that sounded ridiculously formal to someone who had proposed marriage to her. She crossed it out.

"Dear Fletcher." She grimaced—that didn't look right either. "For pete's sake," she scolded herself, "the man's a billionaire! Show some respect."

What was left? "Dear Fletcher Streiker."

"Why are you writing Fletcher Streiker?"

At the voice Adair bolted up, then sank back to the bench. "You startled me, Courtney."

"Isn't he the rich recluse? Another Howard Hughes?" Courtney primly sat next to her.

"I don't think so," Adair hedged. "I don't know that much about him."

"Did you know that the *National Inquisitor* has offered a quarter of a million dollars for a picture of him?" Courtney asked. "Yeech, are you still eating hot dogs? Do you know how much fat is in those?"

"No, I didn't know—"

"So why are you writing Fletcher Streiker?" Courtney asked, taking a bite of to-go salad.

"I . . . wanted to tell him how much I appreciate the things he does for Dallas, like the new arboretum," Adair said slowly.

"Oh, don't bother!" Courtney laughed. "He'll never see your letter. His secretary will read it and write a nice reply and then sign his name. People like that never write letters themselves."

"I guess you're right," Adair said, anxious to drop the subject. She wished Courtney would go eat her healthy salad somewhere else.

Courtney began talking about a new man she had met, but Adair was thinking, *He didn't sign his name, did he? It was all typed. I guess that's so if I showed it to anyone, he could deny having written it. Did he really write it? Or is this still just someone's idea of a joke?*

At that moment she caught sight of a man in a business suit across the access road. He was standing in a parking lot, watching the two women in the courtyard. Adair stood with a quick breath.

"What is it?" Courtney asked, standing as well. Traffic stopping at a red light obscured her view. By the time the cars began moving again, he was gone.

"What is it? Who did you see?" Courtney demanded.

"No one," Adair sighed. "I'm getting positively punchy."

"I'll say. Duane is itching to fire you," Courtney said lightly.

"I know it. I've got to pull myself together," Adair moaned.

"What's bothering you, Adair? You can tell me," Courtney urged sympathetically.

Adair slowly shook her head. "I'm just trying to decide which direction I should go."

Courtney finished her salad and checked her watch. "Back that way, to work. Lunch is over." She authoritatively took Adair's arm. "Come on, I'm not going to let you be late today."

"Thanks," Adair muttered.

She did not look at the letter again, and tried not to think about it until she got home that evening. But the moment she walked into her apartment, she threw her purse on the old secondhand love seat (her living room was not big enough for a sofa), sat down, and wrote:

> Dear Fletcher,
>
> I can't tell you how flattered I am by your proposal. I was a little frightened at first, but your assurances are reassuring.

She scratched out the last clause and wrote in,

> but ~~your assurances are reassuring.~~ you've convinced me I don't need to be afraid. I understand everything that you and Mr. Whinnet have said about why you have to contact me in this way, but from my perspective, I don't even know if you're a real person! Or if you're really who you say you are. I don't mean to impugn the honesty of Mr. and Mrs. Whinnet— they are very fine people—but everything they say about you is secondhand to me. They know you, but I don't.
>
> Which brings me to the main obstacle for me: You say you are ready to marry me, but do you *love* me? I don't see how you could, in spite of what all you know about me. What I have learned about you is interesting, but it's not enough for me to know whether I love you. And I could never commit to a loveless marriage, no matter how comfortable.
>
> I hope I haven't angered you; I felt you deserved total honesty. Whatever does or does not happen between us, you are obviously a good man and I wish you well.
>
> Sincerely,
>
> Adair Weiss

After finishing the letter, Adair heated up canned spaghetti for dinner. While eating, she reread her reply, decided that it was as close as she could come to what she needed to say, and recopied it.

Then she looked up at the kitchen clock. It was 7:30. "Oh no!" she screeched. "I forgot all about my accounting class! It's half over."

She shook her head in despair a moment, then decided, "It's hopeless. I'll drop the accounting tomorrow and try again next semester, when all this is cleared up. Maybe I'll get an easier professor." Still, she winced at the thought of the forfeited tuition.

"Well, what to do with this?" she mused, tapping the letter thoughtfully. She fished Fletcher's file out of the trash can and found the Whinnets' number, which she dialed.

"Alicia? This is Adair. Fine, thanks. I don't know if you knew that Mr. Streiker had written me a note . . . yes, well, I've written a reply, and do you mind . . . ? Yes, I'd like to bring it to you tonight." While she talked, she put the file folder in the nightstand drawer by her bed. "Thanks. Be there in a little while."

As she drove to the Whinnets' home, she was calculating, "Let's see . . . if Charles gives Fletcher this letter in the morning, then he would probably think it over and respond some time tomorrow afternoon, so it would be tomorrow night at the earliest before I got a reply. That's assuming he gives his reply to Charles, but if he uses a courier again, it will probably be day after tomorrow." This line of conjecture sustained her clear to the Whinnets' door.

Charles answered the doorbell. "Hello, Adair. Please come in."

"Oh, no," Adair demurred. "I won't barge in tonight. I just wanted to give you this." She handed him the letter.

He promised, "I'll give it to Fletcher right away."

"Whenever," she said hazily. "Will you ask him something else? Ask him if I saw him across the street from The Rivers branch around noon today."

He arched a brow. "I can answer that: no, you didn't. He was at a board of directors' meeting then, which I attended."

"Oh." Her face fell, then she said, "Why does the board get to see him and I don't?" There was a hint of jealousy in her voice.

"They don't," he smiled. "He was there, but they didn't know it. We conferred with him over the speaker-phone while he was sitting in the next room."

"I see," she said, visualizing a suit in an otherwise empty conference room talking over a speaker-phone to a roomful of people next door. It was a strange picture. "Well, thank you—Charles. Goodnight."

He smiled, "Goodnight, Adair."

Adair climbed the metal staircase and let herself into her lighted apartment. She always left a light burning if she had to be out at night, so that it was not entirely dark when she returned. It was bad enough always coming home to an empty place, where dishes stayed dirty until she washed them and clothes stayed wrinkled until she ironed them; she wasn't about to come home to a dark and empty place.

She threw herself onto the hard love seat to think. She tried to think about Streiker, but her thoughts drifted to Panny on the motorcycle. He said he'd be seeing her—did that mean he'd come by the bank again tomorrow? Smiling, she hugged the sofa arm. Whatever he was hiding behind that helmet included a nice set of lips.

The jangling of the telephone startled her violently. She put a hand on her chest to calm herself down as she went to answer it. Undoubtedly, now that class was out, someone was calling to find out why she had missed tonight. She picked it up on the third ring. "Hello."

"Adair, this is Fletcher Streiker. How are you tonight?"

Adair's throat seized shut for five seconds. "M-Mr. Streiker?" she croaked.

"Please call me Fletcher. You did in your letter, and I prefer it."

"Fletcher," she repeated in shock. *Have I heard that voice before?* she thought.

"I wanted to assure you that I really am a real person," he said humorously, "and to tell you that I wouldn't want a loveless marriage, either. I've waited too long to settle for that. But something tells me we'd be, ah, compatible."

I know that voice. Where have I heard it? She racked her brains for the connection. "Uh, what makes you think that?"

"Go look outside your door," he said.

"Outside my door?" she repeated blankly.

"Yes, I left something there for you."

"Hold on." She put the receiver down and ran to throw open her door. At first she didn't see anything, so she turned on the outside light. There, by the threshold, was a polished rock with a silly face on it. She seized it, gasping, "That *was* him! Panny!"

Adair ran back to the telephone. "I knew it! I knew deep down that was you! I just couldn't believe a big billionaire would be riding around on a motorcycle!"

"Being invisible has its benefits," he chuckled. "So how about it, Adair? Think you could learn to like Panny?"

She felt herself blushing to her toes. "This is all a little heavy. I—have to think about it."

"Okay, just let me know what you're thinking. You can write me, or call me through the answering service listed in the back of the file Chuck gave you," he said.

"Will you come by the bank tomorrow?" she asked slyly.

"Nope. No more kissing until I can finish the job," he said firmly.

She felt a slight tingle. "You're mean."

"And ruthless," he added cheerfully. "I'll do whatever is necessary to have you. Goodnight, Adair."

When Adair crawled into bed that night, she was not thinking about accounting, or her job, or how to pay this month's utility bill. She was hazily imagining life in a mansion with a man who rode a motorcycle and kissed like a dream. She fell asleep before remembering to turn off the lights.

❖

The next morning Adair got to work twenty minutes early and began tabulating the night deposits immediately, without frittering away the minutes before eight chatting with coworkers. When Fletcher came to mind, she thought back to Panny, trying to recall any details about him as someone would scour a beach for small treasures. She was not ready to say that she had made up her mind; nonetheless, she was so productive that Duane momentarily stopped threatening to fire her.

Midmorning, Courtney paused by her side and murmured, "Well! Who's the new man in your life?"

"What?" Adair laughed.

"This is a girl in love. I know all the symptoms," Courtney said smugly, leaning forward on her elbows. "So who is he?"

"I'm not seeing anyone," Adair said truthfully.

"What's the big secret? You can tell me," Courtney chided.

"I *am* telling you, Courtney. I haven't met anyone new." *Technically.*

"Sure. Whatever you say," Courtney turned away, offended.

Adair sighed and went back to work.

Among the many customers that Thursday morning was a young woman who sashayed into the bank around 10:30. Adair, at an inside teller window, glanced up and then gawked. There were plenty of weird dressers in Dallas, but this girl deserved special notice outside of Deep Ellum, Dallas's hot punk rock district. Above her heavy makeup and nose ring, her short yellow hair stood straight up. She was wearing a black rhinestone-studded bra, leopard-print Lycra pants, and four-inch acetate heels. Adair looked her steadily in the eye and said, "May I help you?"

"Yeah," the girl leaned on the counter, slightly out of breath. "I left my bag somewhere. I need some cash. About five hundred."

"Do you have an account with us?" Adair asked delicately.

The girl made a spiteful face. "My old man does. J. Dansforth Peevyhouse." She spat out the name mockingly.

"Just a moment," Adair replied, turning to search on the computer. A few seconds later she shook her head. "I'm sorry, we don't seem to have anyone by that name."

"You dumb Barbie doll!" the girl exploded. "My father has millions in this stupid bank! You'd better check again!"

Adair coolly turned back to the computer. "The only Peevyhouse we have is Arthur."

"That's my uncle. I'll take it from his account," the girl said as if this were a concession.

"What is your name?" Adair asked.

"I'm Poopy," she smirked.

Adair glanced at the screen. "I'm sorry, but 'Poopy' does not have signing privileges on Arthur Peevyhouse's account."

The girl looked irritated, then leaned over and whispered, "Eileen Owsley Peevyhouse."

"Eileen Owsley Peevyhouse doesn't have signing privileges, either," Adair said, looking at the line growing behind Poopy.

"What difference does that make? It's all going to be mine someday, and I need it *now*," Poopy demanded. Charlotte looked over inquiringly.

"I'm sorry, I can't help you at all," Adair said, reaching around her to the next customer.

Poopy knocked her arm aside. "You listen to me! You find my father's account and give me my money or I'll have Sam fire you so fast you won't know what hit you!"

"Sam?" Adair wondered.

"Yeah, Sam Mazzone, the president of this two-bit operation you call a bank!"

Adair smiled at the sudden realization. "Mr. Mazzone isn't president of *this* bank. He's president of First Fidelity and Trust Savings and Loan, across the interstate." Poopy stared at her, so Adair clarified, "You've got the wrong bank."

As the nature of the situation slowly began to sink in, Poopy sniffed, "I knew that," and made as quick an exit as her heels would allow. The long line of customers behind her spontaneously applauded.

The next woman in line smiled, "I wonder if she'll ever get her money," as she presented a check for cashing.

Adair started to voice an opinion, but instinctively changed it to a friendly, "Who knows?" She looked at the check. "Do you have an account with us, Ms. Ducote?"

"No, I don't."

"I'll need to see two pieces of identification, please," Adair requested, and Ms. Ducote opened her wallet. She was short, rather top-heavy, with straight, severely cut brown hair and bright red lipstick.

While waiting, Ms. Ducote idly asked, "Who *is* the president of this bank?"

"Charles Whinnet," Adair smiled briefly, copying numbers.

"Oh, I thought the reclusive Fletcher Streiker was," Ms. Ducote added, a little too casually.

"No, he's not," Adair replied, and counted out two tens and a five to her.

"But doesn't he have some connection with this bank?" the customer asked as she leisurely put away the bills.

"I believe he is chairman of the board," Adair said vaguely. Although suspicious about all these questions, she was not about to get caught in a lie.

"Does he have contact with the employees?" Ducote pressed.

"The chairman of the board? Are you kidding?" Adair laughed. "Thank you, and have a good day."

Ms. Ducote did not leave immediately, much to the ire of the customer behind her, so Adair turned away to replenish the cash drawer. Courtney abruptly backed away from where she had been lingering nearby.

"Has he had contact with you?" Ducote asked suddenly.

"Lady, what is this, Twenty Questions?" the man behind her asked plaintively. Ducote stepped out of the way to let Adair handle his business, but she repeated, "Has he had contact with you?"

"Why do you want to know?" Adair asked, forcefully stamping the back of the man's check.

"I'm a feature reporter for the *North Dallas Expositor*. I'd just love to interview Streiker, but he won't return my phone calls. I need some help getting in touch with him," Ducote said.

"Thank you. Have a good day," Adair smiled at the man as she handed him his receipt. He gave Ducote a dirty look on his way out. Adair turned back to her. "I'm afraid I'd be no help at all. I don't even know what he looks like. Excuse me. Courtney, cover for me here a moment, please." And she went to the rest room just to get away from Ducote.

As she started to leave the break room, she saw Courtney talking with the reporter. Adair held the door open just a crack. Ducote gave Courtney something, then left. Adair backed up into the lounge to think. Did Courtney suspect she was involved with Fletcher? Had she told this reporter? It was really too disturbing to speculate about.

At her lunch hour, Adair found an outdoor pay phone in the complex, out of sight of the bank. She dialed Fletcher's answering service and left the number of this phone. Then she hung up and waited, looking around uneasily for Courtney. It would be just like her to show up about now.

The telephone jangled at her elbow and Adair jumped. "Hello?" she gasped.

"Adair?" Fletcher's voice said cautiously.

"Yeah—hi." She cleared her throat. "I didn't expect you to call so soon. Did I interrupt anything?"

"Well of course you did," he said lightly. "But it can wait. I'm just glad you called."

"You may not be when you hear what I have to say." She took a breath, then told him all about Courtney seeing her write the letter to him, and the reporter this morning at the bank. "I'd hate to think that Courtney is the one who called this reporter, but it sure looks like she suspects I know you," Adair finished anxiously.

"That's nothing but guesswork on her part. Nothing to worry about," he reassured her. "Where are you now?"

"I'm at a pay phone in the complex. The one right outside High Adventure Travel Agency."

"Good," he said. There was a pause. "I'm glad you want to protect our relationship. That tells me . . . you want to pursue it."

"For now," she said in feigned aloofness.

"Um hmm," he assented, and she knew he wasn't fooled.

"Fletcher, is there anyone beside Charles Whinnet who gets to see you?" she suddenly asked.

"Yes, a few people, like Yvonne Fay, my assistant. By the way, any time you need help and you can't get hold of me, you can call her through the answering service or the corporate switchboard."

"Okay," Adair agreed, repeating the name to herself. "Well, I guess I'd better go get something for lunch, while I have time. . . ."

"There's a nice little restaurant right there in the complex. Poco's," he suggested.

"Uh, it's a little pricey for my salary, Fletcher," she laughed uneasily.

"I've opened an account for you there. They'll bill me."

"I can't let you do that," she protested weakly.

"Sure you can," he disagreed. "It's better than having a hot dog every day."

Adair cringed, then asked, "What do you eat for lunch?"

"When I'm in town, I usually eat in the cafeteria right here in the building."

"Oh," she laughed. "Maybe I'll come downtown for lunch some day to see if I can pick you out."

"And get yourself fired by the time you get back from a two-hour lunch? Look, Adair, if you're tired of working at the bank, all you have to do is say yes. Until then, you're better off sticking to Poco's," he advised.

"All right," she groused, adding sincerely, "thank you."

"Can I call you tonight?" he asked.

"Sure, why not?" she said airily.

"Then I will. Bye, Adair."

"Bye," she said softly.

❖

Adair opened the door to Poco's, glancing around at the soft pink and gray decor. The air conditioning felt good, too, after standing out in the noonday sun to talk on the phone during a typically warm October day.

She looked over the buffet. Then, just to make sure, she approached the manager behind the cash register. "My name is Adair Weiss. Do you have an account set up for me?" she asked timidly.

The manager grinned behind a large black moustache. "Sure we do, Miss Weiss. I'm Jaime. You come tell me if there's any little thing you don't like. Now, what will you have today?"

He knows about Fletcher flashed through her mind as she said, "Well, the buffet, of course, and iced tea."

"Very good." They strolled to the buffet table and he handed her a mint green glass of tea. "Help yourself. Plates are on the end."

"Great!" She turned to the buffet with gusto.

After a very satisfying lunch of fajitas, Adair returned to the bank with fifteen minutes left on her lunch hour. She immediately got to work and did not even notice when Duane came in, stared at her, and stared at the clock.

When Courtney came in at exactly one o'clock, she put up her purse and asked Adair, "Well! Where did you eat?"

She saw where I went, Adair thought, answering, "Poco's."

"Poco's! I thought you couldn't afford it!" Courtney teased.

Adair had to think fast. "You know, I decided you were right. It's not healthy for me to skimp on lunch. I revised my budget to cut out some frills and make room for Poco's."

Courtney turned away with a knowing smile, but Adair didn't really care if she believed her or not. Fletcher had made one good meal a day available to her and she was going to take advantage of it.

Then a sly temptation intruded: Goodness gracious, what all *could* Fletcher make available to her? Adair froze with a statement in her hands while the picture of herself in a new convertible played across her mind like a commercial.

"No." She ruthlessly changed channels. "I am not a gold digger."

"What's not a humdinger?" Sharon asked, coming up behind her. "Oh, Adair, look at that. You've got the ATM withdrawals in the wrong column."

"Yes, I was just about to correct that," Adair said hastily. "At least it's not a humdinger like the last goof I made," she laughed weakly. Sharon nodded and moved on.

Adair mentally whipped herself, lectured herself to keep her mind on her work, then immediately began to worry about how she was going to get to the college registrar's office before 5:30 in order to drop her accounting class.

After work, she rushed to the community college to fill out a drop slip before they closed their doors. Then she stopped to pick up a few dollars' worth of groceries (heavy on the carbohydrates) on her way home.

As she pulled into her parking space she noticed a Toyota parked in Ralph's stall, two spaces down. She smiled ironically, "Ralph will be real happy to see that." He didn't even let his girlfriend park her sports coupe in the one covered stall reserved for his precious TransAm.

She wearily headed up the steps with her small sack of groceries, then stopped on the landing halfway up, groping for her keys. Wondering if she had left them in the car, she glanced down toward the parking stalls. Straight down through the Toyota's windshield she could see a woman laid out across the front seat.

Adair ran down the steps and wrenched open the driver's door of the Toyota. The woman sprang up.

"What happened? Are you hurt?" Adair exclaimed, reaching toward her. She noticed that the woman looked familiar.

The woman's pale complexion blushed deeply. "No—I was just looking for—one of my contacts. It popped out on the seat. I found it." She hastily started the engine.

Adair stepped back, open-mouthed. She was sure the woman hadn't been looking for anything on the seat, unless it was with her nose. Now Adair recognized her. It was the reporter from the bank today—Susan Ducote.

Ducote quickly backed out and drove away with Adair staring after her. Then Adair, feeling troubled, went up to her apartment and fixed herself a peanut butter-banana sandwich for dinner.

Shortly after she had rinsed out the dishes, the telephone in the bedroom rang. Expecting Fletcher to call, Adair momentarily wondered if reporters ever bugged telephones. "Hello?" she answered tentatively.

"Hello, Adair. It's Fletcher. Is something wrong?"

"I don't know," she laughed lightly, settling back on the bed. "Remember the reporter I told you about? Well, this evening when I came home, I found her parked near my apartment. She was trying to hide down on the seat! When I asked her if she was okay, she got real embarrassed and drove off."

"Ah," he said. "Congratulations. You're being tailed."

"I was afraid of that. What should I do?" she asked in alarm.

"Everything you normally do. She's not going to find me by following you," he pointed out.

"Can she eavesdrop on our conversations?" Adair asked.

"Only if you talk on a cordless phone—or let her stand at your elbow. It's not worth the mental energy to worry about her, Adair."

"I guess you should know," she murmured, thinking of the large-scale worries he must have to deal with daily. Then she remembered, "I had a wonderful lunch at Poco's today. Thank you very much."

"You're welcome."

"Oh, and Courtney asked me how I could afford to eat there all of a sudden. I told her I was cutting nonessentials out of my budget—like accounting."

Fletcher laughed, "Don't say that in front of my accountants. They're surly beasts." She burst out laughing as he went on, "Accounting is just not your field. I think you might be happier in something more expressive, more creative."

Adair's heart lodged in her throat. "Well . . . now that you mention it . . . I am—I mean, I have been trying to resume ballet. . . ."

As she spoke, a battle broke open inside her. On the one side was her love of dance; on the other was her fear of dependence. Should she let him subsidize this dream, which was otherwise beyond her, and so become indebted to him? Or should she keep a safe distance, not allow him to touch that part of her life, and risk losing the dream forever? It was a terrible conflict.

"That sounds like a fine idea. Do you have a studio in mind?" he asked.

"Uh, Madame Prochaska's is near here," she capitulated.

"Why don't you make arrangements with her, and let me know what you need?" Fletcher suggested. "Then start as you have the opportunity."

Adair was silent, groping for the most gracious way to express her misgivings.

"Adair?"

"Uh, I appreciate that very much, Fletcher. Please don't misunderstand me. I just don't know if I can handle all of the sudden generosity." She thought of the punk-rock poster girl who had been in the bank that day. "I don't want to become a rich witch."

"I see. I understand your concern. I'll put some safeguards in place so that won't happen. Believe me, Adair, I've exercised real restraint in my generosity toward you. There are a lot of things I've wanted to do for you, but haven't."

"You could make me president of the bank so I could fire Duane," she offered.

"That's an interesting suggestion," he said slowly. "I assume your only motivation here would be that Duane is showing some incompetence."

"Nah," she said, doodling in the dust on the bedside table. "He just seems to think I should work all day."

"Then maybe, babe, that's what you'll have to do," he said humorously. His use of this intimate term gave her a tingle that reminded her of a deep kiss in a dark room.

"I want to see you, Fletcher!" she said suddenly.

"Does that mean you accept?" he asked.

"Well, I don't know . . ." she backtracked.

"Don't play with me, Adair—that hurts," he scolded. "I'm very serious about you."

"I know. Just—give me some time," she said, flustered.

"It's yours. Call me if you need me." And he hung up.

———◆———

That night Adair had a vivid dream. She was on stage performing a dance that had been created especially for her. She could feel the dizzying series of pirouettes and the pressure of her toes on the wooden floor. She could hear her controlled, tense breathing under the frenzy of the string section. Somehow, she knew that she was giving the most important performance of her life.

When it was over, she collapsed to the floor, then came up to give her bow, holding her breath in suspense: How would it be received? The lone figure in the auditorium slowly stood and applauded, and his applause filled the building to its rafters. Adair felt a tremendous rush of exhilaration and gratitude simply because her dance had pleased her audience of one.

4

"I tried to call you last night, Adair, but you were on the phone *forever!*"

Adair looked up from the monthly statements in front of her. "I'm sorry, Courtney. What did you need?"

"Would you like to go to lunch with me today? There's a great new Mexican restaurant on Mockingbird I want to try," Courtney suggested, leaning on the counter.

Adair noticed that she was wearing a new sweater, with fingernail polish to match it. "Thanks, Courtney, but with Sharon out sick today, I've been asked to help with these statements. They're due out next week, so I can't stretch my lunch hour any. I'd better stick to Poco's. It's so much closer. Nice sweater."

"Isn't it? I won't tell you who gave it to me," she smirked, running a finger under the cuff. Adair smiled, then gave her a warning glance as Sergeant Charlotte appeared among the ranks. Courtney had started to say something else but took the hint and went back to her window.

Adair did not want to take time to chat with anyone right now.

It was a big opportunity for her to be asked to prepare these statements, and she wanted to do a good job. She also had to complete a certain number of them before noon so that she would not have to work through lunch. She was not only looking forward to Poco's Friday dessert buffet, she was anxious to go see Madame Prochaska.

When noon finally rolled around and Adair pushed aside the statements, she was dismayed to hear Courtney chirp, "Ready to go now?"

"Huh?" Adair said.

"Are you ready to go to Poco's?" Courtney repeated in slight exasperation. "Boy, are you dense today."

"Yes, I guess so," Adair said unhappily.

They walked across the sunny complex to the cool ambience of Poco's. Adair smiled at Jaime, the manager, and helped herself from the buffet table. Then she sat and began eating her taco salad while Courtney paid for her own lunch. When she joined Adair, she noted, "You didn't pay."

"We've worked it out to pay once a month. That helps my budget." Adair was ready with this explanation.

"Oh. How nice." Courtney laid the napkin across her lap.

There followed a strained silence. Adair did not like deceptions, but she didn't dare tell Courtney anything about Fletcher. Still, out of consideration for their friendship, Adair decided to give Courtney an opportunity to clear the air.

"That reporter who was in the bank showed up at my apartment complex yesterday," Adair said casually. "I had the feeling she was watching my apartment. I wonder why. Do you have any idea?"

Courtney stirred her salad around. "No," she said, lifting her dark, shaped brows. She looked at Adair, then away.

"I can't imagine why she thought I knew Fletcher Streiker," Adair continued. "Can you?"

"Of course not," Courtney answered faster this time. Then she made eye contact with someone at the door.

Adair looked over her shoulder as Susan Ducote walked in. She made a show of spotting them and stopped by their table. "Well, it's my friends from the bank. Having a nice lunch?"

"We certainly are! Why don't you join us?" Courtney asked brightly. Adair glared at Courtney as Ducote headed off to the salad bar. "I was just trying to be nice!" Courtney hissed defensively.

When Ducote stopped by the counter to pay, she asked Jaime a question. He looked straight at Adair and shook his head. Adair relaxed a little. He wasn't talking.

"Well!" exclaimed Ducote, setting her salad on the table and pulling up a chair. "It must be nice to eat here every day! You must make a lot more money than I do!"

Only Courtney smiled. "We have friends in high places."

"There's a lot of public interest in people in high places," Ducote observed. She was perspiring slightly as she shrugged off her suit coat and hung it on the back of her chair. "People like Fletcher Streiker are an inspiration to others. And good publicity helps him, too. A positive public image can really open doors." Adair thought the idea that Fletcher needed anyone's help to open doors ludicrous.

"I can accept his desire not to have his picture taken. We don't need that, if we just had some personal anecdotes about the man to give our readers something to relate to. You know—what kind of car does he drive? What does he wear? Even things like, is he a good kisser?" She winked.

Adair set down her tea glass. "What were you doing at my apartment last night?"

Ducote evenly matched her gaze. "You're not the only one who lives in those apartments, you know."

"All right, then, who were you visiting there?" Adair returned. Courtney stared at her in dismay.

"I don't think that's any of your business," Ducote smiled.

"Why not?" Adair asked. "You want to know all kinds of personal things about Mr. Streiker, but you insist on keeping your own life private. I think that's a double standard. I think you people who are free to print whatever you want are just as much public figures as someone like him. Why don't you write about reporters who harass people for information?"

Adair got up and walked out, forfeiting dessert. With only half of her lunch hour left, she prudently decided to postpone going to Madame's studio until after five. Instead, she returned to work on the statements.

Courtney and Adair maintained a cool distance the rest of the afternoon. They spoke to each other only when necessary, and then just briskly. But this posturing soon began to wear on Adair. Courtney had been her first and only friend when she started work at the bank three years ago, guiding her through those first difficult weeks. Adair felt that she had a lot invested in Courtney, and she did not want to see their friendship end in acrimony.

"Maybe I'm wrong about her," Adair reflected, watching Courtney count out change to a customer. Courtney had principles. It was entirely possible that she had nothing to do with steering that reporter toward Adair.

So at the close of the day, Adair caught Courtney in the break room and said, "Please tell me the truth about one thing: Did you put that reporter on to me?"

"No, I did not," Courtney replied, glaring.

"Okay—I'm sorry. Let's just drop it," Adair said.

"Okay," Courtney replied carefully. "See you Tuesday."

Adair paused. "Oh, yeah—I forgot that Monday is a holiday."

Courtney nodded and went to the counter to get her purse. She did not share her weekend plans with Adair, as she normally relished doing. Adair stayed a few minutes to clean up some loose papers and leave a note on Sharon's desk, then went out to her car.

On her way to the dance studio, Adair thought of how nice it would be to talk to Fletcher tonight. She envisioned him calling from a darkened, empty office high atop the Streiker Building, leaning back in a leather chair, laughing in that nice voice. Adair shivered slightly and rubbed the goose bumps on her arm. "Silly girl," she muttered.

She exited the freeway and turned in to the corner plaza where Madame Prochaska's studio was located. A class of young ballerinas was in progress, led by the slender, sinewy Madame, who at forty-five had the body of an athletic thirty-year-old. She wore a black leotard and tights with no shoes, only leg warmers bunched around her ankles. She saw Adair and nodded. Not wishing to disturb the class, Adair stood back quietly and watched them run through "Dancing Snowflakes."

Madame dismissed her students and came over smiling as she smoothed her black hair back into its tight bun. "Adair, darling, it is not time for your class!"

"Yes, I know, Madame. I just stopped by to tell you that I've found a sponsor, and I'll be able to pay you starting Monday!" exclaimed Adair.

"Wonderful! But didn't you know next week I am guest artist at Washington? I will return week after, and you start again then," said Madame. After twenty-five years in the States, she still carried a thick accent like a personality trait.

"Oh," Adair said in disappointment. "Well, that's a wonderful opportunity for you—"

Madame interrupted her to catch a departing student. "Jana, your turnout is much improved. Lovely."

"Thank you, Madame," the child smiled righteously.

Adair resumed, "When I start, how often should I come?"

"We must work you strictly—five evenings a week, at your usual time, to put you in performing condition," Madame said severely.

"Yes, all right. And how much will that cost? So I can tell my sponsor," added Adair.

"Five sessions a week, two hours a session, that is four hundred a month," said Madame.

"Fine," said Adair, hoping that it was. "Break a leg in Washington, Madame."

"Thank you, darling." Madame turned to greet her next group of students, who were teenage girls. They wore the students' uniform of black leotards and pink tights, and as Madame put on a cassette tape, they assembled at the barre to do warmup exercises.

Adair paused to watch these girls with a seasoned eye. Then she left the studio breathing, "It's really going to happen. Thank you, Fletcher."

On her way to her car, Adair paused in front of a shoe store. "All my leg warmers have holes in them . . . my toe shoes have gotten soft. . . ." Before she knew it, she had talked herself into buying several leotards, leg warmers, shoes, and tights. She gulped as she wrote out a check for $116.30.

"I hope I'm not out of line," she worried as she put the packages in her car. But it was not a worry that she could sustain for long. By the time she pulled into her parking stall, she was happily rehearsing what she would tell Fletcher about ballet.

———◆———

After downing a hasty dinner of macaroni and cheese, Adair sat to read yesterday's newspaper and wait for Fletcher to call. By seven o'clock she was growing fidgety. "Isn't this about when he called last night?"

At 7:15 she was doing nothing but staring at the clock. "Something's wrong," she worried. Then she remembered that the last thing he had said was for her to call if she needed him. "Does that mean he's not going to call me anymore? Or did I make him that mad by asking to see him?"

She fretted over this for a while, but impelled by the knowledge that she did not have enough in her account to cover the check she had just written, she decided not to wait for him to call her. She dialed Fletcher's answering service and left her name. By the time she made herself a glass of iced tea, the telephone rang.

Smiling, she took her tea to the bedroom to answer the phone. "Hello!"

"Hello, Ms. Weiss," said a pleasant female voice. "This is Yvonne Fay."

Adair was taken aback. "Who are you?"

"I am Mr. Streiker's personal assistant. He was called out of town on urgent business this afternoon. He left instructions for me to return your calls. Is there anything I can do for you?"

Humiliated, Adair mumbled, "No, I, um, just wanted to tell him about ballet classes." Actually, she just wanted to get off the telephone.

"Did you sign up for ballet at Madame Prochaska's?" the assistant asked encouragingly.

"Uh, yes, I did."

"How nice. When do you start?" Yvonne asked.

"A week from Monday, and I'll go every week night from seven to nine," Adair reported. *Why am I telling her all this?* she thought with irritation.

"Very well." It sounded as though Yvonne were writing it down. "And what is the cost?"

"Oh yes, I forgot about that. It's going to cost $400 a month. And, I, uh, spent $116 on dance gear. I'm afraid I can't cover the check I wrote," Adair confessed, her cheeks burning.

"I will have deposited in your account $516 tomorrow morning. And once a month we'll automatically deposit $400. Will that be satisfactory?" Yvonne asked.

Adair mouthed, "Yes, thank you. Do you need my account number?"

"No, Ms. Weiss; I have it."

The woman's professionalism was warm and nonjudgmental, so that Adair couldn't help asking, "What do you think of this, um, arrangement, Ms. Fay?"

"Please call me Yvonne. I think you are a very lucky young woman."

"You do?" Adair asked hopefully.

"Yes, I do. Mr. Streiker is a very considerate man."

"How long have you been his assistant?" Adair asked.

"Almost thirteen years. I am the first and only personal assistant he's ever had," Yvonne said proudly.

"And . . . you don't mind the thought of his getting married?" Adair asked.

"I think it's about time. As for myself, I've been married for eighteen years to a man I rather like," Yvonne said.

"Oh, good," Adair said, glad to hear the frank tone. She surely did not want to be competing with a long-time secretary for the boss's affections. "I wish I could meet you, at least."

"Certainly. When is convenient for you?" Yvonne agreed.

"But . . . how can you . . . do you meet people and say, 'Hello, I'm Fletcher Streiker's personal assistant'?" Adair asked.

"Oops, there's something more you should know. As far as the rest of the world is concerned, I'm a bookkeeper for the Streiker Corporation. That's all. More than one executive has suggested that I've outlived my usefulness, but no one seems to know who keeps me on the payroll," Yvonne laughed.

"It sounds kind of complicated," mused Adair.

"It sounds that way, but actually it's rather fun. Mr. Streiker and I can walk into the cafeteria together, have a high-powered chicken salad, and nobody pays the slightest attention to either of us," Yvonne explained.

Adair wound the coils of the telephone cord around her finger. "What is he like?" she asked. "I mean, I know you can't tell me what he looks like, but—where did he come from? Where is his family, his home?"

Yvonne hesitated before answering, then began on a tack Adair had only hoped for. "His father, Lieutenant Dan Streiker, was a Navy pilot stationed at Pearl Harbor. He met and married Oona Lani, an island native. They had two children, Fletcher and Desirée. The family moved periodically as Lt. Streiker received new orders, but they always loved the islands best. So when he retired from active service, he and Oona moved back to Hawaii. Mrs. Streiker and Desirée, with her family, still live there. Fletcher went back last year for his father's funeral.

"Fletcher has always seemed . . . different. Even standoffish. He told me that Desirée, six years younger, was usually the one to make new friends, to meet people, to charm strangers on the street. She was so personable and outgoing. Fletcher adored her, but he couldn't be like her. He would read in his room, or go on long hikes by himself. His mother worried herself sick about him, but his dad always said, 'Leave him alone. He's not hurting anybody.'

"He graduated with honors from high school and enrolled at the University of Hawaii, but then dropped out. That upset his dad, but as Fletcher was by then self-supporting, there was not a lot he could say. He only knew that his son had special potential. Once, when I spoke to his mother over the phone, she told me something like, 'I spent too much time trying to make him conform to meaningless standards, when all the while he had the important things in place. He's spent all his life in good-natured rebellion against the tyranny of the unimportant.'"

"That's marvelous," Adair murmured. "That explains so much. Tell me why his sister calls him Panny."

"Panny?" repeated Yvonne. "Goodness, I don't know about that. You'll have to ask him."

"Do you know when he'll be back?" Adair asked.

"I'm afraid I don't. He never leaves an itinerary. Now . . . would you like to meet for lunch? Perhaps I can tell you more," Yvonne said.

"Sure! When?" Adair exclaimed.

"Let's see . . . my husband and I are leaving tonight, and we'll be gone over the weekend. If you like, I can meet you at Poco's next week," Yvonne suggested.

"No! A reporter has been hounding me at work, and she showed up at Poco's today," Adair said urgently.

"Well, if we can't meet during the week, the cafeteria in the Streiker Building is open for lunch on Saturdays. We could meet there next Saturday—the twenty-third," said Yvonne.

"Yes, that will be fine. But . . . if you start talking about Fletcher there, a lot of people are sure to be interested."

"One little preventive measure takes care of all that. Whenever we're in public, never say his name. Just 'he' and 'him.' Keep your voice down and be aware of who's around you. It's not really a problem," Yvonne assured her.

"Okay. How will I know you?" Adair asked.

"Tell you what. Just to be on the safe side, we won't let on that this is a planned thing. You go on in at noon and get your lunch, and I'll find you," Yvonne said.

Adair chuckled, "Undercover, huh? I feel I should wear a trench coat and dark glasses."

"If it's cool and sunny," Yvonne agreed. "Take down my home phone number, just in case." She gave it to Adair, who scribbled it on a gum wrapper and dropped it in her purse. "And I'll see you next Saturday!"

"Thanks, Yvonne," Adair said warmly. "Goodnight."

She cheerfully did some housework, and even handwashed some sweaters in hopes of cooler weather ahead. The next morning, Saturday, she got up with the noblest intentions of filling the time profitably, but found herself lingering over such things as reading the entire back and side panels of the cereal box.

Adair did go to the grocery store, where she picked up a copy of the *National Inquisitor,* telling herself, "I wonder what kind of rag would offer $250,000 for a picture of Fletcher." Glancing through it should have told her, but instead she read every word of fabricated gossip and Elvis sightings, every now and then declaring, "This is pure trash."

She passed Madame Prochaska's studio several times that day, becoming more excited each time, although the studio was locked up and would remain so until Madame returned from her Washington engagement. Adair went so far as to try on her new tights and do some makeshift warmups in her cramped apartment. But before the evening rolled around, she was already bored and wondering how to fill the long weekend with both Fletcher and Yvonne gone.

Sunday was more of the same. Normally, Adair relished Sunday as a true day of rest, sleeping in and forgetting about work. But today she felt sated with rest and vaguely anxious to do something. She went window-shopping at a mall, subconsciously picking out the expensive things she could buy if she did marry Fletcher. A poster beside a music store caught her eye. "Dallas Brass is in town tonight!" she exclaimed. Then she groaned, "They're playing at the Meyerson. A ticket will be thirty dollars." A store employee came out with a black marker and made it all irrelevant: the concert was sold out.

When she returned from the mall, she could not sit in her stuffy apartment for long. With the day partly overcast, and leaves beginning to drift from the trees, it was the perfect day to go jogging around White Rock Lake. But when she got there, she discovered that several thousand people had figured out the same thing. After a few minutes of fighting traffic around the lake, Adair gave up and went home.

Monday . . . more of the same. Adair had been looking forward to Columbus Day. Since only bank and government employees observed this holiday, she always felt some superior pleasure in taking the day off while almost everyone else was rushing to work. But today she woke up bored.

She opened the newspaper over her cereal with a sigh. The State Fair of Texas had begun and would run through the month of October. That sounded interesting. "I'll call Courtney and see if she wants to go," Adair decided.

She dialed Courtney's number. It was answered on the first ring by a soft, sleepy voice: "Hello."

"Hi, Courtney. Adair. Hey, would you like to go to the State Fair with me today? I'll pay your way."

"Adair, are you nuts? It's eight o'clock! Go back to bed!" Courtney said in her regular voice and hung up.

"Well, I'm going anyway. Alone and crowds and all!" Adair declared.

She did go; she paid admission and parking; she patiently waited in line to get in. Then she walked around the grounds with vacuous eyes. The rides made her sick, the food was expensive, the livestock smelled. Finding nothing that could interest her, she left after an hour and a half.

Sitting in traffic on the way home, Adair shook her head in disgust. "What's *wrong* with me? I used to enjoy getting out and doing these things! Everything can't have changed overnight!"

But something *had* changed. Fletcher had proposed to her. And his proposal had opened up the possibility of a kind of life that few people would ever experience. Something in her imagination clung to that possibility, making everything else gray in comparison.

Her common sense railed against the notion of accepting his proposal, sight unseen. But her spirit said, *How exciting. How different. What have you got to lose?* And she knew that she could not go on forever deliberating; the two sides demanded a decision.

Adair went to bed that evening actually looking forward to going to work the next day. *This week,* she thought sleepily, *something's going to happen. Something's got to give....*

◆━◆━◆

Tuesday morning after the Columbus Day holiday, Adair was at work by 7:30. She finished up the statements and placed them on Sharon's desk, then Duane directed her to work the drive-through lane. It was busy, as it was on any day following a holiday, so Courtney was called over to work the second lane.

In between customers, Courtney smirked, "So how was the Fair?"

"It was okay. They had some real interesting exhibits," Adair commented unenthusiastically as she placed a customer's money order in the drawer and sent it out. "Thank you. Have a nice day."

"I'm sorry I couldn't go with you. Bob called that morning and took me to the Adolphus for lunch," Courtney told her.

"That's nice," Adair said.

"We met a lawyer friend of his there. His name's Tom. He's really nice," added Courtney.

"Is that right?" Adair murmured, taking another customer's deposit from the drawer.

"Tom asked me if I knew anyone, and I told him about you. He's interested in meeting you," Courtney said.

Adair did not immediately give an answer, as she was entering the customer's deposit. She placed his receipt in the drawer. "Thank you, sir. Have a nice day."

"I said, Tom is interested in meeting you. He pulls down a hundred and fifty grand a year."

Adair turned her head slightly. "Courtney, I . . . I'm just not interested in meeting anyone right now."

"You don't have to go to bed with him, just have dinner. We'll make it a foursome. At the Mansion on Turtle Creek," Courtney urged.

"It sounds nice, but—" Adair hedged.

"You can't pass up dinner at the Mansion!" Courtney exclaimed.

"I'll let you know," Adair whispered as Charlotte looked over at them.

Later, during break time, Adair paused by Sharon's vacant desk. "Is Sharon still out?" she asked Pat, at a nearby desk.

"Yeah, she had a real nasty viral thing. She hopes to be back tomorrow or the next day," Pat replied.

"Oh," Adair said uneasily. She wanted Sharon to look at the statements before Duane got hold of them. She thought she had better look over them herself then, but the teller lines were teeming and she was called to work drive-through again, where she stayed for most of the day.

Toward five o'clock, Courtney came up with her purse slung over her shoulder. "Well? What about Tom?"

"No, I don't think so, Courtney. I'm just not interested," Adair declined, picking up her purse. She glanced at the statements on Sharon's desk. If she weren't so tired, this would be a good time to go over them.

"Why not? Who are you seeing?" Courtney asked.

"No one. I'm not seeing anyone, and I don't want to start," Adair said irritably. She went on out to her car, promising to come in early tomorrow to check over those statements.

Home for the evening, she heated up a bowl of canned stew in the microwave oven, then sat at the kitchen table and slowly crumbled crackers into the stew until it was almost inedible. "Fletcher must still be out of town, or else he would have called . . .

I think. Even though the last time we talked he said for me to call if I needed him. Well, I don't need him. He can call if he wants to talk to me. If I'm here, I'll talk to him." But the only place she went that evening was to bed.

Wednesday came and went like any other day. Sharon was still out sick, and Adair forgot about the statements. Courtney was cool. Fletcher did not call.

Adair began to feel vaguely troubled. Had he given up on her? Or lost interest in her? Adair tried to pretend that she didn't care, but the thought that she may have been successful in resisting him made her sick to her stomach.

Thursday came and Adair's mind was definitely not at work. She took a message at Sharon's desk from a Mrs. Flaubert Beamer and wrote "Mrs. Fletcher Streiker." Luckily, she caught the error before anyone else saw it; unluckily, Fletcher's name had driven the caller's name from her mind. While working the drive-through, she kept an irrational lookout for men on motorcycles. And once, passing by Duane's office while he was out, she was seized by the desire to run in and call Charles to ask about Fletcher.

Significantly, she no longer fretted about seeing his face. She only wanted to hear his voice—that smooth, sexy voice.

Adair arrived home that evening in a state of high agitation. She paced the small kitchen while she ate tuna from the can. When she went to the bedroom to try to relax and read, she found herself hovering over the telephone like a vulture.

"This is ridiculous!" she shouted. "I'm not going to wait around for him like this!" She impulsively picked up the phone and called Fletcher's answering service. "This is Adair Weiss calling for Mr. Streiker. I'm at home," she calmly announced.

When the telephone rang obligingly a few minutes later, Adair realized that she had not the slightest idea what she planned to say to him. She tried to think quickly as she answered, "Hello?"

"Hello, Adair. It's Yvonne."

"Oh, hi," Adair said.

"I'm returning your call because Mr. Streiker is still out of town.

Is everything all right?" Yvonne asked.

"Yes, fine, everything's fine. A little too quiet. I just wanted to say hello to Fletcher," Adair said vaguely.

"I'll tell him you called. Oh—are we still on for Saturday lunch?"

"Saturday? Oh, yes, lunch at the cafeteria. Sure. Of course," said Adair.

"Good. Is there . . . anything else I can help you with?" Yvonne asked.

"Anything else? Nah. Just wanted to say hello," Adair forced a cheery tone. "Thanks for calling back."

"Certainly. See you Saturday."

"Okay. Bye." Adair hung up, feeling a little relieved and a lot foolish. She somehow found something to do—although afterward she couldn't remember how she'd spent the time—until it was time to go to bed.

Hours later, the shrill ringing of the telephone startled her out of sound sleep. She squinted at the alarm clock's illuminated dial. "For heaven's sake, it's 1:15." She groped on the nightstand for the receiver. "Hullo," she groaned.

"Hello? Adair? It's Fletcher . . . sorry to wake you." His voice sounded distant and crackly.

Adair sat upright. "Fletcher!"

"Yvonne said you called . . . didn't sound too good . . . (unintelligible) . . . a problem?"

"Oh, Fletcher. No, I—I just missed you."

There was some crackling on the line. "What? I can't hear you, Adair."

"I miss you, Fletcher!" she shouted.

"You miss me? How can you? You haven't even met me!" he laughed. He sounded very tired.

"I love you," she said.

"What? Oh, (deleted) this is useless. I can't hear you at all . . . (interference) . . . call you later. Adair? I miss you, too!" The line went dead.

Adair slowly replaced the receiver and turned on the reading lamp. Wide awake, she grappled with what she had said and why she had said it. Did she really love him? Enough to marry him? If she did, then why was she so afraid?

She eased back down on the pillow and pulled the covers up to her chin. What if they did get married, and he found out he didn't like her? What if she couldn't adjust to his lifestyle? What if . . . he found her shallow and self-centered?

Here he is, globe-trotting to help people, and all I'm concerned about is ballet and Poco's, she thought in chagrin. The more she thought about it, the clearer the ugly truth became: Her little world was too narrow for him. It wasn't just the difference in wealth, it was priorities—she could never spend six months in some god-forsaken third-world country establishing a hospital or something. And if they were married, she could never let him go for that long to do it.

Adair reached up to turn off the reading light. "It will never work, Fletcher," she murmured. "I'm so sorry. It just won't work." She clenched her teeth against the ache in her throat and rolled over to try to go back to sleep.

The following morning was Friday, normally Adair's favorite day of the week as she anticipated the weekend (which always turned out to have been more fun in anticipation than in retrospect). But today the ache that had begun in her throat relocated to her stomach. Two bites of cold cereal nauseated her, so she dumped the rest down the disposal.

At 7:30, she called Fletcher's answering service. "This is Adair Weiss. Don't have Yvonne call me. Just leave her a message: I'm not going through with it. I'm calling it off," she said quickly and hung up.

"That was rude," she chastised herself as she found her purse and car keys. "Just like you," she added spitefully. The telephone rang, and she groaned, "I told them not to have her call!" She considered not answering, but then foresaw the possibility of Yvonne calling her at work. "Hello," she answered dully.

"This is Yvonne. What's going on, Adair?"

"Oh, Yvonne, I've been thinking. It's—it's never going to work between Fletcher and me. We're so different. He has such high ideals—such generosity, or something, and I—I don't think I can be like that."

"Adair, you're not giving yourself much of a chance," Yvonne protested.

"I'm afraid Fletcher wants me to be someone I'm not. He'll want someone who shares an interest in his projects, and I just don't know if I can commit to all that."

"You're quite mistaken. Fletcher's not going to absorb you like some big amoeba. Can't you see that by how restrained he's been?" Yvonne said rather sharply.

"Well—just—tell him I'm not going through with it. Tell him not to call me," Adair blurted.

"I'll tell him, but I think you're making a mistake," Yvonne said regretfully.

"I'm sorry. I really am," Adair said firmly, and hung up.

She left for work feeling cold and stone-hearted. The crisp, glowing autumn morning only deepened her rotten disposition. Adair fought back tears on the expressway. "You can't commit to anyone, can you? Not even to a man who wants to give you the world."

Pulling into the bank parking lot, she had to sit in the car a few minutes to compose herself and blot her eyes. "Hot dogs for you today," she told herself sternly as she entered the bank. But when she thought about losing ballet, she almost broke down again.

As if the day were destined to be bad, Duane called her immediately into his office. "You okay?" he peered at her through his glasses.

"Yes," she insisted, blinking. "What did you want to see me about?"

"Did you see the guy who came to talk to me yesterday? Merle Tannahill?" Duane asked, crossing his arms.

Adair felt unreasonably irritated. "Duane, I was so busy yesterday, I didn't notice any of the thousand people you saw."

"He's a reporter for the *North Dallas Expositor*. He wanted to know the scoop on your relationship with Fletcher Streiker."

"I do not have a relationship with Fletcher Streiker! I've never met the man, and I don't intend to!" Adair exploded.

"Okay! Okay! Settle down! I just wondered if you knew him." Duane motioned her down with both hands.

"No, I don't know either man," she said coolly.

"All right, already. Just checking. Go work the window," he said, exercising some control over the interchange.

"Certainly." Adair stiffly marched to the drive-through window. "Good morning," she bared her teeth at the first customer. "How are you this morning?"

Not an hour later Duane came flying from his office and unceremoniously jerked her from the teller window. "Crystal, take over here," he instructed another teller. "Adair, Mr. Whinnet has ordered you to his office downtown *right now*."

"Why?" she gasped.

"To give you a good-conduct medal," he sneered. "Get going! And if you're fired, come back to tell me. I need a party."

Adair hurried out of the bank in utter humiliation. It was Fletcher, surely, taking revenge. Then she remembered the statements she had prepared for Sharon. Had she made some colossal error? What was it—her job, or Fletcher?

The torture track they called an expressway was even more gnarled than usual. Adair had a full fifty minutes to grip the wheel, bite her nails, mutter, and breathe deeply.

She pulled into the downtown building's parking garage on squealing tires and ran to the elevators. It was a long ride to the thirty-second floor. Adair disembarked on rubbery knees.

The exquisitely dressed receptionist looked up. "My name is Adair Weiss. I'm here to see Charles Whinnet," she said in a strained voice that she did not recognize. The receptionist pointed behind Adair with her gold pen, where Whinnet's door stood open.

"Adair?" he called. "In here."

She wobbled in, almost falling when her high heel caught on the fringe of the Oriental carpet. Whinnet was sitting on the edge of his desk, phone in hand. "I told the decorator that those rugs are impractical for an office. That thing is going. Operator? Yes, we're ready here." He handed Adair the phone, walked out of his office, and closed the door.

Dreading what was coming, she put the receiver to her ear. "Hello?"

"Adair!" The voice made her heartsick. "Yvonne told me you called. What are you saying? I don't understand."

"Fletcher," she started crying. "It's no good. It won't work. I can't do the things you do."

"Do what things? What have I asked you to do?" he demanded.

"Fly all over the world—establishing hospitals—rescuing diplomats—"

He started laughing. "You think I expect all that from you?"

"But you do it! And I'd either have to go with you, or let you go alone for six months at a time!" she cried.

He seemed stung. "You don't give me much credit for understanding a partnership. I won't just drag you along—you'll have a voice in whatever we do. And I also think you don't see your own potential. You're the one who organized cosmetic packets for the teenage mothers at Hope Cottage, remember?"

Adair startled. Actually, she had forgotten about the high school senior girls' project, which had since become a tradition. "How did you know about that?"

"I know *a lot* about you! Would I risk proposing marriage to you if I didn't? Stop and think a minute how threatening this is for *me*—the possibility that after baring my soul to you, you might *still* reject me!"

Adair's tears dried up instantly. She had never looked at it that way before. She had considered herself to be the one taking the greater risk for the minor fact that he would not allow her to see him. But now she saw how distorted her perspective had been.

He certainly had more to lose—and had taken the initiative in risking it.

Further, she saw that she had been more in love with what Fletcher could do for her than with Fletcher himself. But it was Fletcher himself she had to accept or reject. His money, much as it was, had to be secondary.

"Adair? Are you there?"

"Yes," she coughed. "I—I'm just so confused, Fletcher. I need time to think."

"So take the time to think about it. I'm not going to pressure you. I'm not going to call you. When you're ready to talk, you have to call me. I'm just going to wait by the phone."

The image popped into her mind of a corporate jet on standby and a corporation at a standstill while its founder sat by the telephone chewing his nails. "Thanks for not applying pressure!" she laughed wryly.

"I won't apply—*undue* pressure," he amended.

"You told me at the beginning that if I asked you to leave me alone, you would," she reminded him.

"Okay, do you want me to leave you alone?" he asked.

She didn't dare play games with him. "No," she whispered.

"Fine, then. I'll be waiting to hear from you."

"Fletcher. . . ." She longed to repeat what she had said early this morning, when he could not hear her.

"Yes?"

Her courage evaporated. "I'm sorry I disrupted your business. . . . Where are you now?"

He hesitated. "I can't tell you that. But if you need me, Yvonne or Chuck can reach me at this time."

"All right. I'll remember that. Bye, Fletcher."

"Goodbye, Adair."

She tiptoed meekly past the receptionist with the gold pen who watched her curiously from under her styled brows. Adair walked into the elevator and stood at the back. The doors slid shut and it started and stopped at every other floor while Adair stood at the back. Finally it opened on the parking level. Two people hurried off, leaving Adair standing at the back. Then the doors shut and the elevator began ascending again, stopping at each floor to conduct transactions in passengers. Adair stood at the back.

At the thirty-second floor she pushed forward to get off. "Excuse me. Excuse me, please." She walked past the receptionist without seeing her and knocked quietly on Whinnet's door.

"Come on in," he called, and looked up in mild surprise as she entered, closing the door behind her.

"I'm sorry to disturb you again. I know you're busy. I have to get back to work, too. Please call Fletcher and tell him I'll marry him." Then she went back out to the elevator to ride it down again.

A dair returned to The Rivers Bank branch shortly before the lunch hour and resumed her position at the teller window. "Thank you, Crystal. I'll take over now," she smiled.

"You'd better go tell Duane what happened first," Crystal whispered.

"Oh, yes. Guess I'd better." Adair stopped by the rest room to splash water on her face and think before she knocked on Duane's closed door.

"Just a minute," he said importantly. About ninety seconds later he opened the door. "Oh, it's you," he said as though he hadn't already known. "What did Mr. Whinnet want?"

"He reprimanded me, but I'm not fired," she said.

"Yet," Duane added meaningfully.

"Yet," she acknowledged.

"Well, get back to the window and help Crystal. We've got the usual rush out there."

"Okay, Duane," she said meekly, turning.

"That must have been some chewing-out," he observed.

Adair barely shrugged.

She went to the window to take care of the second lane of the Friday-paycheck crowd. As she cashed checks and entered deposits, she kept turning over in her mind what she had just done. The reporters for the *Expositor* wanted to know what her relationship to Streiker was. Would they keel over if they knew she was officially his fiancée? She was about to become the wife and partner of a billionaire, and she couldn't even describe him.

"Sure I can," she murmured after a customer asked if she could give him two tens and two fives. *He's funny, and sweet, and persistent, and smart, and generous, and—lonely.* She felt a little thrill inside at this secret she had to keep bottled up. Soon, very soon, she was going to meet him, and actually become his wife. In a way, it was scary, but she had no desire to go back on her decision.

Duane did not let her off the window to go to lunch until 1:20, at which time she dragged herself across the complex to Poco's. Courtney did not accompany her. Adair had not seen her all day.

At the restaurant, she waved at Jaime and made herself a huge *chalupa* from the buffet bar. As she sat, she glanced around warily for reporters or nosy coworkers, but no one seemed remotely interested in her. With her first bite of chalupa, she suddenly wondered, *What now?*

She stared at an errant tomato on the tablecloth beside her plate. *Okay, I've said yes. What happens now? I should have talked to Fletcher myself.* She finished her lunch and quietly sipped her iced tea, but no brilliant ideas seared themselves in her brain, so she picked up her purse and left.

Strolling across the complex, she suddenly came to herself and said, "Why should I go back to work? I'm marrying a billionaire! I can kiss this place goodbye!" Joyfully, she thought of all the parting lines she could give Duane. She sauntered into the bank grinning.

Duane met her in the lobby. In deference to the customers around, he said in a low voice, "Ms. Weiss, please come to my office." She acquiesced, planning her opening line.

Safely behind his closed door, he turned to her and pleaded,

"Adair, will you please, *please* find another job?" Before she could respond, he went on: "You're so bad with numbers it's incredible. You have no interest in banking and no desire to learn. You're nice to people, but that doesn't make up for all your screw-ups. I want you out of my bank! Since Whinnet won't let me fire you, I'm begging you to make life easier for everyone and go somewhere else. They have openings for receptionists downtown—if you'll apply, I'll give you a glowing recommendation. Please, Adair—get out of my life!"

She blinked rapidly. "What's wrong now?"

He went around his desk and picked up the stack of statements ready to go out. "You entered the wrong code and zeroed out every single account you touched."

Adair blanched. "You're kidding."

"Have a look," he said, handing her the stack.

Adair seized the statements and searched the first one. It showed deposits entered, checks cleared, automatic transactions, interest earned—and a current balance of $0.00. The second was the same, as was the third, fourth, and fifth. By pushing the wrong button one time, she had instructed the computer to clear every account.

It was such an obvious error—it would have been easy to catch if only she had bothered to pay attention. But to let it go undetected through several hundred statements—! That was gross negligence. Sick, Adair laid the stack down. What was it she was going to tell Duane before this happened?

"It can be fixed," she declared faintly. "It can be corrected."

"Yes, but it's going to take someone days to go back over each and every one of these accounts and set them straight," Duane pointed out self-righteously.

Adair leaned over his desk and gathered up all of the statements. She took them out to her computer and sat down with them. One at a time, she called up the account on her screen and located the correct current balance. And one by one she began to prepare new statements.

She worked through her afternoon break and never allowed

her mind to wander from the numbers in front of her. She did not even let herself think of the reactions of hundreds of customers had they received statements like these. Her mind briefly lapsed to consider that it must be a terrible burden on Duane to have to check over everything she did, but even then she would not allow herself any self-pity. She just worked on those statements with her full attention.

About the time she began to feel exhausted, she found that not all of the statements had been zeroed out after all—only those which she had apparently worked on at one particular time. But just to make sure, she continued checking each statement.

Adair noticed when her coworkers began leaving at five o'clock, but she was not finished, so she did not move. Pat paused by her side to lean down and whisper, "I just heard Duane on the phone blasting you to Mr. Whinnet." Adair winced. The last thing she wanted was for Fletcher to hear how irresponsible she had been. That gave her renewed vigor to continue checking statements when her stomach began growling at around six o'clock.

Duane came out of his office soon after that. "It's okay, Adair. You go on home; we'll get the rest out Monday," he said. Adair glanced up at him. If she had not known he was setting her up to be fired, she would gladly have taken him up on it.

"I'm almost done," she said. "You can spot-check these if you like, but I'm sure they're right."

"What? Already?" he said in disbelief. Charlotte brought another matter to his attention, and by the time he had returned to Adair's work area, she was placing the dust cover on her computer and cleaning out her drawer. The corrected statements were neatly stacked nearby.

"You leaving?" he asked curiously.

"Yes." Since she did not have an office, there were not many personal items to be removed. She dumped nail polish bottles, tissues, and loose change into her purse. "I'm resigning, Duane. Thank you for giving me the opportunity to work here." She reached out and shook his hand, and he managed a bemused nod. Then she made her final exit from the bank into the cool evening.

As she unlocked her car, she laughed, "Some sendoff! I was going to tell him a thing or two, wasn't I? Instead, I got a lesson in concentration." She took out a tissue to wipe her eyes. Somehow, it was an appropriate end to her employment here, though not the one she would have choreographed. She turned on her headlights and joined the shimmering snake of cars on the expressway.

━━◆◆◆━━

Once in her apartment, Adair put spaghetti leftovers in the microwave oven, wishing she had an answering machine as she glanced inquiringly toward the bedroom telephone.

"Oh well, he knows where to find me." She sat at the table with her plate of spaghetti and liberally piled parmesan cheese on top. Then as she wound the pasta around her fork, she began to imagine how she would meet her intended. Wouldn't it be a scream if he just rang the doorbell? *Hi, Adair. I'm Fletcher. Let's go get married.* Adair laughed out loud, then said, "My goodness, where will we get married? I suppose it doesn't have to be in a church, but will it be a big formal affair?" The thought dismayed her. "Imagine the publicity *that* would generate. No, I bet he'd rather make it small and private, and so would I."

She finished her spaghetti while keeping an ear tuned for the telephone. She washed up the few dishes, then went through her little apartment, straightening it. She knew she would be moving. "Goodbye, little place," she sighed happily. "Thank goodness there's only a few months left on the lease—" then she caught herself and laughed. "As if it made any difference! Fletcher could buy this building out of petty cash!"

She freshened up in the bathroom (in case she had to leave quickly) and then gravitated toward the telephone again. Stretching out on the bed, she propped up a pillow behind her back and picked up a month-old magazine.

Although she did not feel tired, the long hours at the bank today began to have their effect. The words on the page grew fuzzy and Adair closed her eyes. A little while later, half-asleep, she turned off the nightstand light and stuck her stocking feet under the covers.

Later, Adair startled awake and sat up. Her eyes burned from the mascara and her dress was pathetically wrinkled. "I'd better change," she reacted. "I must have dozed off. I wonder how long I slept?" She picked up the nightstand clock. "Oh, it's only 8:30." She started to go to the bathroom when a troubling suspicion began to form. There was no window in her bedroom, so she went out to the living room and saw sunlight streaming from the kitchen window.

"It's morning!" she screeched. "It's Saturday morning! I slept all night! And . . . he didn't call all night."

She stood dejected in the morning sunlight. He had not called all night. Had he gotten the message? Or had he changed his mind? She forlornly pulled her hair back off her forehead.

"I'm supposed to meet Yvonne for lunch today," she remembered. "She'll know. Yvonne will know if he's gotten the message." She headed for the bathroom, then stopped in the doorway. "I can't wait until lunch."

She went back to the bed and pulled Fletcher's file out from the nightstand drawer. Finding the Whinnets' number, she dialed it and chewed on her nails. "Whinnet residence," someone answered.

"Hi, this is Adair Weiss. Is Charles in, please?"

"Just a minute, honey."

And a minute later Charles was on the line. "Hello, Adair! Are you married yet?"

"Uh, no—that's why I was calling. I didn't hear from Fletcher all night long. Did he . . . get my message?"

"Yes, I gave it to him personally," Whinnet said.

"Oh . . . well, what did he say?" Adair asked.

"He was a little surprised, just like I was, but he took your word for it."

"Well, then, I was wondering why he hasn't called or anything," Adair went on.

"I imagine he's making arrangements. Don't worry about him

backing out, Adair. He's gone to too much trouble to do that."

"Oh, okay," she attempted a self-conscious laugh.

"You'll hear something soon. Oh—and our best wishes to you."

"Thank you. Bye." Slightly encouraged, she selected one of her best dresses to wear downtown—one she seldom wore because it had to be dry-cleaned.

When she got to the Streiker Building and entered the twentieth-floor cafeteria, the first thing she did was scan the place for familiar faces. Not seeing anyone she knew, she absent-mindedly selected a seafood plate from the serving line and sat at one of the few empty tables. Generally, the crowd looked to be Streiker employees who had come downtown to clean up their desks over the weekend. She began eating, trying to look nonchalant.

A few minutes later a chic, fortyish woman approached her table, tray in hand. "I think *everybody* had the same idea of Saturday morning catch-up!" she exclaimed. "It's getting *crowded* in here! Do you mind if I share your table?"

"No, not at all," Adair smiled, making room for her.

"I promise to scoot if someone more interesting shows up." The woman gathered her full denim skirt and sat. She wore fashionable clunky earrings and matching necklace, designer eyeglasses, and long pink fingernails. Her short streaked hair was swept up and her slightly lined face showed off a fading summer tan.

"I'm bookkeeper Yvonne Fay." She held out her hand over her tray. "Ms.—?"

"Adair Weiss," she responded, shaking Yvonne's hand and trying not to smile. Yvonne had assumed such a different personality from the crackerjack assistant on the telephone that Adair had not immediately recognized her voice. *This is one shrewd cookie*, Adair thought.

"Well! I'm so pleased to meet you! I wish you could meet my nephew. *Such* a nice young man. He called me this morning and told me he's getting married! Well, I was just so thrilled!"

"Really?" Adair looked around, trying to maintain a facade of disinterest over a pounding heart.

"Yes," Yvonne prattled on, "he was so excited, and so busy trying to get everything in order, that he hasn't even taken the time to call his fiancée. Isn't that ridiculous? I told him that was inexcusable. Don't you think so?"

"I guess so," Adair responded, dipping a shrimp in red sauce. She felt that the color of her face probably matched that of the sauce well enough so there would be no problem if she fainted face down in it.

"Well, I think it is." Yvonne briskly shook down a packet of artificial sweetener for her iced tea. "I asked him when the big event would take place, and he said—now, isn't this just like a man—he said, 'As soon as possible.'"

"Do tell," Adair yawned, but had to close her mouth so she would not throw up from nervous excitement.

"That's right," said Yvonne. She adjusted her glasses and looked over at Adair's plate. "My, that shrimp looks delicious. My nephew loves seafood. He was born in Hawaii, you know."

"That's nice," Adair said.

"I certainly think so. I've been there three times, and it was just wonderful. I think the most romantic thing would be a honeymoon there, don't you?"

For a moment Adair could not reply. She looked down at her plate and Yvonne paused, sensing that she was close to giving away their little game. "Actually, I never really cared for seafood," Adair said abruptly. "But I think under the right circumstances I could learn to like it."

Yvonne's crinkly blue eyes twinkled. "That's the spirit!" She ate her stuffed zucchini over small talk about the heat, the way fall should be, and the color of the aspens in Colorado.

"I've got to remember to pick up my dry cleaning," Yvonne said suddenly as she penciled a note to herself on her lunch ticket. Then she laughed, "Oh, dear! Silly me, that's my bill. And I can't even read it. That's what I get for leaving my bifocals downstairs. Can you look at this and tell me what I owe for lunch?" She handed her tab to Adair.

Adair looked down where Yvonne had written just below the total, *I need your apt. key.*

"You owe $8.19," Adair told her, handing back the tab while reaching into her purse with her other hand. As she unclipped her key from the key ring, she debated, "Well, I can't decide what I should do after lunch. I wonder whether I should go shopping, or to a friend's house . . ." she trailed off.

Yvonne, who was digging around in her own purse, looked up and said, "If you ask me, I think you look tired. I think you should go home and rest." Then, bringing out some bills: "Oh, for pete's sake, all I have is eight dollars. I am so embarrassed to ask, but—do you have any change?"

"Here." Adair placed the key in her hand, marveling at Yvonne's skill at charades.

"You're a dear. Thanks so much. I will certainly pay you back." Covering the key with one hand, Yvonne briskly erased the penciled note as she talked.

"Forget it," smiled Adair. "I enjoyed your company."

"You're so sweet." Yvonne gathered up her belongings. "I'd still like for you to meet my nephew."

"Who knows? Maybe someday I will." Adair watched as Yvonne bustled to the front counter to pay her tab. Adair sipped her tea down to the ice, then dabbed her mouth and pulled out her lipstick. *Now how am I supposed to go home and rest without my key?* she wondered. *Oh well.*

As she got up with her ticket and pushed in her chair, she happened to make eye contact with a man at a nearby table. His gaze would have disturbed her had she not been so confident that even if he had overheard her entire conversation with Yvonne, he still would not know what it meant. She deliberately looked away and took her ticket to the cashier.

She was not pleased that he got up and stood behind her in line, but she pretended not to notice. He was about her height, with permed hair and small eyes. "Excuse me. Miss?" he said.

Adair languidly looked back. "What?"

"Do you work here?"

"No." She turned back around to pay her tab.

"Oh. I thought I'd seen you here before," he said. Adair, concentrating on writing out a check, did not answer. "I'm looking for the office of the president of this company," he continued conversationally, handing her his business card. "The directory lists offices for everyone connected with the Streiker Corporation except its president. I find that strange. You wonder how a CEO runs a company without an office. But there is a penthouse, yet no one listed for that. Isn't that something?"

Adair turned long enough to say coolly, "I don't know anything about it," then walked rapidly toward an open elevator.

While he was paying his lunch bill, she was jabbing the "close door" button on the elevator. Just as he was coming around the corner, the doors finally slid shut and Adair let out her breath.

Only then did she look at the card he had given her. Merle Tannahill, reporter for the *Expositor*. "I should have known," she muttered. "The one who asked Duane about me. Yvonne sure was right." She recalled Whinnet saying that this building was Fletcher's headquarters when he was in town, so it stood to reason that his office was in the penthouse. Apparently Tannahill guessed that she had been there. It was scary when others assumed she knew more than she actually did.

In the parking garage, she wasted no time getting to her car and getting out of there. It had begun to drizzle, and the streets were slick with a film of oil and water. Adair stopped worrying about reporters as she negotiated slippery streets and impatient drivers.

***

By the time she had pulled into her apartment complex, the drizzle had blossomed into rain. She felt under her seat for her umbrella, then dismally remembered it hanging from a coat peg in the break room at the bank. She covered her head with her purse and ran to the manager's first-floor apartment. While she rang the doorbell three or four times, shifts in the wind swept rain under the awning to soak her backside completely.

She had almost given up when the manager finally opened the door a crack. "Hi, Lloyd! I've lost my key. Please come up and let me into my apartment." She tried to smile, wet and shivering.

"Land sakes, Adair, where did you lay it now? You got to hold on to your things. Your insurance won't pay you a dime if somebody breaks in using your key. I've told you that a hunnerd times," he chided her all the way up to her apartment.

"Sorry, Lloyd; it won't happen again. I can get it back—" As soon as she said it she knew it was a mistake.

He gave her a long, disapproving look as he opened her door with his master key. "You young people just invite trouble when you hand out your key to any nice-lookin' Tom, Dick, or Harry. Well, don't you come cryin' to me when you get raped and murdered." With that bit of encouragement, he hustled back down the steps.

Adair sighed, forcing her door shut against the wind. She shed wet shoes and hose all the way back to the bathroom, where she vigorously rubbed her hair with a towel. Then she gazed in despair at her pleated dress, which the rain had reduced to a shriveled rag. In a fit of temper, Adair wadded it up and threw it in the corner of the bathroom.

She pulled on her ratty blue chenille robe and shuffled to the kitchen to fix something to eat. She had been too nervous to eat much an hour ago ("I don't even *like* shrimp"), so she was already hungry again. She pulled out a jar of peanut butter and a box of crackers and sat down at the table.

"Why am I depressed?" she exclaimed. Yvonne had confirmed that Fletcher was acting on her acceptance. Surely she would be hearing something soon.

"Okay," she resolved, munching on a cracker, "I have to take for granted that I'm going to marry Fletcher pretty soon, when he gets everything—whatever that is—set up. So . . . knowing that I'm not going to be here much longer, what do I need to do before I leave?"

She consumed half a dozen peanut butter crackers while she

thought about this. Then she wiped her hands on a dishtowel and, eyeing the dingy floor, conceded, "I need to clean this place up for the next tenant." So, even though she hated it, she tightened the belt of her robe and started doing housework. She washed the dishes, cleaned the counter tops, swept and mopped the vinyl floor, vacuumed, cleaned the windows, dusted, and—after fortifying herself with a cup of coffee and some stale cookies—cleaned the bathroom.

After three full hours she stood back and surveyed the results. "There! It's as clean as can be, considering I haven't moved out yet. . . . Why, of course! That's why he needed the key—to let the movers in. I won't be here!"

She began to pace the floor. "Now, I should pack. I can't pack all of my things, of course, just a few clothes, and my makeup and hair dryer. . . ." She pulled a suitcase out from under her bed and packed as she would for a weekend fling.

"Now what?" she debated, looking out the window at the lengthening shadows on the building nearby. "Should I change? Put on something appropriate for the evening?" That led to the ridiculous mental image of herself sitting around the dinky apartment all night in an evening gown. Then she considered, "What if . . . I don't hear from him all night?" The thought was extremely depressing.

To cheer herself up, she got out her new dance gear. Trying on her toe shoes for the fifth time, she began to think, "At the rate I spend money, I'm liable to spend my tuition before Madame gets back. I'd better go ahead and write her a check for the first month." Which she did, and took it to the corner mailbox. When she got back she even balanced her checkbook in anticipation of a drastic change in its numbers.

That completed, she sat at the kitchen table and watched the buildings fade into the night. Then she got up and went back to the bedroom. She practiced braiding her hair in French braids, then took it all down. She painted her nails as she listened to the radio, but then got bored with it and turned it off. Restlessly, she plopped onto the bed and pulled out Fletcher's file folder from the nightstand drawer.

Flipping through it halfheartedly, she stopped at one article about the completion of a new distribution center for one of the Streiker companies that Fletcher himself oversaw. It said, in part,

> Critics initially charged that the corporation was dragging its feet in starting work on the center, and taking unnecessarily long to schedule contractors and screen applications. However, construction was completed on time and on budget. . . . Six months after opening, when Mr. Streiker invited comments in a company publication, the only substantial complaint about the center which surfaced was that it had filled positions too quickly for all applicants to be fairly considered. Mr. Streiker responded: "As long as some of you are complaining that I dragged my feet and others are complaining that I moved too quickly, then my timing must have been just about perfect."

When Adair finally closed the folder and looked up at the time, it was after ten o'clock. She replaced the folder in the nightstand. Then, on second thought, she put it in her suitcase. She washed the careful makeup job off her face in weary disappointment, put on her nightgown, and climbed under the covers.

Upon awaking the following morning, Adair did not yawn or stretch or roll over or move. She just stared at the wall beside her bed—and might have gone on doing so for hours, except that she had to get up to go to the bathroom.

Once the hard part was accomplished—getting out of bed—she poured herself some cold cereal. Draining the last few ounces of milk from the carton into the bowl, she observed, "That finishes off the milk." Before tossing the carton, she noticed the expiration date: October 24. That was today.

She munched the cereal as she read the box: "FREE!!! Inside this box!!! Super neat diamond* ring!!!" In tiny letters, the companion to the asterisk noted, "*Simulated." Adair suddenly put down her spoon and dug through the box until she found the little plastic package. She ripped it open and let out a mock whistle of admiration at the round-cut plastic gem and gold-toned metal alloy. "Look at the size of that baby! It's got to be a couple of carats, at least." Placing it on her finger, she cooed, "Oh, Fletcher, you shouldn't have. I know I'm worth it, but really—you shouldn't have." She left it on her finger while she ate, stopping periodically to hold her hand up and admire it.

When she finished eating, she rinsed out the bowl and threw on a sweatshirt and jeans without showering, then ran downstairs to get a Sunday *Sun-Times* out of the newspaper rack. After putting on a pot of coffee, she spread out on the couch to read the paper.

She read everything, including sections she did not normally take the time to look at: sports, business, even the classifieds. The Sunday Homes section in particular attracted her attention. The featured Home of the Week was a mansion in Bent Tree, three years old, with over ten thousand square feet—fifteen hundred of them in the master suite closets alone. Adair leaned over the color pictures. "Their closets are half again as big as this whole apartment," she muttered. The house was custom decorated with designer wall coverings and imported marble. And as a special incentive, the bargain purchase price of $3 million included a year's worth of lawn care, valued at $650 a month. "That's more than I pay in rent," she whispered.

Troubled, Adair laid that section aside. Did Fletcher live like that? He could if he wanted to. Could she ever be comfortable with such a lifestyle? *Should* she be? She did not really know how to answer those questions. Part of the problem was her difficulty visualizing herself married to a billionaire. Her disbelieving, cynical side would not accept the assurances of Yvonne or Charles that it was actually going to happen.

When she had finished reading the newspaper, she found a forgotten chicken pot pie in the freezer and stuck it in the oven. "One thing about being rich—it sure would be nice not to have to scrounge around for something to eat every four or five hours," she conceded. But by this time, if the telephone rang she would be surprised.

Adair passed the afternoon in a blank state of mind, eating and lounging. She ran the newspaper down to the recycling bin on the corner, but otherwise did not leave her apartment.

By early evening she was beginning to feel grungy, so she showered and put on fresh clothes. She packed a few additional items in her suitcase, not for one minute believing that she would need it. Then she haphazardly cleaned out the refrigerator. After she threw out all the spoiled, wilted, and stale food, it looked woefully abandoned. As she wiped off the shelves, she observed, "If I don't leave soon, I'll have to go to the grocery store." As much as she disliked food shopping, that was a pretty grim forecast.

She found her way back to the hard couch in the tiny living room and sat and stared. She wasn't really thinking of anything in particular, nor was she waiting with any real expectancy; she was just taking up space until it was time to go to bed.

She roused herself at one point to look at the clock. "It's 9:25," she announced. "Time to go to bed." And because she felt exhausted, that is what she did.

Before drifting off she murmured, "I should have saved the employment section. I may need it since I quit my job. . . ."

The jangling of the telephone jarred Adair from sleep, and she instinctively turned to look at the clock. It was 8:20. She grabbed the receiver and mumbled, "Hello."

"Uh, hello, Adair. Duane. What are you doing this morning?"

Adair sat up groggily. "Why?"

"Well, uh, let me be straight with you, okay? We've got three tellers out sick this morning and I have examiners coming in half an hour. We need you to come in to work right away," Duane said.

"I quit last Friday, just like you wanted me to," Adair reminded him.

"I know, I know. Tell you what. If you'll just come in right now, you can keep your job and I'll throw in a raise. If you don't want this job I'll recommend you to anyone I know downtown. Will you please just come in *now?*" he pleaded.

Adair sighed, "I'll be right in."

"Thank you!" he exclaimed, and hung up.

Adair gulped down a piece of buttered toast and brushed her teeth, excusing herself from a shower since she had taken one the night before. She put on an old hound's-tooth dress that she hated but was too frugal to throw out. Then she ran down to her car in the brilliant October sunshine.

She paused at the car door, remembering her suitcase. "Oh, I won't need that. I'm just going in to work for a few hours. Besides, I can't get back into the apartment with the door locked."

She paused again. "Did I lock the door?" She could not remember. "Better check." She ran back up the stairs and found the door unlocked. She locked it, but before closing it, remembered again about the suitcase. "Oh, for cryin' out loud," she muttered. To silence the mental nagging, she ran in and retrieved the suitcase before locking herself out. Then she threw it in the trunk of her car and proceeded to the bank.

Twenty minutes later she pulled into the parking lot around the line of cars waiting at the one open drive-through window. She ran inside and switched on the green light at the second lane. The other teller was almost frantic. A near collision ensued between two cars as the motorists jumped over to the newly opened lane. A third car got to her window first, and Adair began her first transaction of the new day. "Good morning. How are you today?"

During transaction number three, Duane came over and patted her on the shoulder. "Thanks," he remarked. "I'll be with the boys in the office."

Adair glanced behind him at the suits and briefcases waiting in the lobby. "I didn't know we had examiners coming."

"I didn't either. This is a surprise from the higher-ups," he growled.

Nodding, Adair turned back to her customer. "That's $30.52. Have a nice day."

After seeing Adair arrive, the other teller, a new girl named Marti, relaxed and began to handle the customers more confidently. Before long, Adair was complimenting her on her style.

"Thanks, but I'm just copying you," Marti confessed.

Adair grinned and thought, *She seems nice. Too bad I won't be able to get to know her.* As they worked through the flood of customers together, Adair thought, *Well, why shouldn't I stay? This isn't so bad. And Duane promised me a raise for coming in today!*

She felt a tap on her shoulder, and turned around to see a short young man in an expensive suit. "Ms. Weiss?" he asked. She nodded. "Will you come with me?"

"Who are you?" she said, annoyed over the interruption. "Was that two twenties and three tens you wanted?" she asked the customer in the drive-through.

"Yeah," he answered. She sent the drawer out with the cash.

"I'm Bob McIlvoy, assistant vice-president to Charles Whinnet," the young executive said importantly. "*Now* will you come with me?"

Adair stared briefly at him, then glanced over at Marti. "That's okay; I can handle it now. Thanks, Adair," she said.

With raised brows, Adair got up to go with McIlvoy. As he took her outside, she said, "I need to tell Duane I'm leaving."

"Don't worry about him," McIlvoy answered. He opened the passenger door of a new Mercedes, and Adair got in.

When he had seated himself and started the engine, she asked, "Where are we going?"

"I'm supposed to run you on an errand to—" he let go of the wheel with one hand to draw a piece of paper from his breast pocket "—the Wyrie Medical Center."

"Why?" Adair asked, alarmed.

"I don't know. Don't you?" he asked, glancing down his nose at her as they approached a stoplight.

Her heart began to pound a little harder. "Who sent you?"

"Mr. Whinnet, of course."

━━◆◆━━

Adair sat very still, gripping the armrest with one hand. She didn't know where the Wyrie Medical Center was, so she tried to pay attention to the streets they passed, but as soon as McIlvoy turned from one street to another, she forgot the name of the street they had just been on. She could not seem to hold her thoughts together.

Finally McIlvoy pulled up to a comfortably aging white building. Consulting his paper again, he said, "You go to the eighth floor—suite 803. I'm supposed to wait for you here. Look, how long do you think this will take?" He did not seem enchanted with his role of chauffeur.

"I've no idea," Adair replied, bewildered.

She entered the terrazzo lobby and stepped into an elevator with a mother and a crying baby, who got off on the third floor. At the eighth level, she rounded the corner to suite 803—the office of Dr. Morton P. Diehl.

There were three people in the waiting room, which was clean and airy, but not new. It was decorated in the earth tones that had been popular a generation ago. "May I help you?" asked the receptionist behind a window.

Adair quietly told her, "My name is Adair Weiss."

The receptionist looked down at her appointment book. "Weiss, Weiss . . . oh, yes. Have a seat, please."

She sat, smiling nervously at a bearded man in jeans beside her. Shortly a man in a white coat with a clipboard came to the door and summoned, "Adair Weiss." She got up and followed him down a corridor to an examining room.

"Have a seat, Adair," he said with the air of authority that technicians like to project.

She sat warily on the examining table. *I'm not taking my clothes off, buster,* she thought darkly. But when he began taking out syringes, she exclaimed, "What are you doing?"

He looked up. "Aren't you here for some blood work?"

"Blood work? No!"

"Are you Adair Weiss?"

"Yes," she said.

"Well, Dr. Diehl has ordered blood tests and a series of inoculations. You going on a trip?" he asked amiably, and suddenly Adair understood.

"Who called Dr. Diehl?" she asked.

"I don't know. I just follow the doctor's instructions. Roll up your left sleeve for me, please."

Adair did as he asked and squeezed her eyes shut while he drew blood. Then he loaded another syringe and gave her a shot. She promptly felt weak and dizzy. "You might feel a little puny over the next few weeks. Shouldn't be anything to worry about. But if you start running a fever over 102 degrees, give us a call."

"Thanks," she muttered, gingerly rolling down her sleeve. "Can I go now?"

"Wait outside a minute, please," he said.

Adair made it out to the waiting room and sat limply. About fifteen minutes later the technician came back out and handed her a manila envelope. "Lab results. You're clean," he blithely announced to the entire waiting room.

Adair seized the envelope and hurried out to the elevator. Leaning on the wall as the elevator descended, she looked at the envelope. It had a white address label with her name typed on it. *Why did he give me this?* she wondered. *They never give patients their test results.*

She met McIlvoy at his Mercedes, where he had taken off his coat to wait. The morning was beginning to get warm. "Take me someplace where there aren't any needles," she said, flopping down in the seat.

"The next stop'll be worse," he said, looking over his paper again.

What now? Afraid to ask, she clutched the manila envelope so tightly that her hand started to sweat. But then she remembered the person behind these errands, and she relaxed.

A fifteen-minute drive took them to an upscale office plaza. McIlvoy pulled up to a mauve brick building and told her, "Harbeson Bayles, fifth floor. And would you make it quicker this time?"

"I'll try," she promised, climbing out of the car. This building housed the law offices of five partners, one of whom was Bayles. On the fifth floor, she barely noticed the excruciatingly elegant gray interior, which normally would have intimidated her. Today, however, since she had no idea why she was here except that

Fletcher had arranged it, she entered confidently ignorant. She told the mature, unsmiling receptionist, "I am Adair Weiss, here to see Mr. Bayles."

She sat as the sentry pursed her lips and paged Bayles over the telephone. A moment later he came out, buttoning his suit coat. A fiftyish man with an alert face and comfortable air, he held out his hand as Adair stood. "Ms. Weiss, I am Harb Bayles. Please come back to my office. Would you like some coffee? Anything to drink?" he inquired, pausing by the receptionist's desk.

"Water, thanks," Adair requested.

Bayles motioned to the woman, who got up from her desk to bring Adair a paper cup of water without looking directly at her. Then Bayles directed Adair into his office and shut the door.

"Ms. Weiss, please sit down." He pointed toward an overstuffed leather chair. "Is that from Dr. Diehl?" He reached for the manila envelope, which she reluctantly surrendered.

"Mr. Bayles, I don't really know why I'm here," she said.

"Oh?" He looked up from the contents of the envelope as he settled behind a large desk. "Perhaps you should know that I am Mr. Streiker's personal legal representative."

"Ah," she said. The situation indeed became clearer. She waited tensely as he perused the papers.

"Uh-huh. Okay, very good," he said, returning the papers to the envelope and laying it on his desk. "Everything appears to be in order. Now, I have something for you to sign. . . ."

He began shuffling through another pile on his desk, and Adair thought, *I'll bet you do. The old prenuptial agreement, huh? I should have seen it coming.*

"Here it is." Bayles handed her a single sheet. It was an application for a marriage license, all completed—even her social security number and date of birth were there—except for her signature. She also saw an illegible signature above the typed name of Fletcher Streiker.

"He's already signed it," she murmured.

"Hmm? Oh, Mr. Streiker? Yes. With the required blood tests,

all that remains is the marriage license," Bayles confirmed.

"And . . . when do we get that?" she asked hesitantly.

"I don't know. When you sign that," he nodded at the application, "you're to take it and your medical report with you."

"To where?" she asked.

"Wherever you happen to be going, I'm sure," Bayles responded with a wry grin, leaning back in his swivel chair and clasping his hands behind his head.

"I would think somebody's personal lawyer would know all this," she blurted in frustration.

He rocked easily. "Well, Mr. Streiker is not your average somebody. He calls the shots, and anyone who works for him has to live with that. Frankly, I don't mind. It takes a lot of heat off me. By the way, once the marriage goes on the books, it becomes a matter of public record, you know."

The implications of this fact did not become apparent to Adair right away. *This is it. Are you sure you want to do this?* she thought, gazing down at the paper. Bayles held a pen in view without forcing it on her. Adair stood and laid the application on his desk. Then she took his pen and signed it. As he took up the paper and put it in the envelope with the blood work-up, Adair wondered how much he was being paid to procure that signature. She waited for more papers to follow.

Bayles handed her the envelope and said, "Thank you very much, Ms. Weiss. It's been a pleasure to meet you." He shook her free hand.

"That's it? That's all?" she said, shocked.

"That's all I was authorized to ask of you," he said.

"But—when can I meet Fletcher?"

"I'm sure he'll tell you that himself." His cheerful acceptance of so much uncertainty rankled Adair.

She began to pace, unnerved at the way events were unfolding. "Have you met him?" she asked.

"Not face-to-face. But we communicate frequently, and he has invested me with rather broad authority concerning his affairs. I'm sure that's because," he slowed for emphasis, "I always do *exactly* what he asks of me."

Adair did not really hear him. "What do you think of—all this?" she asked vaguely, meaning, *What do you think of me?*

"I think you are an incredibly fortunate young woman," he promptly replied. "I hope you appreciate that."

Adair nodded slowly. "Thank you, Mr. Bayles."

"Have a good day, Ms. Weiss."

Adair went back to McIlvoy's Mercedes. He revved the engine and swung out onto the freeway. Obviously, he was getting tired and impatient with this business—but oh, if he only knew for whom he was running errands.

Adair looked down at her watch. "It's past lunch time," she hinted.

"We could stop someplace, but I bet Mrs. Whinnet will have something for you," he answered distractedly, watching his rear-view mirror for an opening to change lanes.

"Is that where we're going now?" she asked.

"Yes—no, I have to take you back to the branch to get your car. You're to go straight from there to their house," he asserted.

"After work?" she wondered.

"If I were you, I'd go *now*," he answered testily. "Don't you even know what you're doing?"

"Yes," she nodded. She was surprised at how calm she felt, then attributed that to persistent unbelief. It was still hard to imagine that anything would come of all this.

When he let her off in the parking lot next to her car, she leaned in his window and said, "Thanks, Bob. You'll find out what it all means pretty soon." He shrugged as he pulled away.

But when Adair sat in her car, it hit her: *a matter of public record.* If it *did* happen, she would not need to put an announcement in the paper—anyone looking in the record books would find the reclusive philanthropist's name attached to hers. Then what would she say? What would she do?

Obviously, she could not continue to work at the bank, even

if she wanted. She laid the manila envelope in the passenger seat and started the engine.

Glancing back at the bank, she said, "You begged me to leave, Duane. I hope you can do without me now." And she pulled out onto the freeway.

———◆———

Adair was so preoccupied that she took the wrong exit off the freeway and had to circle back and drive around until she found the street that led to the Whinnets' cul-de-sac. By the time she pulled into their circular driveway, she was nervous and exhausted from a twenty-minute drive that had been stretched into forty.

She walked past a shiny black Rolls Royce parked in the drive. Poised to ring the doorbell, she suddenly gasped and whirled back to look at the car. "It's—his! He's here!" She pressed the doorbell and stood on the porch clutching the envelope.

Alicia answered the door. "Why, hello, Adair. What a nice surprise. Do come in," she said loudly.

"I thought—I was supposed to—" Adair began.

"I know," Alicia whispered. "We believe the house is being watched."

Alicia led her into the gorgeous white drawing room. Charles turned to greet Adair as a balding man in bifocals put down his glass of brandy and rose from the couch. He had a portly, settled air, and regarded her in a most businesslike fashion.

Adair gazed at him and felt a sudden shock of extreme disappointment. He just wasn't what she had expected at all from her blind brushes with Panny. The way he looked was radically different from the way Panny had looked on his motorcycle—and also quite different from how he had felt to her in the darkened conference room at the bank. "Fletcher?" she said weakly.

Laughter erupted around her. The balding man chuckled, "I'm tempted to say yes, Ms. Weiss."

Charles explained, "Adair, let me introduce District Judge Everett Amlin." The judge cordially held out his hand.

Adair was sure her face was purple. "How—how do you do?" she stammered, accepting his hand.

"Very well, thank you." He shook her hand gravely, then took the envelope from her grasp. "Let's see what you have here."

Adair stood like a schoolgirl waiting for a grade while he drew out the papers and scrutinized them.

"Would you like something to drink?" Alicia asked her quietly.

"Huh? No, thanks." Just the smell of the judge's brandy made Adair's stomach churn.

"Well, sit down," Charles insisted, pointing to the couch. "You're not in court."

The judge smiled at her over his glasses and she weakly showed her teeth. Alicia sat next to her and took hold of her clenched hands, stroking them in a soothing manner.

"Very good. Everything's here," Judge Amlin declared, placing the envelope in his leather portfolio. He withdrew another paper and a small book. "I believe we're all set, then. Charles, you stand here, Ms. Weiss here, and Mrs. Whinnet to her right." They lined up as instructed in front of the judge.

He continued, "All right. Let me find it here . . . there we are. Now—Do you, Adair Weiss, take Fletcher Streiker to be your law-fully wedded husband, to have and to hold, in sickness and in health, forsaking all others, till death do you part?"

"Huh? What?" Adair looked disconcertedly behind her. "He's not here! How can we get married when he's not here?"

The Whinnets looked at each other. Judge Amlin replied, "I'm sorry, I thought this was explained to you. You are marrying Mr. Streiker by proxy. Mr. Whinnet is standing in for him."

"But when do I get to *see* him?" Adair wailed.

"As soon as he gets here," Alicia said urgently. "He's literally in the air right now."

"Can't we wait till he comes?" Adair pleaded.

"Ms. Weiss, I have to be back in my chambers in"—the judge consulted his watch—"exactly twenty-eight minutes. If I am going to do this ceremony, it has to be now. So, do you take Fletcher

98

Streiker as your husband?"

Adair's eyes began to water with anxiety. "You mean I have to marry him without even seeing him?"

The judge took off his bifocals. "You don't have to marry him at all. But if you don't take this opportunity, I don't know when we can arrange another."

Adair turned for help to the Whinnets, who both seemed to be holding their breath. "Is he really nice?" she asked helplessly.

Alicia started to say something but Charles forestalled her. "He is everything we said he was," he answered tersely.

"Ms. Weiss, for the last time: Do you take Fletcher Streiker as your husband?" the judge asked, his pale blue eyes fixed on her.

Adair trembled and gulped, "Yes. Yes, I do."

"And Charles Whinnet, as proxy for Fletcher Streiker, do you take Adair Weiss as your lawfully wedded wife, to have and to hold, in sickness and in health, forsaking all others, till death do you part?"

"He does," Charles said.

"Then I pronounce you husband and wife," the judge finished quickly, closing his book.

<hr />

The Whinnets seemed to let down in relief; Adair stood in shock. The judge signed the marriage license he had taken from his portfolio and handed it to Adair. It was dated today; it was recorded in the record books as of today. Adair then realized just how much Fletcher had been doing while she was waiting for him to call her over the weekend.

"Best wishes to you, my dear," Judge Amlin nodded to her.

"Thank you," she answered faintly.

"I must get back to the courthouse now—" she heard him say as Charles ushered him to the front door. "Is she going to be all right?" the judge inquired, glancing back at the lone newlywed.

"Adair? Oh, sure. She's tough," Charles said confidently.

"She'll have to be, now. I'll extend my congratulations to Fletcher."

"Good, Everett. Talk to you later," Charles said.

When he came back into the drawing room, Alicia asked eagerly, "Well? Have you got it?"

"It? Oh, yes, *it*. Yes, I have it," Charles replied, reaching into his pants pocket. He pulled out a small black velvet box, which he handed to Adair. "It's your wedding ring."

Adair opened it. Out flashed the fire of the most beautiful diamond she had ever seen. It was a round cut, set on a slender white gold band. She took it out with shaking hands and slid it on her finger. It was a perfect fit. She tried to hold her hand still, but the trembling made colors explode from the stone. Then she remembered the toy ring from the cereal box she had derisively donned—it was just this size and shape! Only, this one was *real*. It had really happened.

She let herself down to the couch. "What were you going to say, when I asked if Fletcher was nice?" she asked dreamily, gazing at her ring.

Alicia inhaled. "I was going to shout, 'He's *wonderful*. Just *do it!*' But Charles had warned me not to say anything to coerce you."

"Fletch's instructions," added Charles. "He strongly felt that this had to be solely your decision."

Adair slowly nodded, "After I told you yes, on Friday, there were still any number of points—at the doctor's office, at the lawyer's—when I could have backed out."

"But now you're committed, you understand," Charles said.

"Sure. What's the problem?" Adair asked, wondering at his strained tone.

"This, to begin with." Charles ever so slightly drew back the window draperies. Adair peeked out at cars lining the street and a half-dozen people with cameras standing on the lawn. The doorbell rang. "I'm afraid word of your marriage is out."

"So soon? How?" Adair exclaimed.

"It's already on the books," Charles reminded her.

That's right, Adair reflected, furtively watching the growing crowd. *It was recorded as a fact before I ever said my vows to the judge.*

What if I had refused? But I didn't. And there it is.

The good-looking, substantial maid whom Adair had seen before came in. "Mr. Whinnet, can I do what I'd like to all those rubbernecks tramplin' your grass?"

"I doubt it, Jackie, but why don't you move Mrs. Streiker's car into our garage? She'll be staying with us for a little while."

"Fine. Got your keys, honey?" Jackie imperiously held out her hand.

"Yes—" As Adair took her keys from her purse, she slipped the marriage license inside. Then she remembered, "I have an overnight case in the trunk."

"Good thinking," Charles praised her foresight.

Jackie took the keys and stalked out the front door. She brushed aside the throng of reporters and started up the RX-7 with a roar. A few scrambled to get out of the way while Jackie took off on squealing tires toward the three-car garage at the rear of the house.

"She's rather—decisive, isn't she?" asked Adair, watching through a slender aperture in the curtains.

"Jackie could manhandle Godzilla," Charles said with satisfaction. "I'd put her to work at the bank if I didn't need her here so much."

Adair smiled. "She'd make mincemeat of Duane." Then, realizing the folly of maligning her boss, she amended, "Today, anyway, as frazzled as he was with the examiners' coming."

Charles smiled mysteriously, so that Adair asked, "How is it that they happened to come today, of all days?"

He replied, "Who knows? Maybe Fletch took offense at the dressing-down Duane gave you Friday."

"How did he know about that?" Adair exclaimed.

"Just a possibility," Charles insisted.

Before Adair could say more, Alicia came in from the hallway. "Are you hungry, Adair?"

"Yes," she said instantly.

Alicia began apologetically, "We were really caught off guard today . . . Jackie hasn't been able to go to the store, but she did throw together a little lunch for us." She pointed toward the kitchen.

"Sounds great," Adair said as she and Charles followed Alicia through a large country kitchen and sat in a breakfast nook by a bay window. It looked out on a small landscaped area bordered by a high brick wall. Masses of bronze mums filled the garden spot.

A little Border collie with one leg in a splint limped over to nuzzle Adair's leg. She fondly ruffled the dog's fur. "How ya doing, Panny? I figured out that was you I heard here the other night."

While Alicia poured iced tea into tumblers adorned with sprigs of fresh mint, Charles leaned forward to whisper to Adair, "Alicia normally won't tolerate animals in the house. She made an exception for Panny, since we can't put him outside."

"Why not?" she asked, as she loaded her plate from the tray of finger sandwiches and relishes on the table.

Charles started to answer when a movement outside caught his eye. A hand came up and grasped the top of the brick wall. Adair gasped.

Jackie and Alicia turned to look. A head appeared, then the arm of a man hoisting himself up over the wall. He had a camera dangling precariously from his neck. It caught in the vine climbing the wall, and he ripped it free.

Alicia pursed her lips. "He's tearing up my Carolina jessamine."

Adair was half out of her chair, plate in hand, but Charles said, "Sit down. King Herod will be around in a minute."

"King Herod?" she echoed.

From behind the house came a loud, heart-stopping barking. A flash of black surged past the bay window and the reporter jumped back up the wall, effectively tearing down the rest of the vine. A snarling Doberman pinscher lunged up the wall after him and snared his pants leg. The trespasser fell down the outside of the wall as the Doberman came back down the inside, chewing a scrap of fabric as a reward. He trotted away, his stubby tail wagging. Jackie hurried out of the kitchen toward the front of the house.

"We call him King Herod because he's mean and suspicious. Jackie is really the only one who can handle him," Charles said.

Adair watched out the window. "That's why you can't put Panny out back—King Herod would think he was lunch. Why does Fletcher's sister call him Panny?"

Charles looked up. "Fletcher's sister calls him Panny?" he said, and exploded into laughter.

Alicia was leaning forward with a look of amused wonder. "We'd never heard that before," she explained.

"Now you know something interesting to tell the reporters," Charles joked.

Adair laughed nervously and bit into a sandwich, but she found her appetite had faded. "I think . . . I'm beginning to understand why Fletcher avoids publicity. You couldn't even live a normal life having to contend with all that, much less do the things Fletcher does. But . . . after marrying me, what's he going to do now? It won't be hard for them to find a picture of me somewhere. I'll be recognized, so he'll be recognized by being with me. What is he going to do about that?"

"I don't know, but you can rest assured he has thought it out. He must have something in mind," Charles replied.

Adair relaxed enough to finish her sandwich. Jackie came in laughing, "Ooo-weee! Did you see that joker run? They're trying to feed King Herod hot dogs through the gate now. He's just foamin' at the mouth. I haven't seen him have so much fun in a long while!"

"I'm glad we're providing so many people an afternoon of diversion," Charles remarked drily.

"Where do you want Mrs. Streiker?" Jackie asked Alicia.

"The pink room, upstairs, please," she answered, wiping her mouth on a confetti-patterned napkin. Jackie hoisted Adair's overnight bag and left the kitchen.

"Thank you for having me here. I hope it won't be for too long." Adair straightened the diamond on her finger, which had fallen to the side from its own weight.

"I'm sure it won't be, but you're welcome here for as long as need be," Alicia said. Adair smiled appreciatively.

After a moment of reflection, Adair commented, "It's amazing that Fletcher has been able to keep so totally out of the lime-light that they don't even have one single picture of him. Most up-and-coming entrepreneurs don't mind publicity. Did he just always know this was going to be a problem?"

"I doubt it," Charles said, leaning back in his chair as he jarred the ice loose in his glass. "What happened was, he got stung early on. Remember that reporter I told you about, whose feature article on him killed his project? Well, that incident shaped Fletcher's subsequent methods of handling the media."

"I wish I could see that article," Adair mused. Alicia chose that moment to leave the kitchen suddenly.

"I'm sure Fletcher didn't keep it," Charles assured her. The telephone in the kitchen rang. Charles turned his head to listen as Jackie answered it. A moment later she leaned into the nook. "It's one of those newspaper people—" she sighed with annoyance.

"I'm unavailable for comment," Charles said.

"Good, but he wants to talk to Mrs. Streiker," Jackie added.

"She is also unavailable. So are Mrs. Whinnet, and you, and Panny. I believe King Herod has already made a statement," he said.

"Maybe they'll get the picture," she exclaimed on her way back to the telephone.

Alicia then returned and laid a plastic page in front of Adair. Actually, it was an old newspaper clipping encased in plastic. Charles leaned forward. "Where did you get that?"

"Kristin's room," Alicia smiled. "When your daughter was in the midst of her crush on Fletcher, she did a little research and found this. I think Adair is entitled to see it, since she *is* his wife."

Adair began to read. It was headlined, "Hand Up or Hand Out?" with the byline of Wendy Beacham:

It's 5:30 a.m. Fletcher is waiting at the rear door of a local grocery store. It's foggy and cold this morning, and he bounces a little to keep warm in his light khaki jacket and pants. "You don't have to be here," he tells me repeatedly.

But I do. I want to see what gets him up at three o'clock in the morning several days a week.

The produce manager finally appears at the door. "These crates here," he points out. "The bananas, the tomatoes, the curly endive. Not the potatoes—they're going on sale today. And, oh what the h---, take the strawberries, too."

Fletcher thanks him and starts loading the crates on the back of an old pickup.

"This old produce would normally go in the trash today," he explains to me, "although most of it is still good."

As he loads, he throws out the spoiled food, then it's time to crank up the borrowed pickup and head for the next store.

Fletch makes one more stop this morning, then around daybreak takes his pickup load to the housing development on East 7th—the blight of beautiful Barsleigh. There he is met by twenty or more residents who fight for the best of his load until it's all gone. Then they disappear.

"Why do you bother, Fletch?" I ask. "They don't even say thank you."

He loads empty crates back onto the bed of the pickup. "I wish they would thank me," he says. "Appreciation is a valuable asset. But I wouldn't stop because they don't appreciate it. They still need it." His brown eyes reflect the depth of his compassion.

"He has *brown eyes*," Adair said, grasping at this small piece of significant information.

"So now you know," Charles admitted, rolling his eyes.

"This seems like a pretty harmless piece. How did it ruin his project?" Adair asked, scanning the rest of the article.

"As I recall, his little operation depended on the silent goodwill of a number of people. There was a powerful community group trying to move those tenants out and raze the development. When this came out, the group saw Fletcher's efforts as perpetuating the development's existence. He more or less got run out of town," Charles said.

"That's too bad," she observed. "But for all that, at least she could have gotten a picture of him."

Charles squinted. "I believe her camera was stolen from the front seat of the pickup that morning."

"Too bad," Adair repeated. "Wendy Beacham," she noted, to fix the name in her mind.

"Does that sound familiar?" Charles queried with a half-smile.

"No, I don't think so. Should it?" Adair asked.

"She is now the lifestyles editor for the *North Dallas Expositor*," Charles informed her.

Adair's jaw dropped. "The *Expositor*! That's the paper that's been sending out reporters after me! It's not just a coincidence that she works there, is it?"

Charles shrugged, "You tell me. At one point, Wendy and Fletch were dating."

Adair intently reread the article as she finished her lunch and wiped her hands on the colorful napkin. "How did *you* meet Fletcher?" she turned to Alicia.

Alicia looked at her husband and laughed. "It was awful! Charles brought him home for dinner one evening without warning me. That was before we had Jackie or anyone to help me. Kristin was spending the night at a friend's.

"I'd had a terrible day at work, I had nothing to fix on short notice—and then Charles walks in with this strange man. That was just a few days after he had approved the loan for Fletcher and was feeling the heat for it. I resented it terribly—my husband's job was at stake because of him, and here he had the nerve to show up at our front door! Of course, we weren't living *here* then.

"Well, dinner was a disaster. I threw something on the table and sat there seething. Fletcher didn't say ten words. Charles wanted to kill me, I'm sure.

"After dinner when I showed Fletcher to the door, he said,

'Thank you for dinner. You're going to be glad I came over tonight.'

"That made me laugh. 'Why?' I said. And he started telling me all the things Charles was going to accomplish, with his help. I pulled him back inside for coffee, and we stayed up talking until 2:00 a.m. Some of the things he said, sounded—oh, I don't know—egotistical, if you didn't know him. But everything he said turned out to be true. I *was* glad he came over that night, and that I was able to meet him. Fletcher has so much to offer, but most women can't get past appearances to find out—" Charles abruptly swiveled in his chair and Alicia stopped talking.

Adair glanced from one to the other. "What is it about his appearance that puts women off?"

"I didn't say that," Alicia corrected her.

The telephone rang again, interrupting Adair's next question. After answering it, Jackie came into the breakfast nook with a dish-towel in her hand. "It's for Mrs. Streiker—"

"I told you that she is not available," Charles said testily.

"Keep your pants on, boss; it's Mr. Streiker who wants to talk to her."

7

Adair could not believe how nervous she was, taking
this call. "Hello?"

"Hi, Adair. What are you doing this afternoon?"
Fletcher asked.

"Well, uh, I just got married. Did you know about that?"

"Yes," he admitted. "The judge got a message to me just a few
minutes ago. Until then, I wasn't sure that you'd go through
with it."

"To be honest, neither was I. You—certainly got a lot done in
a few days," she observed.

"Thank you."

"But, I was beginning to wonder, when I didn't ever hear from
you . . . so, when can we . . . uh—" She seemed to have trouble
phrasing her thoughts.

"I'm in Dallas now. I want you and Chuck and Alicia to meet
me at the skating rink at the Galleria."

Her heart almost stopped. "When?"

"As soon as you can get out here," he said.

At first she was dumbstruck. Then she blurted, "The house is surrounded by reporters! They'll see us leave!"

He laughed, "Chuck can lose them. Don't worry." When she failed to reply, he asked, "Well? Do you want to see me or not?"

"Yes! Yes! We'll be right there!"

She hung up and started toward the breakfast nook, then gasped as she realized that she had hung up on Fletcher. She hurried back to pick up the phone again, but the line was dead. She returned to the table. "He wants us to meet him at the Galleria right away!"

Charles and Alicia got up. "Okay, that's fine. We're on our way," Charles said calmly. Adair was wringing her hands. "It's okay, Adair," he repeated. "Why are you so uptight?"

"The reporters," she gestured helplessly, "and—the rink is so large! And—I'm going to meet Fletcher in a dress I hate!"

Charles and Alicia laughed until they were breathless. "I don't think—" Alicia gasped, "that Fletcher needs to like your dress enough to put it on."

"I gather he told you to meet him at the skating rink," Charles said, and Adair nodded. "Fine. No problem," he mused, looking out toward the front window. "Jackie! Oh, there you are. Bring Adair's bag back down, please. She's going to meet her husband."

"Wish you folks would get your act together," Jackie scolded gently as she lifted her ample frame up the stairs.

Adair took a few minutes to wash her face, brush her hair, and calm down in the downstairs half-bath. Then she retrieved her overnight bag and purse at the foot of the stairs. Charles smiled and encouragingly patted her shoulder. Alicia descended the stairs, wearing fresh lipstick. "I'm ready," she announced.

They went back to the three-car garage, where Charles opened the spacious trunk of his Mercedes. "Hop in, Adair."

"In the trunk?" she asked incredulously.

"Just until we get past the troops outside," Charles reassured her.

Adair reluctantly climbed in and curled up, clutching her bag. Charles gently shut the trunk lid. Immediately she felt panicky and claustrophobic. But when she paused to consider that she was actually on her way to meet Fletcher, her fears evaporated in the heat of excitement.

She heard the car door slam and the garage door open. She felt the engine start up and the car begin to move. Slowly, it crept along and turned a corner. The smell of fumes became noticeable. Adair held her bag still. The car turned another corner and gained some speed. It stopped, turned left, stopped again, then started and quickly picked up speed. They seemed to be going at freeway speed now. The fumes dissipated.

"Charles? Oh, Charles—are you forgetting something?" Adair remarked. As she shifted gently whenever the car changed lanes or speed, she felt as though she were in the cargo hold of an airplane. She relaxed in the darkness, listening, trying to picture the face she was about to see.

Minutes later they slowed, then turned. They were off the freeway. Now they were turning continuously to the left. They were in a parking garage, probably that of the Galleria. The car stopped. Adair gripped her bag in readiness.

The trunk lid sprang open and Adair rose up, blinking. Charles helped her out. "Are you all right?"

"Yeah, I think so. I thought you were going to let me out as soon as we got past the reporters," she gently accused, looking around the parking level.

"I'm sorry, Adair; there was absolutely no place to pull over. People were all down the block. And since we were so close, I decided to go ahead and just get here," Charles said. "Fortunately, we're not deep into rush hour."

Alicia smoothed out wrinkles in Adair's dress. "Ready?" she smiled. Adair nodded, clutching her bag.

They crossed the street to the double glass doors and entered the mall area. They walked to the railing of the second floor straight ahead and looked down over the skating rink. The mall was crowded for a Monday. Adair looked up at the level above them, then down at the eateries near the ice rink. "Where will he be? On what level are we supposed to meet him?" she asked in sudden panic, forgetting that she was the one who spoke with him on the telephone.

"Let's go down to the first level," Charles suggested.

They bypassed the line waiting for the elevator and took the stairs to the lower level. There they lined up at the railing around the rink, where laughing, gliding, falling skaters filled the ice. One or two daredevils skated too fast in and out of the flow, startling other skaters. Giggly teenaged girls in jeans and big hair were trying to keep their balance and look sophisticated. Moms and dads skated with their future Olympic stars, holding them up on either side. And one man in a business suit skimmed serenely by himself.

Adair turned to Charles. "Do you see him?"

"No," he said slowly. "Guess we'd better split up, since it's hard to see all around from here. Adair, why don't you stay put while Alicia and I go to the other side and look?" Adair nodded.

She watched them work their way around the rink until they were lost in the crowd. She turned to scan the people at tables behind her, then sighed, "This is silly. How am I going to spot him?" But unconsciously she continued to watch any man who looked at her for more than a second or two. When she realized she was drawing unwanted attention that way, she gave up looking and just watched the skaters circle the rink.

"Now, don't overreact and cause a scene," a voice said softly at her side. She caught her breath. It was *his* voice.

❖

Her heart almost gave out. Very slowly, eyes downcast, she turned to look at him. He was resting his elbows on the railing beside her, hands clasped. He was wearing beige cotton pants and a white shirt, tail out. She lifted heavy eyelids to look in his face.

He was gorgeous, in an uncommon way. He had a deep Hawaiian tan with laugh lines around his eyes and mouth. He had thick black hair that needed shaping—and full lips. His mother's Polynesian features dominated his face, but when he straightened up off the railing, he stood at his father's six-foot height. And his eyes were a deep, liquid brown.

"Fletcher," she whispered weakly.

"Hi, Adair," he grinned. "Nice to see you."

"Fletcher . . ." she repeated in disbelief.

He took her hand and regarded the diamond resting on it. Then he showed her the simple, slender white gold band he wore, which matched hers. She held his hand, hardly believing that he was flesh and blood. And had she actually kissed him, or only dreamed it?

"Are you ready to go?" he asked.

She must have indicated that she was, for he picked up her overnight bag with his free hand. "I'm glad you thought to bring this," he said, then let go of it briefly to wave goodbye to Charles and Alicia, across the rink. They waved excitedly and Adair managed some motion with the hand that was not clasped in Fletcher's.

He took her outside the mall to a taxi waiting on the street. "The Streiker Building," he told the driver when he opened the door for Adair. Then he went around to the other side to get in.

As the taxi started off, he sat beside Adair and smiled. After searching briefly for some way to ease her tension, he said, "I like your dress." She burst into tears. The driver glanced into the rearview mirror.

Fletcher laughed and put his arms around her. "I guess it's okay to make a scene now. Am I that disappointing?"

"No! It's just that—I can't believe it, and I cry when I don't know what else to do," she said, furious at herself for babbling. She wiped her eyes with her fingers.

"It's okay," he said again.

She looked at him up close. When he smiled just slightly, the corners of his eyes crinkled. Adair could not take her eyes off his face—the embodiment of the personality she had come to love. If she could have put together a face of her own choosing, it would not have been nicer than the one right here. She had been given all the clues, and yet—she never would have visualized *this* face.

With one arm around her, Fletcher leaned back on the seat

and glanced out the window as the taxi exited the freeway into downtown Dallas.

Adair followed his eyes and observed that it was near five o'clock—streams of downtown office workers poured from buildings into buses and parking lots. *Quitting time,* she thought abstractedly, when she would normally be walking across the parking lot of the bank to her car. Was today Monday? Had she really gone into work this morning? It seemed like a lifetime ago.

"How did you know Duane chewed me out Friday?" she suddenly asked. He smiled and put his finger to his lips, glancing toward the driver. "Oh, yeah," she breathed.

The taxi pulled into the parking garage of the Streiker Building and stopped in front of the elevators. The driver punched his meter and said, "That's a $46.50 fare."

Fletcher helped Adair out, then pulled a crumpled $100 bill from his pants pocket. "Keep the change."

"Hey, thanks, man. Radical." He left the garage on squealing tires, causing the security guard in the booth at the entrance to jump up. When he perceived Fletcher as the cause of the disturbance, he came trotting out toward them. Looking sizable enough from across the garage, he took on some aspects of a gorilla as he came closer to Adair.

"You gotta stop throwing out them Benjamin Franklins. You get people excited, man!" The guard grabbed Fletcher's hand to shake it happily.

Fletcher just grinned. "Adair, I want you to meet Reggie. This is my wife, Adair." The key word sent a thrill up her spine.

The security guard assumed a gentler air. "Pleased to meet you, ma'am." He was so big that he strained the seams of his uniform, which looked incongruous with his black beard and long curly ponytail. A tattoo peeked out from under his short sleeves and a heavy gold cross decorated his chest.

"Nice to meet you," she said, tentatively shaking his football-sized hand.

"He knows you?" she whispered to Fletcher.

"Reggie knows everyone who belongs in the building. He's the best security guard on earth," Fletcher said matter-of-factly. "As of tomorrow, he'll start coming on duty at nine o'clock each night. With you here, I wanted Reggie watching the building at night."

"Sure," Adair acknowledged blankly. As Reggie returned to his booth, she asked, "Where did you find him?"

"Spread out on the side of the highway, left for dead by his motorcycle gang. By the time I finally got him out of the hospital, I had a new employee," Fletcher said. "He used to call himself Cast-Iron, until he found out that he wasn't. So now he goes by what his mother named him."

Fletcher summoned one of the five elevators and Adair seemed to wake up somewhat. "Why are we here?"

"This is where I live," he smiled. "This elevator," he said, standing in front of the one on the far left, "is the only one that takes you all the way up."

When the doors opened, they stepped in and he inserted a round key into the panel. "This is the penthouse key. I've got one like it for you in my apartment." The elevator then took them directly to the very top of the building, the thirty-third floor.

As the doors slid open to reveal the penthouse, Adair looked out at gray industrial carpet and bare white walls. Fletcher walked to a door a few feet from the elevator—the only door Adair saw. There was an electronic lock on this door. Fletcher punched in a code, telling her, "The combination to this lock is 8834. Please remember that: 8834. If you do forget, Yvonne knows it." He pushed open the door and held out his hand.

Adair peeked in through the doorway. She saw a large living area, one whole wall of which was covered with sloped windows. A fireplace, bookcase, and curio shelves covered the opposite wall. The shelves and much available floor space were neatly cluttered with the fascinating objects a much-traveled man might accumulate.

In front of the fireplace were companion sofas of white leather. There was a round dinette between the windows and the fireplace, and beyond that, a kitchen. She felt a twinge of disappointment. Sure, it was a much larger and nicer apartment than hers, but it was no mansion.

Fletcher was watching her as she surveyed her new home. "These are temporary quarters, you understand. I'm going to build a new place for you. There's your elevator key." He nodded toward a glass coffee table supported by stone pedestals. The key lay on the table.

Adair dropped her overnight bag and walked over to the shelves. She curiously picked up a lifelike terra cotta head with a spout at the top. "That's a Mochica portrait jar from about AD 500. They lived on the coast of northern Peru," Fletcher offered. Adair carefully replaced the jar.

Hanging at eye level was a fantastic fragile mask with googly eyes and a lopsided mouth. "That's an owl mask of the Baining tribe of Melanesia. It was used in ceremonies of protection for their children," Fletcher said.

"Did they scare the kids to death?" she wondered, and Fletcher smiled.

There was a jade figure with a skeletal face and red tongue; a heavily scrolled ivory cross; and a stallion rearing in bronze. "You have a museum here!" she exclaimed.

"I know." His tone was slightly exasperated. "I'm not a collector. All these things were given in appreciation for work I've sponsored in some of these areas. I've already donated a number of things to museums, or returned them to their country of origin, but I just haven't had time to clean everything out."

Then she saw placed beside his priceless artifacts her own little collection of mail-order ginger jars. She picked one up, laughing, "What are these doing here?"

"Your apartment has been cleaned out and your belongings brought here. Your utilities have been canceled, and your lease paid off in cash. We've applied for your new social security card and driver's license—they should be coming in a few weeks. Oh—" he reached into his left-hand pocket. "Here's the cash from your checking and savings accounts." He handed her a skinny stack of folded bills.

"Thanks," she said, abashed, stuffing them in her purse. "And as for these—" she contemptuously scooped up the three little ginger jars "—they aren't worth anything."

Deliberately, he took the jars from her fingers and replaced them on the shelf. "They belong to you, and you're worth a great deal."

She stared at him. Was she worth so much? She didn't think so. But he had pursued her without asking her opinion of herself, as if it were irrelevant.

He reached out to run his hand lightly over her cheek and disorderly hair. She glanced down, feeling unbeautiful. His arm was in her field of vision, so that is what she looked at. This was not the arm of a self-indulgent billionaire; it was the arm of a laborer: strong, sinewy, and scarred. He didn't wear a Rolex, just a nondescript black watch. He was a regular human being. His great wealth did not protect him from pain, disappointment, or sorrow. It only meant he had so much more to lose than most people. And he had placed it all secondary to her.

While Adair was contemplating all this, he slipped his arms around her. "Do you want to know the first time I saw you?" he asked.

"Tell me," she said, twining her arms around his neck.

"It was when you came downtown to have your picture made at the main bank for the brochure," he said.

She squinted. "There were so many people around . . . I don't remember seeing you. All I remember is how embarrassed I was over it."

"I remember you. You had on a long-sleeved white dress, and your hair was a little longer than it is now," Fletcher observed.

"I got it cut," she said apologetically.

"And . . ." he murmured, brushing her lips with his, "I couldn't take my eyes off you. I asked Yvonne who you were, and she said she'd find out." His hand stole to the back zipper of her dress.

"When she came back and told me your name, I told her that you were now mine." He cupped her face and pressed her with a deep kiss.

Adair melted into him. He was hungry, but distracted in trying to unzip her dress. Adair had a much easier time slipping his shirt off his brown shoulders. Finally, he reached around her to work on the zipper with both hands. Adair waited, stroking his taut chest.

At length he got the zipper down several inches, far enough to get it hopelessly stuck on the fabric. He stepped back, exhaling in frustration, and Adair took matters in her own hands.

"I hate this dress," she said as she reached back and yanked the zipper apart. Then, smiling, she stepped out of the dress and kicked it out of the way as he lowered her to the zebra skin rug on the floor.

He was gentle but confident, as if helping himself to riches that he had rightfully won. Adair, still overwhelmed by his appearance, gave herself to discovering fully why the man on the motorcycle had excited her so. And he did not disappoint her.

<hr />

Fletcher lay with his head on Adair's chest as she caressed sweat from his temple. She pondered how the most physical of acts could alter her mental outlook so completely. All her fears and reluctance had been swept out of existence. She felt the throbbing of his pulse and the rhythmic expansion of his chest against her body. That he was real was amazing enough; that he was so desirable was astounding. And to top it all off, he was hers.

He looked up at her with a languid smile. "I'm hungry. Want to go eat?"

"Sure," she breathed.

He helped her to a sitting position and she picked up her ruined dress with a wry smile.

"I suppose you'll be demanding a new dress now," he grumbled, glancing over with a grin as he stepped into his pants. "Your clothes are in the closet off the bedroom." He nodded to a door flanked by curio shelves.

Adair opened the door and turned on the light, illuminating a large room with a wood floor and simple, heavy furniture. There were no windows, only skylights. She smiled at the crisp, unmussed bed and crossed to another door, which opened to a dressing area lit by another skylight. Beyond that was a bath and one big walk-in closet with a bureau in the back.

Unknown hands had carefully arranged her things. Her shoes were lined up on shelves and her sweaters stacked in plastic cases. Her clothes hung on one side of the closet and Fletcher's on the other. Neither of them had enough to completely fill the space.

As she pulled out a pair of jeans and a soft sweater, Fletcher, dressed, came to the door. "I hope one closet will do for now. When I built this, I didn't know you'd be sharing it."

Wiggling into her jeans, she glanced up at him. "Considering that it's practically bigger than my old living room, yes, I guess it will do."

He grinned.

While Fletcher combed his hair, Adair brought her purse and overnight bag to the bedroom. She took the marriage license from her purse and placed it in the file folder, then put the folder in the drawer of the nightstand by the bed. Those little scraps of paper that she had once dumped in the trash now took on much greater worth. They represented aspects of Fletcher, some that she did not yet understand.

When he emerged from the bathroom, they took the elevator down to the nearly deserted parking garage. "There's my car!" Adair exclaimed, spotting it at once.

Reggie came out of his booth with her car keys. "Here go. Mr. Whinnet dropped it off just a few minutes ago."

"Thanks, Reggie." She put the keys in her purse. He saluted with two fingers and lumbered back to his security station, carrying his slight limp as a legacy of his former life. Adair watched him, then turned to Fletcher. "Where's your car?" she asked eagerly.

"I don't have one. It's unnecessary," he said.

"Unnecessary!" Adair exclaimed. She could not imagine life in Dallas without one. "Well—where shall we go eat?" She moved toward her car.

"Tell you what," he said, taking her hand to redirect her, "it's not far to West End. Let's walk."

This was a novel and potentially dangerous idea, but anything Fletcher suggested seemed only logical. "All right," she agreed.

They left the garage on foot and headed toward the old downtown section that had been converted from dilapidated warehouses to sleek shops and restaurants. Adair breathed in the cool twilight air and looked up past office buildings at glorious purple and orange clouds—something she did not normally pause to appreciate. She had to trot to keep up with Fletcher's pace, her hand clamped in his. The changing of the guard downtown was at hand; the day people were leaving, and the night people were coming out for play.

After crossing a street and going two blocks over, they arrived in West End. A red trolley car passed by with its cheery *clang-clang*.

"How about here?" she suggested, pausing in front of a popular café.

"Too noisy to talk," he balked, so they went a block over to a small Italian restaurant. There was a line out the door of those waiting to be seated. Fletcher pulled Adair up beside him at the end of the line under an old-fashioned street lamp. As Adair gazed up at him the lamp suddenly came on, turning his skin golden and haloing his head. In this light, he turned his eyes on her and she felt an indescribable thrill.

A girl's voice in the line distracted her. She glanced over the other people waiting, and felt an irrational urge to start grabbing them and shouting, "Do you know who this is? Do you know who is standing in line behind you?" There he was, the most sought-after man in the Southwest, standing quietly and anonymously in line at a restaurant.

The young girl ahead of them whose voice had distracted Adair complained again loudly about the line, "I bet the owner wouldn't have to wait like this!"

Despite the logic of allowing the owner of a restaurant to do things differently than the patrons, Fletcher responded to her, "Oh, I bet the owner probably would anyway, just to see what everybody else has to put up with."

She turned to glare briefly at him and toss her head disdainfully. But she did shut up.

Adair smiled into Fletcher's shoulder. Of course. This restaurant was also his.

Before too long they were seated on the patio at a table for two. "Perfect," Adair purred as she was handed a menu. Above the quaint old street lamp there was a harvest moon on display, now just barely visible above the buildings.

"What would you like?" Fletcher asked her.

"Oh, the lasagna," she sighed happily.

"And I'll have the fettuccine with crab," he said, handing his menu to the waiter.

"Did you see our wine list, sir?" the waiter asked him.

Fletcher glanced inquiringly at Adair, who shrugged self-consciously. "I believe we'll both have iced tea," he said. "Isn't that what you'd prefer, Adair?" She nodded.

A horse-drawn carriage clattered by, and the driver tipped his tall hat to Adair. The evening breeze brought sounds of laughter from the square nearby. Adair breathed in the excitement of the night, and it was not due to food, drink, or sex. It was being the object of a powerful love. She grinned shyly at Fletcher. "This is a dream come true."

"This is just the beginning," he acknowledged.

"If I had known you were going to be like this, I never would have hesitated a minute to accept!" she confessed.

"Like what?" he smiled.

"Well, so . . . sexy!" she said.

He laughed. "Thanks." Shaking out his napkin for his lap, he added, "Yeah, I like you, too. But . . . we'll need more than good sex to weather—"

Adair interrupted him with a revolutionary thought: "You

wouldn't let me see you so I wouldn't be swayed by your good looks! Isn't that right?"

"Partly," he admitted. "Money and looks are both misleading. I can't risk a relationship based on them. I want more. I want your love from the inside out."

"That's what Alicia said—or started to say: that women couldn't get past your appearance to really get to know you. It sounds like—you've been burned before," she ventured.

"Sure. Who hasn't?" he said.

"Could I ask you something?" she said suddenly.

"Of course," he said, steadily looking her in the eyes.

"Am I the first woman who you proposed to in this way?"

"Yes," he said, nodding emphatically. "I tried everything else first—all the accepted, conventional methods. But it always came down to these little power plays to see who had bottom-line control of the relationship. When I saw you, I knew it was worth a radical experiment to see if you could love me on my terms." He paused as their drinks, salads, and bread sticks were brought to the table.

Adair mulled this over. When she saw her expression, he explained, "Look, Adair, I've got no use for people who want personal guarantees instead of a complete relationship. They say, 'I only want enough of you to fill my agenda, so don't bother me with the rest.' Well, I'm not going to sit still for simply being the fulfillment of someone's fantasies."

He sat back and Adair watched him quietly while the waiter set their entrees before them. Then she observed, "You certainly fill my bill. I couldn't ask for more."

He smiled at her in a curious way as he cut his pasta with his fork. "You may have gotten more than you bargained for."

"What do you mean?" she asked.

"That we still have a lot of getting acquainted to do." He offered his tea glass for a toast, and Adair gamely clinked her glass to his.

They ate quietly. Adair tried not to stare at him too much. For all his frankness, there was something elusive about him, something that defied her efforts to know him. He said unexpected things. Then she thought, *Would you rather he be predictable?* She smiled to herself, and Fletcher smiled at her.

"The lasagna is good," she said, feeling a need to explain herself. He nodded.

The trolley clattered down its tracks nearby; Adair looked from it up at the moon. Higher and whiter now, it resembled a sugar cookie.

As Fletcher finished his meal and pushed his plate to the side, he inquired, "Would you like dessert?"

"Oh, I don't know," she sighed over the remains of the lasagna in front of her. "I'm stuffed already."

"Perhaps if we just split a dessert, then," he suggested. "You've got to try the chocolate mousse pie."

"Maybe one bite," Adair conceded as Fletcher looked around for the waiter. "I've got to get my weight down for—" she suddenly remembered with a shock that today, Monday, she was supposed to start back in ballet. At this very moment she was expected at Madame's studio.

Adair shook her head. She was on her honeymoon, for pete's sake! Madame would have to wait.

"You don't want the pie after all?" asked Fletcher.

"Yes, I do—just a little. I just—remembered something I had forgotten...."

She did not explain further, and Fletcher turned back around to look for their server. When he finally got the waiter's attention, he ordered the pie and Adair surrendered the unfinished lasagna.

Then she laughed, "I can't believe it! Was it really just two weeks ago that you first contacted me through Charles? My mother would kill me if she knew I married someone after knowing him for two weeks—without even meeting him! Oh, she'd kill me over the whole thing!"

"Perhaps we'd better go tell her about it, then," Fletcher suggested mildly.

Adair ducked her head. She did not feel ready to face her family, even with Fletcher by her side.

The chocolate mousse pie arrived. "Here—have a bite." Fletcher cut off a corner with his fork and held it up to her mouth.

"Umm, that's good!" She dabbed chocolate sauce from her chin with her napkin. Then taking the fork, she did her part to clean the dessert plate.

"Oh, I ate too much," she groaned, pushing away the plate. "You sure know how to satisfy a girl," she added slyly.

He looked at her over his water glass, and a corner of his mouth turned up. "It's easy when your appetite's been whetted."

They gazed at each other for a few moments, and Adair said softly, "I think I'm getting hungry again." Fletcher immediately turned around to look for the waiter.

They waited a rather long time for their check, and Adair watched Fletcher to see what he would do. When the waiter finally brought it around, Fletcher looked at it and reached into his pocket. "Got a big test tomorrow?"

The waiter reddened. "Yes, sir. How did you know?"

"You don't see many servers trying to study and wait tables at the same time," Fletcher observed, and the student began to stammer apologies.

Standing, Fletcher handed him the check with a folded bill. "Hope you ace it," was all he said as he took Adair's hand to leave.

"Thanks," the waiter mumbled, but did not unfold the bill until Fletcher and Adair had stepped out of the gate. Suddenly he called over the wrought-iron fence, "Mister! Hey, wait! Mister!"

Fletcher and Adair turned, as did a dozen other people. "You come back after tomorrow, and I'll show you service that'll knock your socks off!" the waiter shouted, joyfully waving the bill.

"I'll send someone in my place," Fletcher called back, smiling.

"Who?" the waiter shouted, but Fletcher and Adair had melted into the crowds.

"You won't know who," Fletcher predicted quietly. Adair stared up at him in unabashed admiration.

He walked Adair up the street, where they happened on the trolley loading up. "Oh, Fl—" she quickly caught herself before blurting his name. "Let's ride the trolley!"

He glanced at her, but grudgingly assisted her to board it. When he started digging in his pockets, Adair quickly got out her purse to pay the four-dollar fare. She wished to forestall the likely commotion to follow if Fletcher gave the conductor a hundred-dollar bill.

They sat in the back and watched the lights. The evening had turned quite chilly, and Adair snuggled against Fletcher. Although he still wore the light cotton shirt from earlier in the day, he was not shivering. But he held her close.

Adair's attention was drawn to a group of teenagers at the other end of the trolley. They were jostling, laughing, and posturing, drawing attention to themselves in the sweetly vain belief that they were the most interesting things around. The scene would have looked comical had Adair not recognized herself in there with them. Fletcher was right: the normal dating routine was a circus of acts and a parade of disguises. An unconventional approach was sometimes necessary to stop the pretense before it started. Then you could look at each other and begin to see what was really there.

Adair turned to Fletcher, who brushed wind-blown hair from her face. "If you're done playing tourist, I'd like to go back to the apartment now," he whispered.

"**M**orning, Adair." Fletcher leaned over her, brushing her forehead with his lips. He rose up on one elbow so that she could pull a corner of the sheet up to her chin.

"Mmm," she replied sleepily. An instant later she opened her eyes to stare up at the skylight over their heads. "I'm married to you now." Saying it did not seem to make it more believable.

"That's what I heard," he observed, rolling onto his stomach to look at her more comfortably.

Adair gazed around the clean, bare bedroom, with its white pine floor and slatted ceiling. There was a minimum of furniture in the room, and no art or artifacts. "Does this bedroom belong to you?" she asked groggily. Somehow, it had looked different last night.

"If it doesn't, we've got a lot of explaining to do," he replied seriously.

A muffled clatter from the direction of the living room caused Adair to sit up, clutching the sheet. "There's someone out there!"

"That would be Sugar," yawned Fletcher, reaching for a brown bathrobe on the floor. "She comes on weekdays." He pulled on his robe, then went to the closet and found her blue chenille robe. When he brought it to her in bed, she murmured thanks, embarrassed that she did not have something newer or nicer to wear this morning.

As she turned it around to find the armholes, she casually asked, "You call her Sugar?"

"Everybody does," he said, scooping up clothes from the floor and dropping them into a wicker hamper. "Come meet her."

Fletcher opened the bedroom door and Adair shyly followed him to the kitchen. She caught the aroma of newly baked fruit bread.

"Good morning, Sugar," Fletcher said to a slight woman bending over the oven.

"Mr. Streiker! Good morning." She straightened, pulling off an oven mitt and flashing a bright smile.

"Adair, this is my housekeeper, Sugar. Sugar, this is my wife."

"I am so happy to meet you, Mrs. Streiker. I was just getting breakfast going. Mr. Streiker doesn't normally like a heavy breakfast, just something light, but of course whatever you'd like to have I'd be happy to fix for you."

"What he has will suit me fine. Thank you, Sugar." It didn't seem odd at all to call this pretty lady Sugar. She had fine white angel-hair ringlets curled around a face of indistinct age. She was an easy talker, chatting about personal eating habits while she put a china cup in front of Adair.

"Coffee, dear?" she asked Adair.

"Yes, please. With powdered creamer and a pack of sweetener."

"Dadgumit!" Sugar exclaimed, startling Adair. "I was told you take cream and sugar, so that's what I bought! I don't have that powdered stuff or that 'No-Count Sweet'!"

"Cream and sugar are fine," Adair said hastily. "Just a little."

Sugar fixed her coffee, fussing apologetically, "Mr. Streiker likes his coffee strong and black, and I just knew that wouldn't suit you at all, so I thought it best to get another coffeemaker to fix yours separately. Try this and tell me what you think, honestly now."

Adair cautiously tasted the steaming brew. "I like it. Actually, it's better than the way I usually take it," she admitted.

Sugar seemed greatly relieved. "Oh, you are too kind. Just too kind." Fletcher listened quietly to all this.

After putting out fruit bread, kiwi, and mango, Sugar took up her sweater. "Excuse me, now, the bus comes at 8:40 and I've got some errands to run. Can I get you anything while I'm out?"

"Better bring me a copy of the *Expositor*, Sugar," Fletcher suggested.

She made a face. "That ol' stink rag? Certainly." She locked the door behind her as she left.

With lively Sugar gone, the apartment seemed to settle back to reflect Fletcher's pensiveness. He ate without speaking, as though he had something heavy on his mind, and Adair wondered if he were always so quiet in the mornings. "This bread is wonderful," she noted. He smiled.

After a few moments, Adair asked, "Are you expecting to see anything in the *Expositor* today?"

"I don't know," he replied.

There was further silence. Adair was opening her mouth to say something—anything—when the telephone in the kitchen rang. Fletcher got up to answer it. Adair listened to his end of the conversation: "Hello. Yes. Is that right? What is it?" A long silence. "Okay, I'll see what I can do." Then he hung up.

"Is there a problem?" she asked without concern as he came back to the table.

He cleared his throat. "Yes, there is."

"What is it?" she asked.

"I . . . I'd rather not tell you," he said.

"Why not?" she exclaimed.

"Because . . . you might get hurt," he said slowly. Meeting her gaze, he said, "I have to leave the country this morning."

"You can't be serious," she said.

"I don't know how long I'll be gone," he said.

"You're not serious," she reiterated.

"Sugar will take good care of you. And of course, Yvonne will be there whenever you need her."

"I don't need Yvonne. I'm a big girl," she said defensively.

"Of course you are—"

"I just expected our honeymoon to be longer than a one-night stand," she fumed.

This time he stared her down. "We're married. We're going to stay married. I'll be back. Meanwhile, everything I have is at your disposal. Whatever you need, Yvonne will see that you get it. Understand?"

Adair understood, with a jolt. She was now the wife of a billionaire, and had to start considering what her priorities would be.

Fletcher drained his coffee cup and left the table. Adair heard the shower start in the bathroom. A short while later he emerged in fresh khakis and damp hair. Adair stood. "Fletcher, do you *absolutely* have to leave this morning?"

"Yes," he said heavily, "though I wish I didn't. Are you sorry you married me now?"

"No," she said more reticently than she would have liked. He laughed drily at that. "I simply can't believe I'm losing you so soon," she confessed.

"You're not losing me. I'll be in touch. And I'll be back before long," he said.

She nodded unhappily as he strapped on his plain black watch and placed his wedding band on his finger. He looked at it wistfully. "Guess I'd better get going."

"If you have to," she said dully.

Hesitantly, he approached her to kiss her goodbye. Adair fleetingly considered rebuffing him, but firmly rejected the idea. She opened her arms and gave him a long, caressing sendoff.

"You'll do fine," he sighed. "I know you will, Adair." Holding her face, he reminded her, "You belong to me. I won't forget that; don't you either." He turned and walked out the door.

After it closed, Adair stared at the blank door for about sixty seconds. She was momentarily startled by the sound of a loud engine over her head. "Helicopter on the roof," she said. It faded after a few minutes, then all was silent.

———◆———

"I suppose the first thing I should do is . . . have another cup of coffee." She laughed humorlessly at how quickly her old habit of talking to herself returned. She did it because she was alone so much. And now here she was, alone again.

"Alone?" she continued as she poured the steaming coffee. Its aroma wafted up like a caress. "Well, I have Sugar, and Yvonne, and a couple of billion dollars." She shook her head ironically. She still did not believe it enough to buy anything.

As Adair was lingering over her coffee, Sugar returned. "Yoo-hoo! Mr. Streiker!"

"He's gone." Adair swiveled away from the table. "He got a telephone call and had to leave the country right away."

"Oh, dear. I'm afraid that's not good," Sugar pouted.

"Why?" Adair asked tensely.

"You'd better look at this, sweetheart." Sugar held out a folded newspaper.

With shaking hands, Adair opened it up to see the front-page headline of the *North Dallas Expositor*: "BILLIONAIRE WEDS DALLASITE." The article began:

> The *Expositor* has learned that wealthy recluse Fletcher Streiker was secretly wed yesterday morning to Dallasite Adair Weiss, 24, at the home of Charles Whinnet, 1073 Papillon Court in Dallas.
>
> Ms. Weiss, a teller at the Plano branch of Streiker's Rivers Bank who had reportedly been seeing Streiker secretly for some time, vacated her Wilderness Trails apartment and moved into the home of Whinnet, president of The Rivers Bank. It is unknown where the couple is honeymooning or where they will make their home.

The article went on to enumerate some of Fletcher's known contributions to the city. And there, in all her smiling glory, was Adair in the picture from the bank brochure.

Moaning, Adair laid the paper down. "I should have seen it coming, with all the reporters around yesterday. Fletcher knew. How did they piece it together so fast?"

"People are quick to tell everything they know," Sugar said as she gathered the breakfast dishes from the table. "A court clerk and somebody at the bank could have given them everything they needed for that article."

Courtney, Adair thought dismally, taking her own cup and saucer to the kitchen. Sugar pursed her lips and poured soap into the sink. "It's a shame to see a man's personal life all over the front page like that, especially when it's not even accurate."

"And the one thing he most wanted was to preserve his privacy," Adair muttered, staring down at the newspaper. "What will I do, Sugar?"

"I'm sure I don't know, dear. Mr. Streiker will be helpful, whenever he calls in." This was apparently the routine they assumed during his absences.

"He just now left. I doubt he'll call in for hours, or days," Adair whined. She went to the giant sloped windows, which gave view to half the metroplex. "Since my picture was on the front page, anyone who saw me on the street would know who I am. The only thing I see to do is stay here, out of sight."

Sugar turned from the sink with a quizzical frown. "I'm sure the last thing Mr. Streiker intended was for you to be cooped up forever in this apartment."

Adair shrugged defensively, as there was just the slightest tone of reproval in Sugar's voice. "He may not have intended it, but it looks like that's what will happen!" Since Sugar could not offer more encouragement, Adair decided to go take her shower.

She hung up her robe on a brass hook and looked around the bathroom. It had an open shower area in brown tile, which led to a large oval tub bordered with plants. The floor was pine in here, too. With the morning sun streaming down from the skylight, the room felt almost tropical. Drops of water from an earlier shower looked like a designer touch.

Adair opened a cabinet to get a washcloth and found Ace bandages and Epsom salts. She winced. Apparently Fletcher had suffered a sprain on a recent trip. What would she do if he were hurt or killed on this trip? She would not be able to go to him; she didn't even know where he would be.

She showered despondently, and seemed to be slow and clumsy getting made up and dressed in jeans and a decorated tee shirt. Her new life had lost its focus, and suddenly she could not do the simplest things anymore. Gazing at her fresh reflection, she sighed, "It wasn't exactly supposed to be like this."

After conscientiously cleaning the bathroom sink and counter, she went out to the living area. Sugar looked up from dusting. "Mrs. Streiker, aren't you lovely! Mrs. Fay called while you were dressing."

"She did? I didn't hear the phone," Adair said, surprised.

"Well, no, I guess you might not. The only telephone is here in the kitchen. Mr. Streiker doesn't like them all over the place, and especially not in the bedroom. Anyway—"

"Then how will I hear if he calls at night?" Adair said anxiously. "I sleep so soundly, the phone in the kitchen would never wake me."

Sugar looked mildly concerned. "Hmm. That's a problem. Perhaps Mrs. Fay will have a suggestion. She asked for you to return her call. Her number's by the phone."

"Thanks," Adair mumbled, looking for the telephone. It sat on a stand at the near end of the kitchen cabinets. She dialed the vaguely familiar number.

"Streiker Corporation," answered a bright female voice.

Adair was momentarily caught off guard. "Uh . . . Yvonne Fay, please."

"Thank you." The voice switched off, and a moment later Adair heard, "This is Yvonne Fay."

"Yvonne, this is Adair," she said, not realizing that she was whispering.

"Good morning! How are you today?"

"Not too good. I suppose you know Fletcher left this morning, and—have you seen the paper?" Adair asked.

"Yes ma'am, that's why I called," Yvonne said briskly.

"What will I do?" Adair asked.

Yvonne paused as if shifting the telephone. "I'm sure that's entirely up to you. We'll do whatever you like."

"But if I go anywhere I'll be recognized," Adair said.

"Perhaps," Yvonne allowed.

She started another sentence but Adair interrupted, "Why are you at the Streiker—? You're in this building!"

"That's right," Yvonne said.

"Oh, I forgot. You're a bookkeeper," Adair recalled.

"That's right."

"Oh, this is crazy, me talking at you when you can't answer. Can you come up to the penthouse?" Adair asked.

"Yes, I can," Yvonne said.

"Good. Please come on up here."

"Will do," said Yvonne, and Adair hung up. She went over to pour herself another cup of Sugar's coffee, then paused, cup in hand, by the expansive windows. From here she could see traffic snarled up along Stemmons Freeway, even this late in the morning. The scene reminded her of blood cells traveling single file through capillaries. This poor giant needed help for his blood clots.

There was a light rapping on the door, and she turned as Sugar opened it and welcomed Yvonne.

"Hello, Sugar. How are you today?" Yvonne asked with easy familiarity.

"Well, this morning I'm just fine, but last night, I tell you, I had the *worst* time with my arthritis—I could hardly pick up the phone."

"I am so sorry that it's still bothering you," said Yvonne. She adjusted her glasses to look at Sugar's wrist.

"The aspirin helps, but only for a while, you know," said Sugar, working her fingers to demonstrate her stiffness.

"What does Mr. Streiker say about it?" Yvonne asked.

"Oh, you know, I haven't told him it's acting up again," Sugar admitted. Adair tried to listen patiently, but inwardly she was demanding, *Never mind that! What about me?*

"You haven't!" Yvonne uttered in disapproval.

"I hate to be a bother," Sugar fretted.

"Now, Sugar, you stop being a martyr! He told you that if it didn't improve, you were to go right back to Dr. Forsythe."

"I know, I know," Sugar said, then noticed Adair waiting. "Here's Mrs. Streiker," she said, withdrawing with her duster to the curio cabinets.

"Well! Let me congratulate you now!" Yvonne reached over to give Adair an affectionate hug.

"Thank you," Adair said dismally. "It's not much fun being a bride without the groom."

Yvonne laughed, "He won't be gone long with you here!"

"I guess I'll just have to wait," Adair sighed, dropping onto a sofa and putting her feet up on the coffee table.

"While you wait, have a look at today's mail. I've screened out much of it so you won't be inundated." Yvonne held out several letters.

Adair glanced through them. "They're all addressed to Fletcher. No bills?"

"I take care of all the bills out of a separate account," Yvonne explained, "but I'm sure Mr. Streiker would not object to your opening mail addressed to him."

Adair respected Yvonne's opinion, but she really wanted to talk to Fletcher before doing that. She laid the letters on the coffee table beside her penthouse key.

Yvonne seated herself next to Adair on the sofa. "Adair, could I make a suggestion?"

"Please do."

"I suggest you go about your life and do your normal things," Yvonne said.

"But I *can't!*" Adair pulled her feet down from the coffee table and leaned forward. "I don't *have* my normal life anymore! I lost my job at the bank; I dropped my accounting class, and my former best friend tipped off the newspaper about me!"

"Then make a new friend, start a new class, or get a new job," Yvonne said rather sharply. Adair looked at her in hurt surprise, and Yvonne added, "That reminds me. Alicia Whinnet is having a party tonight and she wants you to come. It starts at seven o'clock."

"Oh . . . I can't . . ." breathed Adair. "I can't go on display as Fletcher's new wife to a bunch of strangers. Surely he doesn't want me to do that."

"Well, I'll talk to Alicia and see what she thinks," Yvonne reluctantly allowed. "Oh, and what about your ballet class?"

"I missed my first class. I'll have to miss tonight, too, if I go to Alicia's party. And if I go tomorrow night, everyone there will know I'm married to Fletcher."

"Adair," Yvonne said, deliberately pushing up her glasses, "believe it or not, some people won't care who you're married to. And some people aren't even going to know who Fletcher is."

Adair studied Yvonne's stern, glittering blue eyes, then smiled sheepishly. "I guess I am overreacting, aren't I?"

"Just a tad," Yvonne smiled.

"And wallowing in self-pity," Adair added.

"For a fleeting moment, there," Yvonne said. "But don't worry. Mr. Streiker's last instructions to me were to help you through this transition, and I'm going to do that—whether you want me to or not."

"Thanks a lot!" Adair laughed.

"You're welcome." Yvonne glanced at her rhinestone-studded watch. "Whoops. I have a departmental meeting in ten minutes. Chin up, Adair. And Sugar—" Yvonne got up "—keep me posted on that arthritis."

"Certainly will," Sugar said from the kitchen, where she was downing some aspirin.

Yvonne left for her meeting. Adair finished her coffee leisurely as she inspected Fletcher's bookcases. He had a lot of books on history, archaeology, and botany; several biographies on some obscure folks she had never heard of; and a few versions of the Bible. There was not one blockbuster novel in this heavy-duty lot.

Adair sighed and turned on the television, which was built into a corner unit facing the dinette. A news network came on. Adair switched. A game show. Switch. Talk show. Switch. Old movie. Switch. Weather channel. Switch, switch, switch. She turned it off and looked out the wall of windows.

"A big city down there and me stuck in this ivory tower," she said, then blushed to remember that she was not alone. She self-consciously glanced over her shoulder at Sugar, who was struggling with a vacuum cleaner. "Let me help you with that," Adair offered.

Sugar amiably brushed her off. "Now, Mrs. Streiker, this is my job. You've got better things to do." Then she involuntarily glanced at Adair as if thinking, *Or you should have.*

Adair let her be and flopped back down on the couch. Over the next long minutes she painted her nails, watched the news to see if they mentioned her (which they did not), and lay on the couch while Sugar worked around her.

She started thinking about lunch when she heard Sugar rattling around in the kitchen. Adair joined her. "What are you planning for lunch?" she asked brightly.

Sugar was struggling with the child-proof top of the aspirin bottle. "I was thinking of a Waldorf salad, Mrs. Streiker—darn! I just can't get this off!"

Adair took the bottle and opened it. "Here. Wait a minute. Didn't you take some only an hour ago?" She looked at Sugar's watery eyes.

"Yes, but they don't seem to be helping." Sugar took a glass from the cabinet and held it unsteadily under the faucet. But when the water gushed in, the glass slipped from her hand and crashed into pieces in the sink. "Oh, dear. Look what I did," Sugar chided, picking up shards with shaking fingers.

Adair stared at her. "Who's that doctor you're supposed to see,

Sugar? I think you need to make an appointment with him."

"I will soon," Sugar promised. She got out a plastic glass.

"I think you need to go today. You can have the day off to go," Adair said.

"Thank you, Mrs. Streiker, but I'm going to have to wait until my next-door neighbor has a day off to take me. You see, I don't drive, and Dr. Forsythe's office is clear in DeSoto." She tentatively filled the glass and swallowed the aspirin.

"Well, for pete's sake, I'll take you!" declared Adair. "You can't do much when you're hurting like that!"

"Thank you, Mrs. Streiker," Sugar said unenthusiastically, "but I can't go today. I don't have an appointment."

"I'll make one for you." Adair lugged the Dallas-area directory out from the telephone stand and plopped it on the counter.

"I can't go today," Sugar repeated, a little desperately. "Payday isn't until Friday, and I just—can't afford it today."

Adair looked up from the phone book. "Don't you have any insurance?"

"I did, but they dropped me. Too many claims."

"Well, then, I'm sure Fletcher will pay for it," Adair said firmly, running her finger down the directory listings. "Forsythe? Quentin Forsythe?"

"Yes," Sugar assented, rubbing her knuckles.

Adair picked up the telephone and dialed. "Yes, this is—" She bit her lip and started over, "I need to bring in Sugar—" she caught herself again. "What is your name?" she whispered.

"Sandra Brigstahl."

"Sandra Bristol needs to see Dr. Forsythe as soon as possible today. Her arthritis is acting up—how to spell it?" She glanced at Sugar.

"B-r-i-g-s-t-a-h-l," Sugar spelled, and Adair repeated it into the telephone. "Okay. Thanks. Oh—where is your office?" She scribbled down directions on a piece of paper near the telephone. "Thank you. We'll be right down."

As she hung up, she said, "His receptionist said to come on

down and he'll work you in. Let's go!" She took up her purse by the door.

"I don't know how to thank you, Mrs. Streiker," Sugar said humbly.

"Don't mention it," Adair said, then thought to check her purse. "Let's see—I have . . . twenty, forty, sixty, eighty, one hundred and change . . . should be plenty." There was an obscure nagging in the back of her brain that she needed something else, but she was in a hurry to go so they could get back and have that Waldorf salad. She zipped her purse shut and headed out to the elevator.

As they got on, she momentarily panicked, wondering what she should do if someone recognized her on the elevator. She briefly considered donning dark glasses, but decided that would look more conspicuous than anything—an idiot wearing sunglasses in an elevator. However, the elevator carried them straight down to the parking garage without stopping at any floors along the way.

Adair walked briskly to her car and got in before opening the passenger door for Sugar. "It should only take us twenty minutes to get to his office," Adair told her.

Twenty minutes later, they were six blocks from the Streiker Building, sitting in traffic. "I should have known," she muttered, inching up to the car in front of her. "Why did I think traffic would magically open up for me as Fletcher's wife?" Sugar smiled weakly, uncharacteristically silent. But the irrational feeling persisted in Adair that she should get *some* consideration for trying to do good.

Another twenty minutes later, after only two wrong turns, Adair pulled up to the medical complex that housed Dr. Forsythe's office. She took Sugar in and paused before the directory.

"I know where his office is—I've been here before," Sugar said.

"Of course you have," Adair said, embarrassed. Sugar led the way down the hall to a sleek waiting room with chrome chairs and gray carpet.

She gave her name to the doctor's receptionist, who responded, "Oh yes, Sandra, the doctor will be with you as soon as possible.

Please have a seat."

Adair noted the time—12:15. Expecting to wait, she plopped into a chair and picked up the nearest magazine. It was one of those slick women's magazines that portrayed glamorous women in high-powered careers. One lead article promised to divulge, "How to Make Love Last."

"Tie him to a chair," Adair grumbled. A gentleman sitting nearby shifted. Chagrined, she swore to conquer her habit of talking to herself.

After flipping through the magazine, she tossed it on an end table and looked around. Sugar was wincing, rubbing her hands. Adair went back to the receptionist's window. "How soon can we get Ms. Brigstahl in? She's really in pain."

The receptionist looked sympathetic. "Just as soon as possible. Dr. Forsythe knows she's here."

Adair nodded and began to return to her seat. Then she drew a quick breath. Lying on a table was a copy of this morning's *Expositor,* folded so that half of her face showed.

Adair walked around it and sat opposite her picture. What to do? Pick up the paper and hold on to it? Tear out the picture? Throw the paper away? While she was thinking about it, a man reached over and picked up the newspaper. As he turned it to the front page, Adair froze. He glanced at the headlines, then discarded the first section in favor of the sports pages.

As nonchalantly as possible, Adair picked up the front section and slowly opened it so that the offending picture stared straight up at her. Then she quietly dug in her purse for a pen. Surreptitiously, she defaced the picture with a beard and mustache, horns, and assorted curlicues. She replaced her pen, pretended to read the paper for a while, then placed it face down on the end table. She folded her hands to wait serenely.

And wait, and wait. She glanced at her watch at 1:00, when her stomach began to growl. *Why didn't I take time to eat something before we left? I knew we would have to wait.* She leaned over to Sugar. "When was the last time you were here?"

"About two months ago," Sugar replied faintly, all her spunk dissolved in pain.

The receptionist left for lunch, and Adair determined to do the same. She whispered to Sugar, "I'm famished. What would you like to eat?"

"Nothing, dear. I think the sight of food would just make me lose my breakfast right now. But you go ahead and get yourself something," Sugar encouraged her.

Adair watched one patient being summoned to an examining room as she thought it over. She did not really want to leave Sugar to wait by herself. An elderly patient left and a new one entered the waiting room and sat gingerly. *Things seem to be picking up now,* she thought. *Maybe the doctor just now got back from lunch.* She waited a while longer, trying to recall any fast-food places she had passed on the way here.

About the time she had decided to go find one, the nurse came to the door and summoned, "Sandra Brigstahl." Sugar got up stiffly with a grateful glance at Adair, who beamed at her. *Won't be long now,* Adair rejoiced. Her watch said 1:50.

Someone picked up the defaced newspaper and Adair smiled at the Rousseau print on the wall. She studied the light green squiggles on the silver wallpaper to avoid looking at the other waiting patients. She certainly did not want anyone staring back at her.

An important-looking gentleman sat down one chair over. He leaned toward her and said, "Excuse me. Do you have the time?"

"Yes, it's just two o'clock," Adair answered.

"Thank you," he said, eyeing her. She looked away, then picked up the women's magazine. "I consider myself to be a fairly astute observer of people," the gentleman said.

"Oh?" she smiled disinterestedly, trying to focus on the magazine print.

"Yes, and there is something quite obvious about you," he said.

"Oh yeah?" She belatedly turned the ring around on her finger to hide the stone.

"Yes. It's obvious that because of the way you avoid looking at people, you are a repressed individual," he said.

She shrugged, "I'm trying to get help for that."

A woman sitting on his left made it a point to look over, and he said no more.

Smiling, Adair looked down at the magazine in her lap, which she had opened to the article on "How to Make Love Last." She skeptically began to read:

> When that special guy sweeps into your life with champagne and flowers, after the heady romance of endless nights and hour-long phone calls, how do you make sure you're not just a two-week diversion for him?

Adair's rumbling stomach interrupted momentarily.

> The answer is to provide another diversion yourself! Change your makeup one week; your hair the next. Pick up a book on his interests and leave it where he'll see it. Try a new dish or a new wine on him. Surprise him with little gifts, or a romantic note in his briefcase, then don't be home when he calls! Change enough and he can't get bored!

"That's schizophrenic," Adair snorted, flipping the magazine closed. "All the pathetic little stratagems in the world won't keep someone around who's lost interest."

She shifted to take some weight off her posterior, numb from sitting. *So what does make love last? How do you prolong that desire, that yearning?* She turned her ring back around to look at the magnificent stone. *Doesn't a certain amount of it come from frustration—from not being able to have all you want of that special person?* She thought about Fletcher's departure earlier that morning.

The door to the examining rooms opened and Adair sat up. Another patient came out. Adair eased back into the seat and tried to recapture her train of thought, but it was gone. So she stared at the squiggly patterns on the wallpaper and wondered why they made little tiny wallpaper patterns that drove people crazy who had to look at them for more than fifteen minutes at a time.

Did Fletcher love her? Yes, he must. Did she love Fletcher? Last night, in his arms, she wanted him forever. Today, she was just . . . numb. Like her rear end.

She shifted again and dismally checked her watch: 3:08. *If I sit here much longer I'm going to need a doctor to detach me from this chair,* she thought. She got up simply to replace the magazine in the waiting room rack, then stood over it a moment to stretch her legs.

A preteen girl nudged her gently in order to get a magazine. "'Scuse me."

"Sorry." Adair stepped aside, then went back to the chair that was by now custom molded to her posterior. She closed her eyes for just a moment. The next thing she knew, Sugar was lightly tapping her shoulder. "Missus? I'm all done." Adair sat up blinking and looked at her watch. It was 4:15. "Here's the bill," Sugar said apologetically, handing a form to Adair. "He ran a lot of tests and gave me a shot of cortisone and all these pills—we don't even have to go by the pharmacy," Sugar began detailing to Adair.

"I'm glad you're feeling better," Adair murmured as she groggily handed the form to the billing clerk and opened her purse.

"That will be $167," the clerk said brightly.

"What?" Adair gasped.

"One hundred sixty-seven dollars," the clerk repeated, slowly.

"I have . . ." Adair pulled out her bills, "I have one hundred and . . . twelve dollars. Can you bill us—" She caught herself. Bill whom? She had promised Sugar that Fletcher would pay for it. But the clerk pointed to a prominent plaque that read, "Payment for professional services is expected at the time they are rendered."

"Here's twenty dollars," Sugar offered quietly. "That's all I have."

Adair took it. "That makes $132.00. Can you write a check, Sugar? Fl—uh, my husband will reimburse you."

"I don't carry a checkbook, Missus. The Mister just gives me cash for household expenses."

Adair stood thinking while the clerk waited, tapping her pencil.

"Look," Adair said, "Ms. Brigstahl is an employee of the Streiker Corporation, and I know she has health benefits. Please call them and—" Adair gave her the number, instructing, "ask for bookkeeper Yvonne Fay. Explain the situation to her, and I know she'll arrange for the other thirty-five dollars."

The clerk looked skeptical, but turned away to dial the number. Adair, slightly faint, leaned back against the counter to wait.

A moment later the billing clerk hung up and returned to the window. "She says that Sandra is covered, and she's sending over a courier with the cash."

"Good," Adair said in relief. The clerk stamped the long form and gave it to Sugar, saying brightly, "Have a nice day." Adair looked at the clerk with sinister thoughts.

On their way to the car, Adair sighed, "It sure will be nice to see that Waldorf salad."

"Mrs. Streiker, I would love to make it for you, but the bus comes by the building at 4:40. Another bus doesn't come until almost 8:00, and my husband—he really expects me home, though I do so appreciate your taking me to the doctor today."

"No problem," Adair said in disappointment, then added, "I'll get you to the bus stop in time. If I don't, I'll drive you home." She gunned the Mazda out into traffic.

As they pulled up to the Streiker Building, they saw the yellow-and-white bus pull up behind them. "There it is! Thank you, Missus! See you tomorrow!" Sugar exclaimed, hurrying out of the car. Adair waved warmly as Sugar boarded the bus.

<hr />

Parking her car in the building's garage, Adair could think of nothing but raiding Fletcher's refrigerator. Only when she locked her car and headed for the elevator did she begin to realize something was amiss. She slowed gradually to a stop.

"The elevator key!" she exclaimed in a whisper. "I don't have it. Did Sugar take it? Or is it in the apartment?" She could not remember. But she could not get up to the penthouse without it.

"Wait—I remember seeing it on the table. Could I have put it in my purse?" She stopped where she was to dig through her handbag. Not finding it, she returned to her car to dump everything out of her purse to search for it. It was not there.

Adair paused over the scattered contents of her bag and checked her watch. It wasn't quite five o'clock. She got out of her car and trotted to the security guard's booth. There was a younger man in it who wore his revolver prominently on his hip.

"Where's Reggie?" she asked, leaning her head in the booth.

"He comes on duty at nine," replied the security guard. "Can I help you?"

Good—he doesn't recognize me. "Yes. I need to contact someone in this building. Can you call up Yvonne Fay? She's in bookkeeping."

"Sure." The guard turned to his telephone and Adair relaxed against the booth. He had a sandwich out on the counter, which she would have seriously considered stealing except that she was an elevator ride from her own new home. His gun, incidentally, was not a deterrent.

The guard hung up. "I'm sorry, but Mrs. Fay has left for the day. Is there anyone else you could talk to?"

"Oh . . ." Adair trailed off. Anyone else? Charles Whinnet? She looked over to his reserved parking place, which was empty.

"Oh, dear. I guess I'll have to bring Sugar back here after all. I'll have to find out where she lives, first. May I use the phone?"

"Sure." He stepped aside and picked up his sandwich. Adair winced.

She lifted the receiver and reasoned, "She just got on the bus. She hasn't had time to get home yet." After a moment's thought, she dug out the gum wrapper with Yvonne's phone number and dialed it. The line was busy. "At least she's home," Adair said hopefully. She depressed the hook, then dialed information. "Yes, I'd like the number of Charles Whinnet, please."

"I'm sorry; that number is unlisted," the operator replied.

"Ugh." Adair hung up. "Do you have Charles Whinnet's home

phone number?" she asked the guard.

"I'm afraid I can't give that out to anyone," he replied with a half-smile.

She sat weakly, and her eye fell on his sack supper again. "Could I—I hate to ask this, but I haven't had anything to eat since breakfast. Could I have one of your Twinkies?"

"Here—take them both," he offered.

"Thank you!" She inhaled them. Then she began thinking that since he was obviously a nice person, perhaps he could help her in a more direct way. She would try telling him the truth. "Do you know Fletcher Streiker?" she ventured. "I mean, have you ever met him?"

"Lady, *nobody* here has actually met Fletcher Streiker." He smiled at her naiveté.

"Well, actually, I have. Have you seen today's *Expositor*?" she asked, and he nodded. "That was me on the front page. I'm Adair Weiss, the one who married him."

"I noticed from the article," he said, leaning on the counter with a knowing look, "that Mr. Streiker never confirmed that story, and neither did Mr. Whinnet. Since that paper has never been exactly a lighthouse of the truth, the feeling around here is that the story was generated by the paper in order to get access to Mr. Streiker."

"It's in the record books," Adair protested. "Judge Everett Amlin performed the ceremony."

"Judge Amlin's office would not comment," he observed.

"Well, of course he's not going to comment! But all you have to do is check the records—"

"I don't have to do anything but ask you to leave," he said, straightening and crossing his arms on his chest.

"Right. Okay. I'm leaving," she said, backing out of the booth. "Thank you for the Twinkies." She went to her car and pulled into the street under his cool eye.

As she cruised down the block, she encouraged herself, "Reggie comes on at nine. If I can only find someplace to go until then. . . .

146

Ballet! I've got pointe class tonight!" But all her gear was up in the apartment. Adair considered what Madame would do if she showed up at her studio hungry, without shoes or tights, and generally unprepared to dance. "She would throw me back out on the street," she admitted—and who could blame her? Madame was a dance teacher, not a social agency.

"Well, I've got to find something to eat before I die," she moaned, thinking Poco's was much too far away. Straight ahead she spotted a nightclub's marquee: "LADIES: No cover, first drink free."

Adair turned into the club's parking lot and sat in her car. She did not really want to go in here, but. . . . She checked her purse: there was exactly thirty-five cents, a bunch of invalid checks, and no credit cards. She reluctantly locked her car and went in.

It was dark and smoky, with loud, grating music from a jukebox. Candles in red glass globes flickered on small tables, representing someone's idea of romantic decor. She took a seat at the bar and reached for the dish of nuts. A bartender with a trendy haircut and gold chains smiled. "What'll you have, Angel?"

"Umm. . . ." Alcohol on an empty stomach made her wretchedly sick. "A diet cola, please. First one's no charge?"

"That's right. And I bet you won't pay for a drink all night long," he grinned.

You got that right, she thought, scooping up another handful of nuts. The bartender brought her a small cola with two cherries on a pick. Adair ate the fruit and took a large drink, then glanced at her ring. Feeling it unwise to parade her rock in downtown Dallas, she slipped it off and put it in her pants pocket. "We could use some more nuts," she said, passing the empty dish to the bartender.

"That's funny. Most people think there are too many nuts around as it is." A cologned man in a print shirt, mostly unbuttoned, sat next to Adair.

"Possibly," Adair murmured, watching the bartender refill her dinner dish.

As he replaced it on the bar, the unbuttoned man intercepted it and held it away from Adair. "Say please," he grinned.

"Please put the dish down," said Adair, mentally adding, *before I kill you.*

He put it down only to make a bolder move: "Care to dance?"

Adair looked up with a caustic remark on her tongue, then wisely changed her mind. "Yes, I'd like that." As they started toward the small dance floor, she said, "By the way, if my boyfriend comes in, don't let him bother you. He's not really crazy. I mean, he got a bad rap on that assault conviction. The other guy started it."

Suddenly Unbuttoned saw someone he knew on the other side of the room. "Catch you later, honey." And he left her standing on the floor.

Adair returned to the bar to fetch the bowl of mixed nuts and took them and her cola to a dark corner table. Her watch said it was only six o'clock—three hours until Reggie came on.

Without warning there was plopped down in front of her face an edition of that morning's *Expositor,* with her photo smiling up at her. Adair almost choked on a nut as she looked up.

"That looks just like you," observed an unsmiling man in a blue sports coat.

Adair calmly picked up the paper and pretended to look over the article. "Right," she laughed sarcastically. "If I had just married a billionaire, what would I be doing by myself in this place?"

He drew up a chair and sat down. "You look like the kind of chick to get hooked up with a rich guy. Girls like you don't give regular guys a chance—you have to go for the big money. The rest of us can just go to hell, as far as you're concerned."

Adair tried to smile engagingly. "That's not true; I—"

"Like the slick way you ditched that guy who tried to dance with you. You like playing games. Can you play rough?"

Adair studied him before answering. Was he dangerous, or just desperate? The bartender came by her table. "He bothering you, Angel?"

"No. Thanks," Adair said with a quick smile up at him. She turned back to the malcontent. "Why do you have to play rough?"

"'Cause I'm not rich," he said spitefully. "I'm just a regular guy, and the good-looking women are only interested in money."

Adair chose not to pick an argument with him about the relative fairness of a man choosing a girlfriend based on her looks as opposed to a woman choosing a man for money and said, "That's not fair, and it's not true—at least not for everyone. We're interested in men who are interested in more than making themselves feel good. Sometimes we play these little games to protect ourselves. It's pretty scary when a man comes on like a Mack truck. Most girls don't want to play rough."

His eyes flicked down a little. "Yeah."

"Look, I have to be honest with you. I *am* married. My husband and I are having problems, but I think I'd like to work things out with him. He's really just a regular guy, you know."

"Yeah," he muttered.

She stood up. "I hope you find someone who can appreciate you for who you are. It was nice talking with you." She held out her hand and he hesitantly shook it. Then she turned and walked out, ran to her car, jumped in, and gunned it out of the parking lot.

D riving down Preston Road, Adair glanced at her watch and moaned. It was only 6:45. "At least Yvonne *has* to be off the phone by now," she declared, pulling up to a convenience store.

She dug the last quarter out of her purse and dialed Yvonne's number at one of the outside pay telephones. It rang! But after the fourth ring, there was a click and Yvonne's voice said, "I'm sorry, we are unable to come to the phone right now. After the beep, please leave your name and number and we will return your call as soon as possible. Thank you."

As Adair listened with a sinking heart to this message, she saw a car with four young toughs pull up to the convenience store. She turned her back and slouched. "Yvonne, it's Adair. I, uh. . . ." Three went past her into the store, while the fourth sat at the wheel of their loudly idling car. What kind of a rational message could she leave? She glanced at the boy in the car. He was watching her.

On a survival impulse, Adair hung up and went straight to her car without looking into the store, fully aware that she had spent her last quarter. She drove slowly down the thoroughfare past six intersections. A police car with screaming sirens passed her going in the opposite direction.

Adair pulled into a grocery store parking lot and put her head in one hand, close to despair. "Now what?" She had barely an eighth of a tank of gas. "I can't drive around until nine o'clock!"

Then she thumped herself on the head. "Dumbbell! Alicia's party! I'm supposed to be there tonight anyway!" She turned her car back down the thoroughfare. Passing the convenience store, she saw three patrol cruisers clustered around it.

Greatly heartened, Adair drove to the Whinnets' lush, well-lighted neighborhood. As she approached their house, she slowed. There were a lot of cars parked along the street. Valets were parking them. She stopped in front of the Whinnets' house to watch people in evening clothes going in. She was still in jeans and a glitzy tee shirt.

"Here for the Whinnet party, miss?" A smiling valet tapped on her window.

Adair startled. "Uh—no."

She drove on down and parked several blocks away, feeling foolish and ashamed. Why did she say that? She *was* here for Alicia's party. So what if she wasn't in evening wear? Alicia wouldn't care. Still, Adair waited until a glittering threesome had gone inside before she approached the door. As the night wind picked up, she was glad to be wearing pants, at least.

A strange man answered the doorbell. "Name?" he said politely, clipboard in hand. He glanced at her casual attire.

Intimidated, Adair mumbled, "Adair Weiss."

He glanced down his list. "I'm sorry; your name doesn't appear." He began to close the door.

"No, wait! Streiker! She'll have me down as Adair Streiker. Mrs. Fletcher Streiker."

"Sure," he said, not bothering to check his list again.

"Would you look—or ask Alicia—wait, you!" But he had shut the door in her face.

The irony of the situation was not lost on Adair, since she had told Yvonne that she did not want to come tonight—not as Fletcher's wife, anyway. She began to shiver, then had to step out of the way for a couple to get to the door. The woman looked briefly down her nose at Adair, who stared back defiantly. Retreating down the sidewalk, she noticed that they had no trouble getting in. She was momentarily furious with Alicia.

She looked around. "If I can get to the back door—to Jackie— she knows me." Adair began to slink around the side of the house. As she approached the back wall, she was jolted by a sudden barking. "King Herod!" she gasped. "I forgot all about him!"

Adair quickly backed away, then went out to the street and on down to her car. She drove by the house again, slowly, then pulled into a neighbor's circular drive to watch for Alicia or Charles to come to the door. The neighbor's floodlights came on, so Adair drove off.

Not knowing where else to go, she went back to the Streiker Building and parked along the opposite side of the street. It was now 7:30, and the building was mostly dark. Adair sat in the car and looked up at her inaccessible home on the thirty-third floor.

She sat in the dark car and waited, slouched down in the seat. After a while a patrol car passed her, then stopped and began to back up. Adair quickly started her car and drove off with a friendly wave. She circled the block a few times, then parked again near the entrance of the Streiker garage. She thought about trying to park in the garage, but could not work up the muscle for another confrontation with the security guard. So there she sat.

Waiting for an hour and a half at night on a downtown Dallas street was no fun. Tired, cramped, and ravenous, Adair counted minutes as she warily scanned the street. There were a lot of street people out here. They wandered in and out of the shadows, some dragging belongings, some hardly able to stand. For the most part they ignored Adair, but still they frightened her—they looked so dirty, and ravaged, and lost.

She looked across from them to Fletcher's building. He had

the means and the compassion to help every single one of them. So why didn't he? Was it because his security guards wouldn't allow them access? But Fletcher had eyes; surely he knew they were here. Did they refuse to let him help them? Adair knew that, often, the people who needed help the most barricaded themselves from anyone trying to give it.

A sudden pounding on the passenger window startled her. A homeless man was pressing his face against the glass. "I want five dollars!" he shouted.

Adair swallowed nervously and leaned over to roll down the window a crack. "I don't have any money," she began, "but I can introduce you to someone who can help you find a job and a place to live—"

He suddenly began cursing and grabbed at her face through the window opening. She screamed and pulled back, but he caught a batch of her hair and jerked her toward the window. The instant she yanked free she cranked up the window, pinching his fingers. Then she started the car with a roar. As she fled, he shouted and spat.

Adair circled a long block and came back, only to find him sitting on the sidewalk in the same spot. She drove by without slowing. "I can't wait here until he leaves," she said, shaking all over. Her head hurt where he had pulled her hair.

But Adair's biggest shock was the realization that in his ravings, the man had been cursing Fletcher. He was quite aware that Fletcher lived in that building. That in itself was a strange comfort, because it told her that Fletcher had attempted to reach these people—even now he was probably still working on it. And she was glad, because there was nothing she could do for them without him.

Then she thought of Fletcher's answering service. Surely they could reach Yvonne or Charles . . . or Fletcher. Did she really want him to know she had gotten herself locked out of the apartment all day? And maybe all night?

"Not for several years, at which time we can laugh about it," she said without laughing. So she decided against calling the answering service. But maybe she could reach Yvonne, who was certainly at the Whinnets' party. Since Adair was not there, Yvonne probably knew something was wrong. Adair momentarily wondered whether she should have been more forceful with the bouncer at the door. But she never was very good at crashing parties.

She shook her head and continued her original line of thought: Yvonne was bound to check her answering machine. Adair needed only a place to call her and a place to wait for her. Adair *had* to wait downtown, so she could watch for Reggie. Besides that, her gas indicator was hovering on empty. Now, to find a free telephone.

Adair drove a short distance to a service station and pulled in. She went inside and found the attendant. "Excuse me. I've gotten myself in a predicament, and I need to use a phone, but I'm out of quarters. Could I use your telephone to make a local call?" She pointed to the desk phone behind the counter.

"Sure. One call," he answered.

"Thanks." She dialed Yvonne's number. The recording came on again. Adair took a breath and said quickly, "Yvonne, I've locked myself out of the apartment. I'm waiting outside the garage." Then she glanced self-consciously at the attendant, who was shaking his head and smiling. She returned to her car and drove back downtown. To her relief, the homeless man was gone.

Close to nine o'clock, she saw a car enter the garage. She perked up. A few minutes later another car exited, and she recognized the driver as the daytime security guard. "Reggie's here!" she squealed, starting her engine. She pulled into the garage and peered at the booth. Yes! It was Reggie!

She parked and ran to the booth. "Reggie, I'm so glad to see you! I'm Fletcher's wife—remember?"

"Sure, Mrs. Streiker. How're you tonight?"

"Terrible! I can't get to my apartment! I don't have a key! The elevator key!" she cried.

"No sweat, ma'am." He unlocked a cabinet and reached into the back. Adair trembled in relief as he pulled out a round key on a chain. "You'd better hold on to that one until you get another, then bring it back to me."

"Thank you, Reggie!" She plopped a kiss on his cheek and hurried to the elevator. As it ascended to the topmost floor, she felt as if she were going to heaven. At the penthouse, Adair burst out of the elevator and came to her apartment door—with its coded lock. She stopped dead.

"What is the code?" she asked herself sternly. She squeezed her eyes shut, trying to recall it. "Eight . . . blank . . . blank . . . four." Tentatively, she punched in 8044. Nothing. She tried 8054. Nope. 8034. No. "Oh, I'm wasting time trying this. I'll just have to go back down and ask Reggie."

So she returned to the security booth, where Reggie looked up from his closed-circuit television monitor. "Something wrong, Mrs. Streiker?"

"Reggie, I don't remember the door code. To unlock the door. What is it?"

His ruddy face wrinkled. "Gee, Mrs. Streiker, I don't know that."

She stared blankly at him. "You don't? Then who would? Oh, Yvonne! I still have to call Yvonne!" She picked up his telephone and dialed. A minute later she hung up again. "It's busy. She's either home, or her machine's taking a message and she's still at the Whinnets'. Reggie, *please* give me Charles Whinnet's home phone number!" Adair pleaded.

"Sure, Mrs. Streiker." He opened a loose-leaf book and pointed to a listing. Adair dialed the number, beaming gratefully at him.

The telephone rang twice. "Whinnet residence."

"Oh, a human voice! Jackie, it's Adair. Is Yvonne over there?"

"She was, but she left some time ago, honey," Jackie said.

"Oh . . . then . . . let me speak to Alicia, please."

"Hang on," said Jackie.

A moment later: "Adair! I was really disappointed not to see you tonight. Why did you come to the door and then leave?"

Adair stuttered, "Well—that gorilla at the door wouldn't let me in!"

"By the time he cleared your name with me, you'd left. Why did you leave?" Alicia sounded as if she were the injured party.

"Oh, I'm sorry, Alicia. Today has just been a nightmare. I've gotten locked out of my apartment. Do you or Charles know the door code to Fletcher's apartment?" Adair asked.

"I don't—let me ask Charles," Alicia said, leaving the telephone. When she returned, she said, "He doesn't know either, but he says Yvonne knows."

"Yes, I know; her line's busy," Adair said wearily.

"Come here for the night," Alicia said.

"I haven't got the gas to make it over there. I'll be okay. Thanks, Alicia. Goodnight." Adair hung up, then sat heavily on the stool in the cramped little booth. "I can't believe this," she whispered. "This has been the worst day of my whole life."

Reggie, like most men, could not bear to see a woman cry. "You just wait right here, Mrs. Streiker. I'll call Mrs. Fay until I get an answer."

"Okay, Reggie," she murmured. Her head leaned back on the window and her eyes closed, and he draped his jacket over her.

<hr />

Somewhere in a fog Adair heard Reggie talking loudly. "Shhh," she said unconsciously.

Then he was gently shaking her. "Mrs. Streiker . . . Mrs. Fay is on the line."

"Huh?" She opened bleary eyes. "Mrs. Fay?" Adair bolted up and grabbed the telephone. "Yvonne!"

"Adair, where have you been? I've been trying to call you all day! You were supposed to be at the Whinnets' home tonight! Where did you go after the doctor's office?" Yvonne demanded.

"Oh, Yvonne, I got locked out of the apartment. I don't remember the code to get in!" Adair cried.

"8834," said Yvonne. "It's 8834."

"8834. Thank you," Adair said, her eyes watering fiercely.

"Go on up to bed, and I'll call you tomorrow," Yvonne said.

"8834. Okay," Adair said, hanging up. "Goodnight, Reggie," she mumbled. "8834."

"Goodnight, Mrs. Streiker," he said tenderly.

"8834," Adair said on the elevator. She looked one last time at her watch. It was 10:15.

At the apartment door, Adair punched in 8834. And it opened. She slowly entered and closed the door behind her, not really believing that she was finally in. Then she headed straight for the refrigerator. As she opened the door, a sudden warbling almost knocked her over. She lurched to the telephone, gasping, "Hello."

"Hello, Adair. I'm sorry to call so late."

"Fletcher," she whispered.

"I just got through sitting on a plane for about eleven hours." He sounded as though he were stretching. "I'm one tired and cantankerous old man. I hope you've had a better day than I had."

"Oh, Fletcher! I miss you so!" Adair burst into tears. "I love you. I really do. You don't have to go away to prove anything."

"Why do you say that?" he asked.

Adair brought herself under control and cleared her throat. Since she did not know why she had said that, she changed the subject. "Umm, Sugar's arthritis was bothering her a lot today, so I took her to the doctor." No way was she going to tell him the rest of it.

"Good. I appreciate it," he said. "I hope you didn't have any problems getting back in. When I left this morning, your key was still sitting on the coffee table."

Adair took the receiver away from her ear to look. Sure enough, there was the key sitting on the glass table.

"That's okay. Reggie lent me his key."

"Good. And you remembered the door combination?"

"Actually, no; but Yvonne told me," she said. It all sounded so simple now.

"Ah, good," he said. A moment's pause. "I was afraid after I left, that you might have second thoughts . . . it's probably not going to be the kind of life you envisioned, and it won't always be easy.

But, whatever happens, I'll be there when you need me. Well, maybe not always exactly *there*, but, within reach. . . . Do you know what I mean?"

"Yes," she said, barely suppressing an ironic laugh, and then a yawn.

There was a moment of silence, as if he were waiting to hear something. Then he said, "You're tired. Go on to bed, babe. I'll talk to you tomorrow."

"Okay. Goodnight, Fletcher." After hanging up, she stood in front of the refrigerator and ate whatever she could find for about thirty minutes. Then she went to bed without even washing the makeup off her face.

It was the coffee that brought Adair to consciousness the next morning—that wonderful aroma creeping into her sleep. She felt for her watch on the bedside table and opened one eye to look at it. A quarter to nine. Rising stiffly, she wondered why she was so chained to the clock.

She took a moment to wash off yesterday's mascara. Then she came out of the bedroom, patting her swollen eyes dry. Sugar was working away in the kitchen: "Good morning, Mrs. Streiker. Did you have a nice time at Mrs. Whinnet's party? I tell you, I feel so much better today. Why, like I told Mr. Streiker—"

"Did Fletcher call this morning?" Adair asked abruptly.

"No, last night. And when I told him how kind you were—"

"Wait a minute," Adair said, confused. "When last night did you talk to him?"

"Oh, he called me at home about 7:30, I suppose. And I told him how kind you were to take me to Dr. Forsythe, and wait with me all that time, and I felt you were hurting with me, and then to pay for it and hurry me back so I wouldn't miss my bus. I told him all about it, and he said he was so glad you were here to take up the slack, or something like that."

"He didn't mention it," muttered Adair, pouring herself a cup of coffee. As she sipped the coffee, she looked out over the sky-line awash in morning light. Remembering how forlorn she had felt on the street last night gave her greater appreciation for her new home. So what if it wasn't a mansion? It was comfortable, safe, and roomy. She went over to the curio cabinets to take a closer look at some of the objects. Above all else, the apartment reflected an interesting man.

The telephone rang and Sugar answered it. "Yes, she's up. All right; I'll tell her."

Adair turned. "Do I need to get dressed?"

"Only if you want. Mrs. Fay is coming up for a moment."

This one time Adair accepted the propriety of receiving company while she was in her ratty bathrobe, and used the next thirty seconds to get herself another cup of coffee.

Sugar answered the light knock on the door. In came Yvonne, looking as chic as ever. "Good morning, Adair. I hope you got some rest last night."

"Thanks to you, yes," Adair admitted. "Have a seat."

Yvonne gathered in her midcalf corduroy skirt and sat next to Adair on the white sofa. "Did Mr. Streiker reach you?" she asked while accepting a cup of coffee from Sugar. "Thank you."

"Yes, he did. Don't tell me you talked to him as well!" said Adair.

"Yes, he called three times—once over to the Whinnets'. He was quite concerned when he could not reach you here." Yvonne paused to sip her coffee.

Adair squinted, trying to sort out all these calls. "When did he call you?"

"The first time, about four o'clock, right before you had the doctor's office call—that was a smart move, by the way. When he called the Whinnets' home around seven, I was able to tell him that you had taken Sugar to the doctor. But since you weren't there and he still couldn't reach you, I began trying to find you. I finally had to leave the party early—by the way, you were on the guest list as April Joyce. I had told Alicia of your concerns, and she came up with a pseudonym.

"Oh—I got only part of your two messages—the last one was something about waiting at a garage, but we couldn't figure out which garage you were at. I thought you might have had car trouble, so I called every garage between Dallas and DeSoto."

"I meant the Streiker parking garage," Adair interjected. "The first part of that message was that I'd locked myself out."

"I realize that now," Yvonne responded.

"Anyway, when did he call again?" Adair asked.

"He called the last time around ten, and I made him give me fifteen minutes before he took further action. The instant I hung up, Reggie got through. I suppose I had better get call waiting on my line," Yvonne mused.

"'Further action'? What further action do you mean?" Adair asked in slight alarm.

"Oh, well, Fletcher has all kinds of options. I don't know what he had in mind for last night," Yvonne said matter-of-factly.

"Why didn't he tell me all this when he called?" Adair asked.

"Well, really, Adair, what would that accomplish but to make you feel foolish? Or that he was checking up on you? And . . . did you tell him that you were locked out of the apartment all day?"

"No," blushed Adair.

"Well, he's not going to beat it out of you," Yvonne said with a wink at the absurd. She smiled over her porcelain cup. "This is delicious, Sugar."

"Thank you, Yvonne!" came Sugar's voice from the kitchen.

Adair was studying the worn edge of her old chenille robe.

"Are you upset?" Yvonne asked.

"No," Adair coughed. "I'm . . . a little jealous that you know Fletcher so well."

"But I'm not married to him. Now, the first thing to do," Yvonne resumed in a businesslike manner, "is to make sure you don't get locked out again. Do you have your key?"

"I have Reggie's, in my purse," Adair pointed.

"Here's yours, Mrs. Streiker." Sugar came over with another

key on a gold chain. "This is the one Mr. Streiker left for you. I found it on the table this morning."

Embarrassed, Adair took the key. After all that, she still had forgotten to put it in her purse last night.

Yvonne resumed, "Okay, do you remember your door code?"

"8834," Adair replied immediately.

"You know my telephone number, so. . . ." Yvonne pulled out a piece of paper and scribbled on it. "Here is Sugar's home phone—Brigstahl. Pete Brigstahl. And the Whinnets'. And mine, just in case you forget it." She stopped to dig in her leather tote. "Here is Mr. Streiker's bank card—these middle digits are his personal identification number—so you'll have access to the cash you need."

Adair meekly took the paper and card. Yvonne drummed her fingers on her chin. "Anything else you can think of that you need?" she asked. Adair shook her head.

"All right, then, I'll get back to work." Yvonne stood up. "Believe it or not, I really do perform bookkeeping for the company."

Adair smiled feebly as she walked Yvonne to the door.

Yvonne paused. "Would you . . . like some advice?"

Adair looked up. "Tell me."

"Mr. Streiker has very definite notions of privacy, I guess you noticed. That extends to you. What I mean is, he won't invade your privacy with a lot of questions. I imagine he wanted to know very much where you were all that time, but he wouldn't put you on the spot by asking. He would leave it up to you to mention it. Next time he calls, I'd tell him everything that was on my mind—everything that went wrong, everything that worried me. You'd be surprised at how much he can do, even long distance." She opened the door. "He'll probably call in the evening, being pretty much tied up during the day. If you want to hear from him, you ought to be home at night."

Adair nodded. "Thanks, Yvonne. I will be." She closed the door and trudged to the shower. She stood under the warm water and let it run down her face and hair to bathe away the embarrassment of yesterday's fiascoes.

Still, she had had something to do yesterday, even if it was not a lot of fun. How was she going to fill today? Or tomorrow? Or the next day or the next, until Fletcher came home?

When Adair finally emerged from the bedroom, she found Sugar putting on her sweater. "Where are you going?" Adair asked.

"I'm out of walnuts for the Waldorf salad," Sugar said apologetically. (*Of course you are. I ate them last night,* Adair thought.) "The bus should be by in about fifteen minutes, so I'm going to run to the market for some."

"Oh, for pete's sake, I'll go get them," said Adair. "I've got a car and nothing else to do."

"That would be very kind of you, Mrs. Streiker," Sugar said, taking off her sweater. "I do need to get some laundry done. Oh—and would you mind picking up whipping cream too?"

"Not at all," Adair said. She stopped at the door to make sure she had her key, her bank card, and her list of phone numbers.

"Thank you so much. Take your time now—I'm in no rush," Sugar said. Adair smiled at her. Sugar really looked relieved that she did not have to go out right now.

Adair left the apartment and pushed the button to summon the elevator. As she waited, she glanced around the hall and saw a doorway. "Stairs!" She banged her forehead in exasperation on the wall. "All that time I was scrounging for a key, I could have taken the stairs!"

She went over and opened the door. It was a stairwell, all right, but it led only up. Puzzled, Adair took the stairs up one flight to another door, which she opened.

This led onto the roof of the building. She stepped onto a large, multilevel deck surrounded by potted plants and leading to a lap pool. A gazebo stood on one side of the deck and a tennis court on the other, protected by large green wind screens. On the far side of the gazebo was a greenhouse. Adair peeked in at the variety of tropical plants. Beyond the tennis court was a helicopter pad, with a sleek blue helicopter sitting on one side. "Well, of course, that's where he left from the other day."

She wandered over to look at the sparkling pool, admired the marigolds and chrysanthemums planted in half-barrels, and paused in the gazebo. There were two deck chairs and an arm-side table with a telephone. She picked up the receiver and pushed the button marked "Intercom."

"Yes? Mrs. Streiker?" Sugar answered.

"How did you know it was me?" asked Adair.

"I assume you're on the roof. The intercom rings differently from an outside line," Sugar said.

"Well, isn't this something! I'm glad to know about all this!" exclaimed Adair.

"I'm sorry; I thought Mr. Streiker already showed it to you," said Sugar.

"No, he didn't. I guess he didn't have time before he left." Adair felt a slight pain in her chest. "Well, I really am going to run those errands now."

"Fine, Mrs. Streiker."

Adair hung up and went back down the stairs to the elevator, which took her, as always, straight to whichever floor she indicated without stopping on the way.

In her car, she drummed the steering wheel, thinking, "Let's see. . . . I could go back inside to use the automatic teller in the lobby, but there's a drive-through teller on the other side of this building, and there's a grocery store in the little shopping center on Redwine. Poor Sugar, to have to take the bus to run errands."

Adair started the engine and drove to the money machine. Just in case she needed extra cash, she withdrew fifty dollars. "Got to get gas," she reminded herself, glancing at the fuel gauge.

Mimicking Fletcher, she dropped a twenty to pay for a twelve-fifty fill-up, then went on to the market, where she picked up whipping cream and shelled walnuts. Passing the nut bins, she slowed. Pistachios. She loved them, but never could afford them. Grinning, she picked up the scoop and a paper sack. By the time she reached the checkout, she had to pull out another twenty-dollar bill, although this time she got a few dollars in change. "Looks like I need to get more cash," she said happily on her way to the car.

Driving a roundabout way home on the freeway, she passed NorthPark Mall, with its wonderful little expensive shops. Her foot automatically eased up on the accelerator. Then she shook her head. "What am I doing? I'm running an errand for Sugar." She continued home.

But all the way back she argued, "Why shouldn't I get some new things? Fletcher would let me, and I need them. I really do need a winter coat." She began to get so excited that she failed to notice her speedometer inching up. A bright flash in the rear-view mirror caught her eye, and she gasped. A police cruiser had his lights on directly behind her. She pulled onto the shoulder of the freeway, panicky thoughts racing by: *He's going to ask for my driver's license. Does he read the* Expositor? *How will this reflect on Fletcher?* The absurd headline appeared in her mind: BILLIONAIRE'S WIFE STOPPED FOR SPEEDING. Another instant later, the patrol car passed her in pursuit of a Corvette.

Adair sat numbly at the wheel, breathing gratitude. Then, mindful of her close call, she cautiously edged back into traffic.

Her high spirits returned as she pulled into the Streiker garage. Bounding into the elevator, she pulled out the round elevator key. But before she had a chance to use it, a man suddenly stepped onto the elevator with her. He was tall and good-looking, with close-cropped curly hair. He wore an expensive Italian suit. Adair paused, her hand curled around the key.

He pushed the button for the twentieth floor, then asked her, smiling easily, "Which floor?"

"Uh—yeah, twenty, that's it," she stammered, glancing away. "Have I seen you somewhere before?" she asked suddenly, surprising herself.

"Maybe," he answered as the elevator ascended. "Fletcher and I are old friends. Oh, by the way, congratulations. Or shouldn't I say, best wishes?" His smile was pure and disarming, but Adair had trouble looking him in the eye.

She floundered for a response while the elevator stopped and the door opened. "Who are you?" she asked as he stepped out.

He turned back to smile at her, and the door shut between them. Adair stood immobilized until the elevator began to ascend again. She quickly used her key to make it override other summons and take her straight up.

Her door was unlocked. "Sugar?" she called. "Here are the things you needed."

"Thank you, Mrs. Streiker. That was so kind of you." Sugar came out from behind an ironing board.

Adair saw with a pang of guilt that Sugar had been ironing Adair's cotton separates, which had been hanging wrinkled in her closet for so long that they were now out of season. "Thanks for doing my ironing," Adair mumbled.

Sugar took the groceries to put them away. "That's my job, dear. Pistachios! How nice."

"Yes, I guess it is. . . . Sugar, I'm going to pick up a few things for myself now. Do you need anything from NorthPark?"

"NorthPark? Heavens, no," laughed Sugar. "You go on now and have a good time."

"I will," Adair said, relaxing. She realized that she had been tensed up ever since getting off the elevator.

<hr />

On her way to the car, Adair thought out loud, "So he saw my picture in the paper. I knew that would happen. So what?" *But who is he? Why did I think I had seen him before?* she wondered.

She shook off the questions in order to concentrate on something more important, like what she should buy. Seeing the daytime security guard settling into the booth, she drove in a wide arc to avoid him, in case he remembered her from yesterday.

She drove an ultra-conservative sixty-five miles per hour to the mall, allowing traffic to whiz by her on the left. But she felt vindicated on seeing a Porsche being pulled over.

She parked in the shade at the mall, since the summer sun seemed determined to hang around through the fall, and breezed into a main entrance. Her first stop was at an automatic teller machine. After she had keyed in her desire to withdraw cash, the machine inquired, *Amount?* She keyed in 50, but her finger stayed an instant too long on the zero key. *$500.00 entered. Correct?*

"Okay," she agreed, and the machine gave her a stack of twenties.

Then came the hard part—deciding where to start. Adair strolled down the walkway, eyeing decorations. Halloween was approaching, so a lot of stores had set up the obligatory skeletons and the dismal black and orange streamers. Childless Adair had a difficult time understanding the appeal of Halloween. She thought it was silly for adults to dress up in costumes, and she hated gory horror movies. The whole thing seemed like a prank that had gotten out of hand. She walked quickly past the displays, feeling irritated that they were taking up space.

Adair slowed in front of a little boutique with crystal chandeliers, wall-to-wall mirrors, and clothing creations displayed on stands, not racks. For someone whose most frequent shopping outlet was Goodwill, Adair did something bold. She went in.

A saleswoman with black-ringed eyes and inch-long fingernails met her immediately. "May I help you?" she asked, discreetly sizing up the customer. Her eye landed on Adair's ring.

"I need a new coat," Adair said, fingering the sleeve of a sweater. It was on sale for $250.

"Wool, leather, or fur?" inquired the clerk, steering Adair to a back corner.

"What have you got in fur?" Adair asked automatically.

"We just got in a wonderful new shipment." The clerk began pulling out a luxurious harvest. "We have mink, chinchilla, otter, and fox. I assume you want a full-length," she said, implying that anything else would be substandard.

"Shurtainly," Adair said, then reddened at her slip. Her old, poor self had started to say *sure* while her new, rich self was saying *certainly,* and the two had come out as one word.

The salesclerk pretended not to notice. "If you're concerned about appearances, I have to tell you that this winter it's mink. *Everyone* will be wearing it. You just won't fit in without at least one good mink." She unfurled a beautiful black coat, glistening and incredibly soft.

"How much is it?" Adair asked, lightly caressing its folds.

"This one is a steal at $5200," the clerk said emphatically. "Try it on."

Adair slipped her arms into the mink and wrapped it around her. At once she was adrift in bliss.

The saleswoman turned her around to a mirror. "It's made for you. You look like a million dollars. *He'll* appreciate that," she purred, stroking the fur. "You can charge it."

"No," Adair objected. "I'll pay cash. But I have to go get it. I'll be right back."

She slipped out of the coat and flew down to the money machine, where she punched in a demand for $5000. Then she drummed her fingernails on the machine while it processed her request. A moment later the response flashed: *Request denied. Withdrawal limit exceeded.*

"What?" gasped Adair. Lowering her sights, she then asked for $1000. And after making her wait again, the machine indicated, *Request denied. Withdrawal limit exceeded.*

Fuming, Adair went to a nearby telephone and dialed the corporation's number. "Yvonne Fay," she growled into the receiver.

Seconds later: "This is Yvonne Fay."

"Yvonne, what is going on? I can't get enough money for a new coat!" Adair exploded.

After the briefest pause, Yvonne said crisply, "Hold on, please." A moment later she said in a muffled voice, "What's the problem, Adair? Can't you get a coat for a thousand dollars?"

"A thousand dollars?" Adair repeated blankly. "Is that all I can withdraw?"

"Yes, in one day. Haven't you talked to Mr. Streiker about this?"

"No," Adair snapped. "He's not available at the moment. So maybe you can tell me why I have a thousand-dollar-a-day limit."

"I understand it's because you requested it," Yvonne said calmly.

"I have no idea what you're talking about," Adair assured her.

"All I know is, he said something about how you were afraid of becoming a 'rich witch.' So he set the limit to help you."

In a flash Adair recalled the girl at the bank. And she saw how very much she herself sounded like that girl, demanding money from an account not even her own. When she found her voice, she said, "He's . . . that's right. I'm sorry I bothered you, Yvonne."

"That's what I'm here for," Yvonne replied cheerfully.

Adair turned in deepest humiliation from the telephone and walked the length of the mall to a department store. With the cash she had, she found a royal blue wool coat with a matching hat. When she left, she still had two hundred dollars in her purse.

Adair was reasonably careful driving home from NorthPark Mall, but she kept discovering that she had made turns or stopped at red lights without remembering that she had done so. As she entered the garage, she pulled the visor down to block her face from the security guard and vaguely wished for a more private entrance to her home.

When she got on the far left elevator, two other people hurried on with her. After a bemused pause, she got off at the lobby level. But every time she attempted to board the elevator, people kept getting on with her so that she did not have it to herself, and she did not wish to advertise her use of the penthouse key. It seemed to be the end of lunch hour for a number of Streiker employees—everyone was going up or down. Adair rode the elevator from floor to floor, growing increasingly exasperated while her packages grew heavier.

At one point Adair got off on the fourteenth floor and leaned against the wall while shifting her packages. A young woman who had also disembarked hesitated, looking back over her shoulder.

Adair smiled reflexively.

"You're the one who married Mr. Streiker, aren't you?" the girl asked. "What's your name again?"

Surprised, Adair said, "Uh, well, yes, I am. I'm Adair."

"Oh, yes." The girl nodded thoughtfully. She looked at Adair's packages. "I see you've been shopping."

Wondering at the faint disapproval, Adair looked down at her boxes with coat and hat. "Yes, I have." She stopped short of explaining that she needed a winter coat.

"Don't you think that as Mr. Streiker's wife, you have better things to do than go shopping? Considering all the worthwhile things that he does, shouldn't you be giving your time in charitable service rather than going out spending money and enjoying yourself?" the young woman asked.

Adair felt broadsided. "I don't think—"

"Just asking." The girl smiled in a smug, sarcastic way and turned down the hall.

Adair chewed her lip as she returned to the elevator and jabbed the down button again. All at once she hated this building and everyone in it. She could understand now why that homeless man had attacked her last night.

When she got to the lobby level again, she had an idea. She discreetly summoned every elevator in the lobby and waited near the far one. It worked. She was able to hop on and use her key before anyone else could make it to the door. With tired arms, she entered her apartment and tossed the packages on the closest sofa.

Sugar came out from the bedroom. "Did you find anything at the mall?"

"A winter coat," Adair smiled feebly, opening the box to show her.

"Oh, that's so nice. Such a pretty color. Practical, though, and not terribly extravagant. Mr. Streiker will like it," Sugar commented.

"I hope so," Adair said sincerely. She looked inquiringly toward the kitchen.

"I have that Waldorf salad ready, if you'd like some now," Sugar offered.

"I sure would," Adair admitted. She sat at the glass dinette near the windows while Sugar served her coffee, salad, and hot rolls. "You're a wonderful cook," Adair reflected.

"Thank you. That's my job, and I enjoy it." Sugar left in response to the buzz of the clothes dryer.

Adair ate rather dejectedly. Sugar had her job and did it well. Yvonne knew her job inside and out as liaison to Fletcher. But what was Adair's job? What was she supposed to *do* as Mrs. Streiker? Sure, she could have a good time on a thousand dollars a day, but her Puritan heritage would not permit her such self-indulgence—not to mention what Fletcher would think of it. When she was struggling to support herself, she had no problem filling her time. Every moment was dictated by necessity. But now that her basic material needs were met, what was she supposed to do with herself?

She finished her salad, but continued to gaze over the hazy Dallas skyline. After some thought, she went to the kitchen telephone and called Yvonne. "I hate to bother you again—it's Adair—but could you come up to the penthouse when you have time?"

"Yes. Give me about fifteen minutes," Yvonne replied. Adair hung up feeling hopeful, so she helped herself to more Waldorf salad.

When Yvonne came to the door, Adair opened it, since Sugar was still back in the laundry room off the kitchen.

"Good afternoon," Yvonne smiled, then noticed the packages. "Did you find a coat?"

"Yes; I think I got a good buy," Adair said a little anxiously.

"I'm sure you did," Yvonne said as she sat. She didn't show any real curiosity to see what Adair had bought. "What's on your mind?"

"I was hoping you could give me some advice," Adair began uncertainly, sitting across from Yvonne.

"Regarding . . . ?"

"Well, regarding what I should do," said Adair. "I was thinking about volunteer work with one of the social agencies, or maybe at a hospital, you know. . . ." Her fragile train of thought derailed under Yvonne's gaze.

"Is this something you have a burning desire to do?" Yvonne asked.

"Well, I don't think I can know that until I try it. And I really feel I should be doing something worthwhile."

Yvonne smiled faintly. "Your intentions are certainly good. But I believe you're going to have to ask Mr. Streiker about this. He may want you to remain somewhat anonymous, for now."

"Oh!" Adair had forgotten. "Yes, that may very well be."

"I'm sure he'll call you tonight, and you can talk it over with him then," Yvonne said reassuringly. Then she looked up toward the kitchen where Sugar had brought out a basket of clothes to fold. "How is your arthritis today, Sugar?"

"I tell you, today it just hardly bothers me at all. I don't know why it flares up sometimes, but today I feel just great," Sugar said happily. There was certainly no mistaking whether she was feeling good or bad.

"I'm so glad." Yvonne gave Adair a mysterious little smile. "I suppose I'd better get back. Someone lost last quarter's municipal taxes in the computer and I've got to dig them out." She stood up, then paused over yesterday's mail still on the table. "One thing you *can* do is look through this mail."

"Sure," Adair said noncommittally.

Before she left, Yvonne had one last word of encouragement. "Don't worry, Adair. You'll get the hang of it soon."

"Get the hang of *what?*" Adair asked into the air after Yvonne had departed. She sat listlessly on the couch for a while, then got up to stare out of the huge windows. A gray autumn rain had begun to fall from low clouds. Adair shivered. For having so many people, Dallas could be the coldest, loneliest place.

For the first time, she felt a sense of regret. She regretted her decision to marry Fletcher. She regretted tying herself up with anyone else's priorities and timetable. She regretted having lost her independence to gain him.

Adair barely heard the telephone ring and Sugar answer it. "Why, yes, she is," Sugar said excitedly. "It's Mr. Streiker!" she called to Adair.

The wife slowly took the telephone, trying to repress the sudden elevation of her heartbeat. "Hello," she said quietly.

"Adair? How are you holding up?" that warm voice asked.

"Okay," she said nonchalantly. "I'm doing fine."

"Good. I was thinking about you—thinking that it took a lot of courage for you to make a leap into the dark the way you did. Right now things probably don't look much brighter. Yvonne thought there might be some things you wanted to talk about."

"Well . . . where are you?" she asked.

"I can't tell you," he said.

"Then what did you want me to ask you?" she snapped.

"Just tell me what's on your mind," he said.

"Okay. Why did you go off and leave me?" she demanded.

"I had to. I wouldn't unless I absolutely had to," he replied.

"Oh, Fletcher, I just—I just don't know what to do with myself. I made a total fool of myself to Yvonne. I tried to withdraw too much money to get a fur coat, then I screamed at her because I couldn't get enough, when I didn't need it anyway."

"Were you able to get a coat?" he asked.

"Yes," she admitted.

"Are you happy with it?" he asked.

"Sure. It's very nice," she said.

"Then don't worry about what Yvonne thinks. She's there to help you. What else is bothering you?"

"I had a heck of a time trying to get to the apartment," she remembered. "People kept getting on the elevator with me, and I had to keep getting off until I could catch it empty."

He laughed. "Try this for now: ask Reggie to turn on the 'out of service' sign on the elevator. Then it won't operate except with the penthouse key. How's that?"

"Fine," she said, relieved. Then she remembered something else. "There was a man on the elevator—a tall, nice-looking guy—who called me by name, and said he was an old friend of yours, but I didn't get his name."

"Any number of people would have seen your picture in the paper, and they can *say* anything. I don't want you to hide, but I do want you to be wary," he said.

"So you saw the paper," she mused.

"Yes. Yvonne faxed it to me," Fletcher told her.

"Why does she get to know where you are when I don't?" she asked, hurt.

"Because she is not—as vulnerable," Fletcher replied.

Adair was taken aback. "If I'm so vulnerable, why don't you come protect me?"

"You'll be fine as long as you do what I ask. And I couldn't do any more for you if I were right there by your side," he assured her.

"And just what is it that I'm supposed to do?" she asked in frustration.

"Well, for starters, you can go see Wendy Beacham at the *Expositor*. Tell her who you are and ask her to leave you alone."

Adair was silent for a good ten seconds. "You must be joking."

"No, I'm quite serious."

"I can't do that! She'll—she'll devour me!" Adair exclaimed.

"I doubt that," he said calmly.

Adair grappled with his request. "Will she listen to me?"

Fletcher hesitated before answering, "Yes."

"All right," she said without conviction. "If you want me to, I'll do it." She glanced at her watch.

As if seeing that, Fletcher said, "You needn't go now if you don't feel prepared."

"I might as well," she allowed, "before I chicken out. When will you call again, Fletcher?"

"I can call tonight, if you'll be home."

"Yes, yes, I will," she promised.

"Tonight, then. . . . I love you, Adair," he said quietly.

"I love you, Fletcher," she dutifully replied. Distracted by the prospect before her, she hung up.

Then immediately she remembered, "No! Oh, no! My ballet class is tonight!" She quickly picked up the phone again, but the line was dead.

In exasperation, she found Madame Prochaska's number and dialed it. Madame was not at the studio yet, so Adair left this message on her answering machine: "This is Adair Weiss. Madame, it's not working out for me to come to class at night. Can we schedule a special day class? I can pay more now than I could before." Then Adair left her new telephone number.

She hung up, troubled. How ironic that what little she had to do conflicted. Sugar smiled at her sympathetically. "Would you like a glass of mint tea?" She already had a glass for herself.

"Maybe later. I have to go somewhere for Fletcher," Adair said listlessly.

"He always has such good reasons for what he asks—the only problem is, he doesn't usually explain them!" Sugar laughed.

That elicited a wan smile from Adair, as well as some curiosity. "How long have you worked for Fletcher, Sugar?"

"Goodness, let's see." Sugar fluffed her white ringlets back away from her forehead. "It'll be four years next March. Four years for him personally, but I worked seven years before that as a night maid for the company."

"How did you start as his personal housekeeper?" Adair asked.

"Well, that's so strange. I started having trouble with my arthritis the last year I worked for the company. I had a lot of pain, and I found that I couldn't pick up trash cans or push a vacuum cleaner. My disability started piling up, and my boss threatened to fire me. That scared me to death, 'cause my husband is disabled with a bad back and we had a boy in high school, looking to college. My husband was just adamant that he go to college—you know how men are—and I just didn't know what we were going to do if I couldn't keep working.

"So I sat down and wrote a letter to Mr. Streiker himself, without ever having met him. I told him how much I needed the job, and that I could still work if I had help paying for medical treatment. I told him my arthritis acted up when I was tired, which made night work hard, but that I was a good cook. For some reason, I felt he should know that I'm a good cook.

"Then a few days later Yvonne called me to the conference room on the tenth floor—that room with the big table and all those plush chairs. When I went in, there was Mr. Streiker himself, holding my letter. He said, 'Can you really cook?' And I told him my favorite thing in the world is to piddle in the kitchen. He said, 'How would you like to come work for me?'

"Well, I couldn't believe it. I was so shocked, you could have knocked me over with a feather. But I started for him that very day." Sugar shook her head, smiling, and sipped her tea.

"Sugar—do you mind if I ask—I'm wondering if your arthritis interferes with your housekeeping?" Adair asked delicately.

"Well, yes, sometimes I'm not able to do all that I want to do, but Mr. Streiker tells me not to worry about it, just do what I can. And I do, and it seems to work out all right. He doesn't go around leaving big messes and he never complains about what doesn't get done," Sugar said fondly.

"I'll try not to make it any more difficult for you," Adair added. She liked Sugar, but she wondered why in the world Fletcher couldn't find someone who could do the job. If he hired all of his employees out of pity, his company would fall apart.

Then Adair looked around the apartment. As large as it was, it *was* spotless, wasn't it? The clothes were clean and ironed, and the refrigerator *was* well-stocked, wasn't it? Sugar might consider herself inadequate for the job, but Adair had no business fault-finding. The snide girl who had accosted Adair over her shopping trip sprang to mind.

"You do your job well," Adair insisted, then asked, "how much does he pay you?"

Sugar's cheeks grew pink. "More than I'm worth. He's very generous. . . ." As she saw Adair waiting for an answer, she added, "Seventy thousand a year, Mrs. Streiker."

Adair would have been shocked had she not already witnessed Fletcher's generosity. "No, I'm sure you're worth it. I wouldn't tamper with your pay. I wouldn't dare."

"You're too kind," Sugar murmured into her tea.

Not really, Adair thought. Of course she considered the pay excessive, but she meant it when she said she would not dare think of cutting it. As Sugar had said, Fletcher had his own reasons for what he did, and Adair did not pretend to understand them all.

She looked at her watch. "I guess I'd better go now if I'm going to do what Fletcher asked."

"Whatever it is, I'm sure you'll handle it just fine," Sugar said confidently, taking her tea back to the kitchen.

"If I did my job as well as you do yours, I'd have nothing to worry about," Adair replied. Her eye fell on the untouched mail, and she remembered something. Finding blank stationery in the desk drawer, she wrote out a note to Reggie, asking him to turn on the "out of service" sign on the far elevator. Then she put his elevator key with the note in the envelope and addressed it in large letters to REGGIE.

"Sugar, could you do me a favor? Please take this to the security guard in the parking garage, and ask him to give it to Reggie when he comes on duty tonight. I . . . I don't want the guard to see me."

"I'll do that right now," Sugar said.

"Thank you." Adair inhaled deeply, then said, "I'll be gone when you get back."

When Sugar had left, Adair stopped in the bathroom to freshen up. These little rituals of brushing her hair and putting on lipstick fortified her to face unpleasantness down the road.

She left the apartment, leaving it unlocked for Sugar, and rode the silent elevator down to the garage. As she was getting into her car, she saw Sugar leaving the security booth. Adair let the engine idle while she considered the best route to the *Expositor*'s offices. "No matter which way I go, it will take a good thirty minutes to get there," she advised herself. "What the heck—I need the time to think of what I'm going to say."

<hr>

But when she pulled into the newspaper's parking lot half an hour later, her mind was still a blank except for the question, *Why am I doing this?*

It made no sense at all. The only thing that pried her out of the car seat was that Fletcher had requested it. Yes, she was mad at him for leaving, but she still experienced palpitations whenever she thought of him. She locked her car and walked up to the front door of the *North Dallas Expositor*, circulation 353,000.

An exiting photographer held the door open for her, and she fleetingly smiled at him. The front receptionist was talking on the telephone when Adair approached. The receptionist paused to eye her questioningly, and Adair asked for "Wendy Beacham, please."

"Second floor, first office to the right," the receptionist answered briskly.

Adair turned to the elevator, amazed that she had not even been asked her name. On the second floor, she stepped out to find a large open area to her left, crowded with desks and computers. From the appearance of all the backs hunched over keyboards, she inferred that deadlines were at hand. Adair turned to her right, to a door that said, "W. Beacham, Lifestyles Editor." After several false starts, Adair knocked.

An indistinct reply came that sounded more like "What is it?" than "Come in," but Adair went in anyway.

The office was small and cluttered, with several moribund plants, a coffee maker still heating the early morning's coffee, and a woman typing rapidly at a computer terminal. As she glanced up impatiently, Adair felt a twinge of disappointment. She looked so— fragile, and childlike. She was small and slender, with prematurely graying hair and large eyes. Any makeup on her face would have seemed superfluous.

"Ms. Beacham?" Adair asked.

"Yes, and I'm *extremely* busy," the editor answered, then muttered to herself as she corrected an error on the keyboard.

"I'm sorry to barge in like this; I'll only be a moment." Adair inhaled. "My name is Adair Streiker."

The editor's fingers froze and she swiveled abruptly. "Streiker's new wife! That's right—I thought I knew you." Her eyes darkened with intensity. "Here—sit down." Wendy yanked a book off a nearby chair.

"Like I said, I'll only be a moment." Adair sat on the edge of the chair. "I've only come to ask you to—leave us alone. To not pursue stories on us."

"If you didn't want to be interviewed, why did you come here?" Wendy asked with a smile.

"I had been hiding from you. I'd been afraid to even leave the apartment since you ran my picture on the front page—" Wendy made a quick note and Adair regretted her mention of *apartment* "—and so Fletcher suggested I come ask you to leave me alone. That's what I'm asking."

"I can appreciate your desire for privacy, but anything a man like Fletcher Streiker does is newsworthy, particularly when he marries a local woman," Wendy said logically.

"Is your vendetta against him also newsworthy?" Adair asked.

"Vendetta?" laughed Wendy. "I haven't got a vendetta in the world. I consider myself lucky to have known him once, before he got rich and famous."

Adair sat still, trying to weigh carefully what she said. She was acutely aware that any comment of hers might very well appear in tomorrow's paper. "All right, pursue Fletcher. But please leave me alone."

"Unfortunately, publicity is one thing that comes with the vast amount of territory you gained when you married him," Wendy said gamely. "But if you will tell me just a few things, I will take the reporters off your case."

"I'll consider answering some questions," Adair said cautiously.

"Fair enough. Where is Streiker now?" asked Wendy, holding her pencil ready.

"He's out of the country. I don't know precisely where," Adair answered.

Wendy raised an eyebrow. "What is he doing?"

"I don't know. He wouldn't tell me what he's working on."

"Doesn't he confide in you at all?" asked Wendy.

"Yes, but on very selective things. Almost nothing about his work, unless it's a completed project," Adair said.

Wendy twirled the pencil, which had not made any further notes. "I see . . . and what do you plan to do in your new position as Mrs. Fletcher Streiker?"

"I don't know yet. I'm trying to figure that out," Adair said with unfortunate honesty.

"Well," said Wendy, laying down the pencil and settling back, "it's obvious that we don't need to dog you. You're just an orna-ment in this relationship and have no influence at all. You don't even know what's going on. I didn't realize, after the enlighten-ment of the women's movement, that there are still women around who are content to be prostitutes their whole lives. Thank you for stopping by." Wendy turned back to her computer.

Adair was almost knocked senseless. She wordlessly left the office, and only dimly perceived leaving the building and getting into her car. She drove home perfectly at the speed limit, parked, and walked right into the elevator standing open like a grave.

Eight-eight-three-four opened her apartment door. "I'll probably never forget that number now, even if I never use it again," she told the empty hallway.

Sugar looked up from the kitchen range as Adair came in. "Hello, Mrs. Streiker! How did it go?"

"Fine. Fine, Sugar," Adair said without pausing on her way to the bedroom. She found her old sturdy suitcase in the closet and pulled it out onto the bed. Then she began critically selecting only the most essential clothes from her meager wardrobe. "I will not be anyone's knickknack," she told a purple sweater.

———◆———

She heard the telephone ring in the kitchen but ignored it. Presently Sugar knocked on the bedroom door. "Mrs. Streiker? Telephone."

"Is it Fletcher?" she asked unemotionally, poised over the suitcase.

"No, ma'am, it's Mrs. Clay Shaw," Sugar said through the door.

"Mrs. Clay Shaw? What does she want?" asked Adair.

"To talk to you, Mrs. Streiker," Sugar said.

Adair hesitated, then put the sweater in the suitcase and left the bedroom, closing the door behind her. She took the telephone as Sugar returned to the range. "Hello?" said Adair.

"Is this Adair Streiker?" asked a soft, childlike voice.

"Yes. Who is this?" Adair said firmly.

"Oh, thank goodness!" sighed the girl. "This is the first time I've ever had to get hold of Panny in a real emergency, and I knew he wasn't there, but he told me about you, and that if I needed him to call you!"

"Is this his sister?" Adair asked.

"Yes, I'm sorry—this is Desirée Shaw. I'm calling from Honolulu."

"Oh?" Adair said.

"Our mother has just had a heart attack. She's in critical condition here at Pacific General Hospital. They want to do an emergency coronary bypass on her, but the hospital wants fifty thousand dollars up front before they'll do it. We just can't scrape up that kind of cash right away. We need Panny's—I mean, Fletcher's—help."

"I'll have the money wired to the hospital immediately," said Adair. "Pacific General in Honolulu."

"Yes. She refused to go to the veterans' hospital," said Desirée.

"Call me back and let me know how she's doing," Adair requested. "I expect Fletcher to call in tonight."

"Yes, I will. Thank you so much, Adair. I'm so grateful that you were there when he wasn't."

"You're welcome," Adair said, a tight feeling in her stomach. As she hung up and dialed, she said, "Sugar, can you listen in to this? I can't explain right now, but I want you to hear it." Sugar looked up from her saucepan.

"Yvonne Fay, please," Adair said into the receiver.

Five rings later a woman's voice answered, "Accounting."

"Yvonne Fay, please," Adair patiently repeated.

"She's away from her desk at the moment. Can I help you?"

"No," Adair said crossly, hanging up. She paused, then dialed again. "Charles Whinnet, please," she told the telephone.

A secretary answered, "Mr. Whinnet's office."

"Charles Whinnet, please," Adair said, slightly exasperated.

"He is in a meeting. May I have him return your call?" asked the secretary.

"No. This is Adair. It's an emergency. Please call him to the phone," she insisted. Sugar leaned forward.

"What's the emergency?" the secretary asked skeptically.

"None of your business! This is Mrs. Fletcher Streiker; this is important, and I want you to call Charles to the phone *right now!*" Adair demanded.

There was a brief pause. "Yes, Mrs. Streiker," she said quietly, and put Adair on hold.

Waiting tensely, Adair glanced up at Sugar and winked. "Time to pull out the big guns."

Whinnet came on the line. "Adair? What's wrong?"

"Charles, I couldn't reach Yvonne. Fletcher's sister called me from Hawaii. Their mother has had a heart attack, and she is in critical condition waiting for an emergency coronary bypass. The hospital won't operate until they have fifty thousand dollars in cash."

"Which hospital?" he said, slightly muffled, as if moving.

"Pacific General in Honolulu. It's for Mrs. Dan Streiker's coronary bypass," she enunciated.

"They'll have the money within minutes," he said.

"Thank you. Sorry to disrupt your meeting," Adair said.

"That particular meeting was a total waste of time. I was looking for a way out of it. Fletch won't put up with that kind of nonsense," he said vehemently. Adair laughed. He added, "Keep me posted on her condition."

"I will. Bye." That accomplished, she hung up.

"How fortunate you had just walked in the door!" exclaimed Sugar. "Mr. Streiker's mother could have died waiting for that money!"

"I don't know that she hasn't already. But I'm glad I was here, too." Adair returned to the bedroom and stood over the suitcase. Slowly, she folded a favorite pair of brown cotton pants (ironed by Sugar) and packed them with the purple sweater.

Sugar knocked at the door again. "Mrs. Fay is here," she said through the closed door.

Adair gave up and came out. "Hello, Yvonne."

"Adair," Yvonne nodded, then readjusted her designer glasses as she looked at Adair. "Here's your mail."

"Thank you," Adair responded mechanically, taking the letters Yvonne held out and depositing them with the others on the desk awaiting Fletcher's return.

"You had better look through those. Some of them are for you," Yvonne advised.

Adair obediently picked up the first envelope, addressed to "Mr. and Mrs. Fletcher Streiker." Opening it, she found a wedding card signed, "Affectionately, Jack and Marie." Adair did not know them. She replaced it on the top of the stack and did not reach for another.

Sugar came out from the kitchen. "I'm sure Mrs. Streiker will come through just fine," she said, as if continuing a conversation.

"What?" asked Yvonne.

"Why, Mr. Streiker's sister called . . . oh, excuse me. Did you tell Mrs. Fay?" Sugar asked uncomfortably.

"I was about to," Adair said hastily. "That's right—Desirée called to say their mother had just suffered a heart attack, and needed fifty thousand dollars for emergency surgery. I couldn't get hold of you, so I called Charles to wire it."

"Good," said Yvonne. "Good thinking, Adair. Now perhaps you're getting an inkling of what you're supposed to do."

Adair blinked at her. "No, I don't understand anything at all."

"Why, it seems you're needed to act in Mr. Streiker's stead when he's not available. I don't have the authority to send fifty thousand dollars anywhere without consulting him; but as his wife, you do," Yvonne replied.

"But look, I can't withdraw more than a thousand dollars a day," Adair argued.

"Excuse me—did you or did you not authorize a fifty-thousand-dollar wire transfer?" Yvonne asked.

"Yes, I did . . . at least Charles said it was as good as done," Adair said, and the telephone rang. She and Yvonne turned as Sugar hurried to the kitchen to answer it.

"Hello? Yes, she's right here. Mrs. Streiker."

Adair went to the telephone without wasting time asking Sugar who it was. "Hello."

"Adair? This is Desirée," said the little girl's voice. "We got the money, and Mother is in surgery now. We won't know for hours how she's going to be, but I wanted to thank you for getting the money here so quickly. Fletcher will be grateful, too."

"I'm glad I could help," Adair said mildly.

"Oh, how selfish of me!" Desirée suddenly exclaimed. "In all the fuss over Mother, I forgot to congratulate you! Mother got so excited when Fletcher called to tell her he was finally getting married, she almost went to Dallas by herself. And she never leaves the islands, never, not since before Dad died. But Fletcher told her to wait, and he'd bring you to Honolulu. When can you two come?"

"I haven't the faintest idea," Adair said lightly. "I have no idea where he is now or when he's coming back."

"You know, that's just like him. Once, about seven or eight years ago, he called me from Port-of-Spain, Trinidad, and left the phone number of his hotel. That night a bomb went off in the hotel, and several people were killed. Fletcher told me later that he was the target—that a coincidence kept him from being killed. He seemed to think his call to me had been intercepted. Since then, he hasn't told Mother or me where he goes. We just have to wait to hear from him.

"It was kind of a relief, too, not to know anything, because for the longest time reporters were hounding us about what he was doing or when he was coming to the islands. I was always so afraid I'd say something more than I should have. But when they found out we really didn't know anything, they quit bothering us. I haven't heard from a reporter in years. Oh yes—except yesterday. One called yesterday from Dallas to ask if I knew that Fletcher had just gotten married."

"From the *Expositor*?" Adair asked.

"Could have been. I don't remember. It was five o'clock in the morning here when she called. I think Clay was kind of short with her," Desirée replied.

"Uh huh," Adair said, listening.

"I know it must be difficult adjusting to the way Fletcher does things, seeing how it's so different from what you'd expect. But, he's just so—pure. You know what I mean? He's the same all the way through, inside and out. He doesn't have hidden motives. When he tells you something, it's the truth. If he loves you, he'll move heaven and earth for you, Adair. And he can. You're not going to find many people like that."

"I understand," Adair murmured. "Would you mind telling me—I was curious as to why you call him Panny."

"*He* told you that, didn't he?" Desirée laughed. "He's never told *anyone* that. When I was about three—Fletcher would have been nine—we went to a friend's ranch, where there were horses. Our friend offered to let us ride, but I had never seen such big animals up close and I was scared to death. Fletcher got on one and showed me they were okay. Then he held me in the saddle with him. I started calling him *paniolo*—Hawaiian for 'cowboy'—and that got shortened to Panny. I used to call him that whenever I needed him to be my big brother. I guess I slipped and used that name when I called you, didn't I?"

"That's okay," Adair smiled. Then she stirred, adding, "Please call me back when your mother is out of surgery."

"Okay, but it may be late. It's noon here, so it must be about— five o'clock there."

Adair looked at the clock. "That's right."

"Rather than call in the middle of the night, why don't I wait till first thing in the morning?" Desirée suggested.

"I appreciate that, but I'd rather you call me as soon as you know something. I don't know when Fletcher may call, and I want to be able to tell him she's all right," Adair said.

"Oh, you're right. Thanks so much, Adair. You're lovely. Tell Fletcher I love him and you."

"Okay," Adair smiled, and hung up. She shrugged self-consciously to Sugar and Yvonne, "I guess you heard. She's in surgery, and they won't know anything for hours."

Yvonne nodded. "I'll check back with you in the morning."

She was half-smiling, Adair thought, as if she knew everything Desirée had said about Fletcher.

"I need to go make a note about a little fifty-thousand-dollar withdrawal before quitting time," Yvonne said, turning to the door. "Have a nice evening. And go through your mail."

"All right, all right," Adair relented.

Sugar waved goodbye to Yvonne and exclaimed, "Goodness! I got so caught up in all the excitement that I left that pan on the stove!" She ran back to the kitchen to check it, and Adair went back to the bedroom and shut the door.

She opened the suitcase and stared down in it. Grudgingly, she saw that Fletcher knew exactly what he was doing in sending her to Wendy Beacham. It was a humiliating but liberating experience to confess her ignorance to Beacham. It accomplished exactly what they had hoped: to discourage her from harassing Adair. As much as it stung to be called a prostitute, did it *really* matter what Beacham thought? Adair knew that Yvonne did not think that, nor did

Desirée—and especially not Fletcher. They seemed to consider her capable of learning to carry on a piece of his business.

And how much independence had she really lost by becoming Mrs. Streiker? What freedom was there in being chained to a job she hated? She was always going to be chained to something, wasn't she? Otherwise she would go through life without moorings. Then what was there better to chain herself to than Fletcher?

Adair slowly closed the suitcase, but left it out. "I can't leave anyway, until Desirée calls back. I asked her to call back." Besides, there also remained the question of what Sugar was cooking for dinner.

✦11✦

Adair wandered into the kitchen as Sugar was cooking dinner—roast tenderloin in a fresh mushroom sauce, for Adair alone. Sugar was preparing ingredients Adair had never seen before. "What're those?" she queried, watching Sugar mince some small vegetables on a cutting board.

"Shallots. Listen, dear, since these recipes make so much, I'll put leftovers in the freezer, labeled with cooking directions, so you'll have something to eat when I'm not here."

"Aren't you eating with me?" Adair asked forlornly.

"I wish I could, but you know that if I don't catch the 4:40 bus to get home, my husband starts to fret," Sugar reminded her.

"Oh, yeah. What are *those*?" Adair asked.

"Dried morels. They're nightshade. Related to the mushroom," Sugar answered while chopping them.

"Oh." Adair was sincerely impressed by her knowledge of food. "Sugar, isn't it tiresome to cook and clean here, then go home and cook and clean for your husband?"

Sugar paused with a handful of morel. "Tiresome? Heavens,

no! I love to cook. It's so creative. And my husband does a lot of cleaning at home, especially when my arthritis is acting up. Tiresome? Oh dear, that would be so ungrateful to tell myself this work is tiresome when Mr. Streiker takes such good care of me.

"You see, neither my husband nor I has any health insurance. We're both what you call 'uninsurable.' Because of our medical bills, even with the salary Mr. Streiker pays me, it's still hard to get by. If he didn't help us out, we'd never make it. We'd have to go without treatment.

"So when that old self-pity starts creeping in—'oh, poor little me, with all this pain, having to do housework for a living, at my age, my husband with a bad back and can't work at all'—well, I just squash that like a bug. I've no right to feel that way! *Everybody* has problems and pain—some worse than mine—but not everybody has Fletcher to help them! Whatever happens to me, I know he will always step in and pay for the doctor and the medicine, and a roof and groceries. So as long as I'm able, I'm going to do the very best I can for him." She opened the oven door to check on the beef.

Adair was struck silent in admiration for Sugar's perceptive outlook. And she was sure that Sugar's confidence in Fletcher was well-placed. It was apparent about him from the beginning that he took care of people who had nowhere else to turn—if they let him. But he did it his way. He demanded some effort in return. And because Sugar was able to do what he needed done and do it well, then she could take his support without shame.

While the tenderloin finished roasting, Sugar steamed broccoli and cauliflower. Adair drifted to the windows to look over rush-hour Dallas. An unexpected feeling of contentment came over her to look from her ivory tower on the city below, knowing that she no longer had to scrap for herself. But she also knew it did not mean the fight was over. It was just not solely her interests at stake any more.

"Everything's ready, Mrs. Streiker," called Sugar as she came out of the laundry room with her cardigan. "I just have time to catch the bus for home. Don't you worry about cleaning up anything in the kitchen—it can wait till tomorrow. I'll be looking forward to hearing how Mrs. Streiker came through her operation."

"Okay, Sugar. Thanks," Adair said. And then she was alone.

Sugar had left out a dinner plate and utensils for Adair to help herself from the aromatic dishes on the rangetop. Adair speared a slice of tenderloin and heaped vegetables and bread around it. She took her plate to the dinette and sat down.

Since she was eating alone—again—she looked around for something to read. She glanced at the mail on the desk, but reached instead for the remote control, turning on the television to watch a mildly entertaining rerun of "The Beverly Hillbillies."

After finishing her meal, Adair sat limply and stared with vacant eyes at the loud commercials with sultry faces and lots of skin. Finally, she touched the control to turn the television off. Quiet rushed in to fill the void.

She sat there a long time, staring at the golden reflections of the late afternoon sun on the ball of Reunion Tower. Most of the other buildings were taller than the Streiker Building, but they were far enough removed so no one was staring down on the roof or through the windows. Only Reunion Tower was close by, and anybody desiring a peek into the penthouse from there would have to be on top of the ball with a pair of binoculars. As a matter of fact, this building was situated so that the view to the west was unobstructed, affording a spectacular sunset vista every day. "Fletcher thinks of everything," she murmured.

She roused enough to take her plate to the sink and put the leftovers in the refrigerator. Taking Sugar at her word, Adair did not clean up the kitchen, though she felt guilty leaving it dirty. Then she wandered back over to the desk and reluctantly picked up the small stack of mail, taking it to the table.

There was a large envelope sent via overnight express from Honolulu. Adair smiled as she opened it, and withdrew a small, delicate painting from a cardboard sheath. It portrayed a bird of paradise perched on the stem of a red hibiscus. On the back was lettered, "To Adair and Fletcher. Aloha, Desirée." It appeared that

Desirée herself was the artist.

Adair studied it with satisfaction, then propped it up carefully against the books on the shelf so that she could see it.

Then she picked up the next envelope, also sent express mail. It was addressed to "Mrs. Fletcher Streiker" with a fountain pen, and printed on the back was a street address in Honolulu. Adair opened it and read:

> My dear Adair,
>
> You cannot imagine my joy when Fletcher called and told me you had agreed to be his bride. Desirée always had perfect confidence that he would find someone to love him for himself and not for his gifts, but I was afraid to hope for that. He has always marched to a different drummer, and that can be difficult to follow.
>
> Fletcher tells me you are very beautiful and independent. He promised I will meet you soon, but I could not wait to find out more about you. I am anxious to know how Fletcher overcame his natural reserve to propose to you. You must be very special. He has met many beautiful and independent women before who did not interest him. He often complained that they were manipulative. I am so pleased you are not like that!

Adair got cold chills when she read that sentence. Then she read on:

> Oh dear! Enough of Fletcher's past girlfriends! I meant to write to welcome you into our family. Whoever my son loves, then I love, and I know when I meet you I will be very glad that he waited for you. I feel in some way that I already know you.
>
> Fondly,
>
> Your mother-in-law, Oona

Adair studied the letter in wonder. Were such premonitions possible? Rereading it, she felt an outpouring of warmth toward Fletcher's mother who, though not always understanding her son nor always agreeing with him, always loved him.

Standing and stretching, Adair put the letter under Desirée's painting and paused to make herself a glass of iced tea. It seemed to be warm tonight, though she could not open the windows to tell.

Adair took her tea back to the table, where she picked up the next letter. Immediately she recognized Courtney's round handwriting on the envelope, which was addressed to "Adair Weiss-Streiker." Inside was a studio card that depicted a curvaceous blonde in fishing gear posing beside a man in a business suit, dripping wet, hanging from a line in his mouth. The inside of the card read, "Heard you hooked a live one. Congrats!" It was signed by almost everyone who worked at The Rivers branch, including Courtney and Duane.

"How tacky," muttered Adair. "Just like that group." Before signing her name, Courtney had written an urgent "Call me!"

"She wants to know if he has a brother," Adair sniffed, then chided herself for being ungracious. Still, she tossed the card in the trash can.

The telephone rang. Adair jumped up, ran to the kitchen stand, and caught it on the second ring. "Hello!"

"Adair, it's Alicia. Did I catch you at a bad time?"

"No," Adair panted, then realized her heart was pounding furiously. "Not at all."

"Charles told me about your call today. How is Fletcher's mother?"

"Uh, I don't know yet. Desirée called back around four o'clock to say that they'd received the money, and she was in surgery, but they wouldn't know anything for hours." Gradually, Adair's heart rate settled down.

"I see. Well, can I do anything for you?" Alicia asked.

"No, thank you, Alicia. But I'll call you tomorrow to tell you what I know."

"Good. Do that. Um, have you heard from Fletcher today?"

Adair said, "Yes, he called early this afternoon, and promised to call again tonight."

"When he does, will you tell him that Charles needs to talk to him?" Alicia asked.

"Sure," sighed Adair. "I'm his message center."

Alicia laughed, "Actually, you're the one he's sure to contact first."

"What happened to his answering service?" Adair asked, remembering its existence.

"Adair, he set that up exclusively for you," Alicia said.

"Then maybe I can still reach him through it," mused Adair.

"Maybe. I don't know. If—you can't reach him and you need to talk to someone, call me," Alicia suggested.

"Thanks. You're probably the first one I would call if I needed to talk. But I'm okay. Really," Adair insisted.

"All right, then, I'll expect to hear from you tomorrow about Mrs. Streiker," Alicia said.

"You will," Adair promised. "Goodbye."

She hung up and went straight to the bedroom, where she pulled the file on Fletcher out from the bedstand drawer. She found the number for the answering service, which she took to the kitchen telephone and dialed. It had been disconnected.

Disappointed but not surprised, Adair returned to the table. The three remaining letters were all addressed to Fletcher. Yvonne had sufficiently convinced her to open them, but before she did, she felt that she needed a break. Almost as soon as she thought about going up on the roof, she was climbing the short stairway to the rooftop door. The first thing she intended to do there was check the telephone in the poolside gazebo to make sure that it was working.

The early evening darkness was a little scary, and she had to feel around for the telephone on the table. In so doing, she touched a button and the lap pool lit up. Adair startled, then squinted down at the panel she had found. Of course. There was a light switch for the gazebo, the deck, the tennis court, and the helicopter pad. She turned on the lights and picked up the telephone receiver to hear the reassuring dial tone. Then she left all of the rooftop lights on as she went to the parapet to look over the city of Dallas.

The wind was strong and cool. She held on tightly and did not lean far out on the four-foot-high wall. But the lights! It seemed as if she were looking over half the world. The lights shimmered, converged, and faded into the distance. Was there a more beautiful sight anywhere in the world? She could make out the lights of the Dallas/Fort Worth Airport, but beyond that—what were those far lights? Chili? Trinidad? Or any one of a thousand exotic places Fletcher had been? But no—since she could not even see to Fort Worth, how much farther away must Trinidad really be? How far away was Fletcher?

The largeness of the world almost overwhelmed her. She turned off all the lights and retreated from the rooftop back to the smaller, more manageable space of the apartment.

◆◦◆

Resolutely, she seated herself at the table and picked up the first of the three letters to Fletcher. This one had no return address. The typed text of the letter read:

Dear Mr. Streiker:

In your best interest, I feel you should know what type of person you have just married. Adair Weiss has been known to make herself available to men with money. It is well known that she would not go out with men below a certain income level. However, she did string men along who she thought could help her. Among them are Duane Minshew and Charles Whinnet. Ask her how she got her car.

Sincerely,

A Concerned Friend

Adair felt cold and nauseated. Her immediate impulse was to shred the letter into a thousand tiny pieces. Lies! . . . mostly. That part about the car. . . . She did get the car from a man whom she knew rather well—but he didn't give it to her because . . . and that was five years ago, when she was young and desperate. There had been no one since then. No one. And she didn't *use* men.

"Who would say such a thing?" she moaned. *Courtney*. It had to be Courtney. She knew about the car. Did Fletcher know where her car had come from?

Shaking, Adair laid the letter aside. She could hardly bear to look at the other two. After staring at the envelopes for a solid minute, she opened the smaller one. It said:

Congratulations. Your little wife is so lovely. How much are you going to let her in on? I'm watching.

DL

That was almost worse than the first, if possible. Adair suddenly realized how much she had simply taken Fletcher's word for—well, everything: why he wanted to marry her, why he had to leave, even what she should do. Too distraught to mull it over any more, she placed that letter on top of Courtney's. Then she ripped open the third letter in reckless dismay. The text was printed in block letters on a smudged sheet of lined notepaper:

Dear Mr. Streiker:
  I don't really know why I am writing to you, I have never done this before. I have read about in the newspapers how you help people sometimes, and I guess what I am asking for is your help. I wouldn't blame you if you threw this letter away because you don't know me and you don't owe me anything.
  I guess I have made some mistakes in my life. I better say I know I have made mistakes. My wife left me because of my drinking and I guess I went crazy.

In a month I'll get out on parole if I can get a job. I don't have family or friends here. I don't know anyone who will hire me. You have a big company and I know you must have a lot of people work for you. I have experience in construction and plumbing and I took a course here in electronics, which is the future. If you hire me, I will work hard for you. I have been dry for 18 months.

Thank you,

Russell F. Cooper #203306555
Gatesville, Texas 76500

Adair reread this letter several times with a mixture of pity and skepticism. Then she put it on the pile with the others. "Those he'll need to hear about when he calls," she said. Though her stomach knotted at the prospect of reading one in particular to him, it hardly crossed her mind to withhold anything. He'd certainly find out anyway.

"He'll need to hear about those, and his mother, and—what else? I'd better make a list." She found a pen and notepad in the desk and wrote out:

1. Fletcher's mother. Desirée will call.
2. Mail.
3.

She tapped her pen. "There was something else—" With a pang she remembered that day's visit with Wendy Beacham. "How could I forget that?" So she added to her list:

3. W. Beacham.

She put all the mail together with Oona's letter, Desirée's painting, and the list, and placed the neat pile on the table. Then she sat down and stared at it.

She got up to look at the clock—7:40. "Forty minutes into my ballet class," she noted. "Madame hasn't called me back! Well, I'm going to interrupt her class, then!" She marched to the telephone and dialed the studio's number. The answering machine came on, but after the beep Adair said, "Madame, please pick up the phone. This is Adair Weiss and I really need to talk to you. I'm going to stay on the line until you pick up the telephone."

A few seconds later an irritated Madame said, "Adair, what is it?"

"Madame, I've had a terrible conflict come up with evening classes. I can't take them at night anymore. Please schedule a class for me during the day—please!"

"This is impossible. I have my young ones come at day. All pointe classes are in the evening," Madame said crisply.

"But Madame—"

"Adair, you must decide what is most important to you. If this other thing is more important, then forget the ballet. You will never succeed unless dance is most important thing in world to you. I will not waste my time with less dedication than that." And Madame hung up.

Adair burst into tears. Now that she finally had the money to pursue her dream, she had lost the opportunity. "No, I haven't!" she declared savagely. "There are a thousand dance teachers in Dallas who will give me all day for what I can pay them!"

But . . . could *she* give all day? What if Fletcher wanted her to be available to do something else?

She held her breath in the agony of decision. Madame was right—excelling at ballet required that it be the all-consuming passion of her life. But Fletcher expected to have that position himself, and it was he who made ballet possible at all for her. What could she do when two compelling loves demanded all or nothing of her?

Adair let her breath out. There was no competition. It was useless to choose the gift over the giver. Without the giver, she would have nothing at all.

"The one dream that gave me hope . . . that made me get out of bed in the morning to face another day," she reflected through tears. "Time to let it go." So, in her despair, she strangled the ballerina and left her crumpled in tulle. It hurt as much as if flesh-and-blood hands were at her own throat, and she cried until her head throbbed. Then she quieted down, wiped away her own tears, and went into the kitchen to prowl for a snack.

The dirty dishes proved too big an obstacle, however. Despite Sugar's promise to do them tomorrow, Adair rinsed them and put them in the dishwasher, then cleaned off the counters. Only then was she able to help herself to some chocolate creme cookies in the refrigerator.

As she wiped her hands, she looked wearily around the apartment. She began to feel the desire to escape her confining tower life. But there was no place for her on the outside anymore. So she escaped to the only place she knew: the rooftop. Knowing it was probably cool up there, she got a blanket from the bedroom closet to take with her.

Adair turned on the rooftop lights and spread her blanket on a chaise lounge by the lap pool. Then she lay down in the blanket to look up at the starry night sky. After a minute, she turned off the lights so she could see the stars more clearly. And there they were, more than she had ever seen, dancing. Whether anyone was there to watch them or not, they danced every night for the joy of it. . . . Adair closed her eyes in pain.

<hr />

A sudden warbling startled her into a sitting position. Blankly, Adair tried to remember where she was. The telephone in the gazebo warbled again loudly. Shedding the blanket, Adair ran in to grab it. "Hello?"

"Hello, Adair. I must have woken you. Sorry."

"Fletcher . . . I just dozed off. . . . What time is it?"

"Ah, 10:20, your time. I'll try to call earlier next time. How are you, babe?"

"Not—not very well. I'm lonely, and I get more confused all the time," she said, tears coming to her eyes.

"I don't blame you. I'm not very happy myself," he replied.

"There were some things . . . Yvonne brought the mail, and I left it downstairs. I have to go downstairs to get the mail," she said disjointedly.

"Are you on the roof?" he asked.

"Yes," she said tentatively.

"Oh, well, just hang up and go down to the kitchen phone. I'll stay on the line."

"Are you sure?" she said anxiously.

"Yes," he laughed. "Go downstairs."

"Okay. Hang on." She eased the receiver down on the base and flew downstairs to the apartment door. She collided with it when it did not immediately open. "I don't remember locking it! Now, the code is—" Her mind went blank.

She laughed. "8834, dummy!" She punched it in and ran to the telephone, scooping up the pile from the table on the way. "Hello! Fletcher?"

"I'm here."

"Oh, good." She found she needed a moment to collect herself.

"Anything happen today?" he asked casually.

"Yes. Desirée called. Fletcher, your mother had a heart attack, and she had to go into emergency surgery. But the hospital wouldn't operate without fifty thousand dollars up front. So I authorized Charles to send the money. Desirée called back about four—Dallas time—to say that she was in surgery, and she would call back when they were finished. I haven't heard from her yet."

There was a brief silence. "Thank you, Adair. You did . . . great," he said in a quiet voice.

"Please remember that when I read you the mail," she said, her hands getting cold.

"Oh? What came?"

"Well, your mother sent a perfectly lovely letter to me—about how she's so glad you got married and wants us to come see her. . . . Will you go to Honolulu now?" she asked.

"Not without you. And I can't come get you yet." His voice was so quiet, he sounded almost depressed.

"Well . . . and Desirée sent a painting—it's beautiful. Is she an artist?"

"Oh yes," Fletcher said, perking up. "She did the illustrations for the ornithological book on my shelves. She's the finest bird illustrator since John Jacobin."

"You're not proud of her, are you?" laughed Adair.

"A little," he admitted. "What else came?"

"Well . . ." she looked. "Congratulations from Jack and Marie."

"Who are they?" Fletcher asked.

"You don't know?" she exclaimed.

"No, I don't think so," he said.

"Neither do I!" she said. They shared a laugh over this. Then Adair turned her eye on the rest of the mail and stopped laughing. "Fletcher, some letters came addressed only to you, but Yvonne told me I should open them. I'm sorry now that I did."

"Why? What did they say?" he asked.

She braced herself, then read him the short typed letter from "A Concerned Friend." She kept her voice as steady and impersonal as possible until she had read it through.

"Okay," said Fletcher. "You can throw that away."

"Just like that?" she asked. "I mean . . . do you know how I got my car?"

"You mean from Lance Heinrichs? That was not really a wise relationship, Adair. Do you know that he's in prison now for dealing cocaine?"

"No," she gulped.

"Definitely not a profitable relationship," he murmured. "But at least you did get the car out of it. Anyway, don't worry about the content of that letter. If I were you, I'd be more concerned about which one of my friends wanted to sabotage my marriage."

"I know who," Adair said bitterly. "Courtney Amsterdam."

"You think so? I don't know. Did she ever see you talk with Chuck?" asked Fletcher.

Adair thought back carefully, then replied, "No, I don't believe she did. But Duane asked me what I had on him."

"Hmm. That's interesting. Would Courtney accuse you of stringing along Duane?"

"Of course not. Neither of us considered him worth the effort. But *Duane* once accused me of that. . . ." Adair thought out loud.

"Looks like you may have figured out who my concerned friend is. But don't be hasty," he said.

"All right," she said cheerfully, mentally strangling Duane.

"Anything else?" he asked.

"Yes." With a little more confidence, she read him the note from DL. It was his turn to do some explaining.

But all he said was, "Okay, you can toss that, too."

"Uh . . . are you going to tell me who DL is?" she asked.

"No."

"Why not?" she pressed.

"Because it's a burden you don't need. He's no one you should be concerned about," he said.

"I believe you," she said. "But—it does kind of pique my curiosity, to know what you could 'let me in on.'"

"I *will* tell you that DL doesn't know nearly what he thinks he knows. He's a fraud and a liar, and I don't want you taken in by him." He sounded not quite angry, but very decisive on that point.

"Okay, okay," she said, hastily dropping the note in the trash can.

"Now, what else?" he asked.

Not quite believing how rapidly he made decisions, and not knowing what to expect next, she read him the letter from Russell Cooper. After she had finished, Fletcher was silent for so long that she finally said, "Hello? Are you there?"

"Yes," he said. A few beats later he added, "I think I will let you handle that one."

"What?" she asked, uncomprehending.

"I will let you decide what to do about that letter," he said.

"Me?" she echoed, shocked. "Fletcher, I can't! I have no idea what to do!"

"Yvonne can help you," he said.

"But, Fletcher! Wouldn't it be dangerous?"

"No more dangerous than a single woman living alone in Dallas," he said seriously. "I trust you to use good judgment."

"I don't know if I trust me," she muttered, then remembered: "Alicia said Charles needed to talk to you."

"All right, I'll call him when we're through talking."

"Oh, Fletcher, don't you have any idea how long this will go on?"

"Probably an hour, at this rate," he said drily.

"No, no. How long you will be gone. Can't you give me a date to hang on to?" she asked.

"If I did, it's bound to be wrong, because I'd only be guessing. I can only tell you it will be as soon as possible," he promised.

Adair sighed. She could not maneuver him into coming back now any more than she could maneuver him into letting her see him before they got married. That thought reminded her of something else. "Fletcher, in the letter from your mother, she said something about how you always disliked manipulative women, and how glad she was that I wasn't like that. But . . . I am, aren't I? Haven't I tried to manipulate you?"

"I haven't given you much of a chance to," he chuckled. "And a lot of that may be due to the insecurity you feel. The more secure you feel in our relationship, the more you'll trust me and the less need you'll feel to move me around."

"But, the point is, I'm not different from the others. I've *tried* to manipulate you," she confessed with brutal honesty.

He paused. "The difference is, you accepted me on my terms despite your desire to be in control."

That was true. She did not like to relinquish control—to give up her own schedule, her own agenda, her own dreams. . . . She thought of ballet and her eyes began to water. Squinting to contain the tears, she saw number three on her list: W. Beacham.

"I went to see Wendy Beacham like you asked me to," she said briskly.

"Oh? How did it go?"

"She chewed me up and spit me out," Adair said.

"How do you mean?" he asked.

"She told me that I was an ornament and a prostitute and nothing more," Adair said evenly.

"Uh huh. Sounds like Wendy has gotten kind of bitter," he said.

"I'd be bitter, too, if the man I once dated became a billionaire," Adair said, half in jest.

"It was Wendy's choice to break up. She felt I was too rigid and demanding," he said.

"You do lay out some pretty hard choices," she admitted.

"I've only made you decide what's important to you. I won't make the choice for you, but you see it's got to be done if you want to accomplish anything. You have to decide what in your life is worth sacrificing for. Wendy chose to sacrifice for her career," he observed.

"What have you sacrificed for, Fletcher?" she asked, thinking she knew the answer to be his wealth.

"Frankly, I've put my neck on the chopping block for you, Adair," he answered.

Although her first inclination was to respond, *Yeah? How?* she refrained, saying instead, "I'm sure you have."

"You don't see it yet, but you will. I'll see to it that you understand everything," he promised.

Adair could not say how much she cared at this point, but she had no strength for argument. All at once she felt drained. "Thanks," she whispered.

"You should hear from me again tomorrow night."

"I'll be here," she said faintly.

In a voice that cracked, he said, "Sleep tight, Adair."

⇥12⇤

By the time Adair had showered and dressed the next morning, Sugar was almost finished baking a fresh batch of croissants. Adair could smell them from the bedroom.

"Good morning," she greeted Sugar as she entered the kitchen and poured herself a cup of coffee.

"Oh, good morning, Mrs. Streiker." Sugar turned from the oven. "I'm so sorry. I should have known better than to leave that mess last night. I've gotten fat and lazy. From now on, if I can't finish everything in time to catch my bus, I'll just stay late and take a cab home."

Adair listened to this speech with her coffee cup poised at her lips. When she finally realized what Sugar was talking about, she laughed and took a sip. "Forget it. I didn't clean up much. I need to do a little something around here; I really do. Otherwise, I'd feel too guilty."

"All the same, I have to stay on top of it better," Sugar insisted.

Adair drifted over to the table where she had left out the mail. The letters from "DL" and "Concerned Friend" were in the trash can, as instructed. She pensively took up the letter from convict Russell Cooper.

"Did you hear from Mr. Streiker last night?" Sugar asked.

"Yes, I did." Adair half-turned. "He's doing fine, though of course he wouldn't tell me where he is or when he'll be back."

"Well, that just makes for a fun surprise when he does come home," Sugar said.

Adair had to think about that possibility. "It's only been—what's today? Thursday? He just left Tuesday morning. Last night he talked like it might be a while before he gets back," Adair told her.

"He always talks like that—'I just don't know when I'll be back'—then poof! One day he walks in the door, right out of the blue. Keeps you on your toes," Sugar said as she busily dropped hot rolls into a bun warmer.

There was a tap on the door. Adair went over to open it herself, letter in hand. "Yvonne! Good morning. Come in." Adair pulled her inside and shut the door. "Coffee for Yvonne, please, Sugar," she said as she steered Yvonne to the couch.

"My, how nice it is to be welcome," Yvonne cracked bemusedly, settling in her suede dress. "Thank you, Sugar," she said over the coffee. "Here's your morning mail, Adair." Yvonne placed several letters onto the coffee table.

"Ugh. I don't want any more mail," Adair said, making a face. "But I want you to look at this." She gave Russell Cooper's letter to Yvonne, who adjusted her glasses and held it up to read.

Meanwhile, Sugar asked, "How is Mrs. Streiker this morning?" Adair blinked at her. "Oona Streiker," Sugar clarified. Yvonne glanced up from the letter in her hand.

Adair sat open-mouthed. "I—I don't know. I haven't heard! Oh, good heavens. Desirée must have called some time during the night, and I never heard the phone. Can we see about getting an extension in the bedroom?" she asked Yvonne, who nodded. "Today?" Adair implored. The thought of missing a late-night call from Fletcher made her sick.

"Yes," Yvonne said, laying the letter down and removing her glasses. "Don't worry, I'm sure Desirée will call back later in the morning. Now, I assume you've shared this letter with Mr. Streiker."

"Yes, and he told *me* to handle it!" Adair exclaimed, expecting to shock Yvonne.

But she only smiled. "So what are you going to do about it?"

"I haven't the faintest idea. It's a little threatening," Adair said.

"Being approached by an ex-convict for a job? For someone in Mr. Streiker's position, it's not that unusual. I suppose he wants to initiate you in how to handle these requests."

"That's like putting a child behind the wheel of a car on North Central and telling him to drive," Adair responded.

Yvonne smiled in such a way that made it unnecessary to say that Adair was exaggerating.

"Well, it seems that way to me," Adair mumbled.

"Take it in pieces, then. What should you do first?" Yvonne said.

Adair thought it over. "Check him out to see if what he says is true?" she guessed.

"Sounds good to me," Yvonne said, putting the letter in Adair's lap.

Adair placed the letter atop the unopened mail, then allowed several seconds to pass quietly while Yvonne sipped her coffee. "Do you know a DL?" Adair asked suddenly.

"DL?" Yvonne's shaped eyebrows gathered. "No. Oh, wait—do you mean Darren Loggia?"

Adair dug the note out of the trash and gave it to Yvonne. She read it impassively, then folded it carefully. "What did Mr. Streiker tell you about this?"

"He just said to throw it away. He wouldn't tell me anything," Adair said.

Yvonne parted her lips, but then raised an eyebrow and shrugged, unwilling to fill in the gaps that her boss had left open.

Adair asked cunningly, "Who is Darren Loggia?"

Yvonne glanced up guiltily.

"I think I'm entitled to know," Adair pointed out. "He knows all about me."

"As long as you don't try to *do* anything about him. If you got too close to him, he'd eat your lunch," Yvonne said.

"I can keep my distance easier if I know who to stay away from," Adair parried. "Who is he?"

Yvonne sighed and took off her glasses to clean them. "He used to be Mr. Streiker's best friend. They were roommates at the University of Hawaii and, when Mr. Streiker started up a landscaping firm, Darren was his first employee.

"Just when the business was beginning to take off, Darren and a woman employee filed a complaint with the EEOC charging Mr. Streiker with sexual harassment. Of course, it was a total fabrication designed to get the boss out of the business—and much later the woman involved dropped the charges—but by then the damage had been done. It was in all the newspapers and Fletcher was forced to leave the business.

"It ran all right without him for a while, but Darren was not the manager Fletcher was. When the business folded, Darren blamed his old friend, and has since been looking for every opportunity to get revenge."

"Like Wendy Beacham?" Adair asked.

"Wendy's emotional baggage is nothing compared to this. I believe Darren is unbalanced. His swipes at Fletcher have become bolder and more dangerous. Obviously, he read about your marriage in the newspapers. You are the best opportunity he's ever had to hurt Fletcher." At Adair's shocked expression, Yvonne emphasized, "You must not talk to him or have any contact with him at all. You're no match for him, Adair."

Adair pondered all this while Yvonne drank her coffee. "Who was the woman who filed the complaint against Fletcher?"

Yvonne paused. "I don't remember her name. I have no idea where she is now. She just let herself be used as plaintiff in exchange for promises of advancement. The ironic thing is that she got nothing for her trouble. The company folded a few years after Fletcher left and she was out of a job."

"I see," Adair reflected. She held up her coffee cup to let Sugar refill it.

"I think I've said enough for now," Yvonne concluded, rising to her feet. "You might keep me posted on what you find out about Mr. Cooper—and, of course, Mrs. Streiker."

"Of course," Adair said vaguely, deep in thought.

———◆———

After Yvonne had left, Sugar asked, "Would you care for another roll, Mrs. Streiker?"

"No, thanks," Adair said, absently waving Cooper's letter. "I don't really want to do this. I'd rather go shopping." She looked up enticingly at Sugar. "Want to go to Valley View with me?"

"Oh, Mrs. Streiker, you're such a card! Teasing me that way! I know you're not about to run out to the mall when Mrs. Shaw might call."

"Oh, yes. You're right. Well, since I know she won't call this early, I suppose I should go ahead and check out this Cooper guy," Adair said.

She went to the kitchen and dialed information for the number of the Gatesville prison. With that, she dialed the prison and asked for the warden.

"Warden Peale," answered a male voice.

"Warden, this is Adair Streiker, calling from Dallas. An inmate of your prison, Russell Cooper, has applied to work for my husband's corporation. What can you tell me about him?"

"Cooper? Oh yeah, Russ Cooper. He's okay, Mrs.—Striper, you say?"

"Streiker."

"Yeah, Mrs. Streiker. Russ is okay, ma'am, as long as he's sober. One of the conditions of his parole is no alcohol."

"I see. When will he get out?" she asked.

"Ma'am?"

"When is he scheduled for parole?" Adair repeated.

"Russ was paroled about two weeks ago, ma'am," the warden replied.

"He was? Well, where is he now?"

"Let me check. Hold on a minute." The warden put her on hold and Adair looked down at the letter in her hand. "Okay, ma'am, his address is 2481 Pine Street, Houston."

"Houston . . . all right," said Adair, scribbling it down. "Do you have a phone number there?"

"No ma'am, no phone. He checks in with his parole officer once a week, on Monday," he replied.

"In Houston?" she asked.

"Yes, in Houston."

"Does he plan to move to Dallas?" Adair asked.

"I wouldn't know that. But he can't go anywhere without informing his parole officer."

"What is the parole officer's name?" Adair got her pen ready again.

"Uh, Don Calvecchi." And the warden gave her his Houston telephone number.

Adair thanked him, hung up, and dialed the parole officer. "Don Calvecchi, please," she said primly.

"Speaking," he said.

"Mr. Calvecchi, this is Adair Streiker of Dallas. Russell Cooper has applied to work for my husband's corporation—"

"He has? Where?" Calvecchi interrupted.

"Dallas."

"Dallas? He's already got a job here, at Roy's Body Shop. He hasn't told me anything about moving to Dallas."

"Well, I guess he wrote my husband before getting the job at Roy's—"

"Who is this, again?" he asked.

"This is Adair Streiker. Mrs. Fletcher Streiker."

"No kidding? How're you doing?"

"I'm fine, thank you," Adair said, wishing to wind up this conversation. "Since Mr. Cooper already has a job, I don't think we need to pursue it any further."

"Would you really hire an ex-con?" Calvecchi asked.

"Yes, if everything checked out," Adair answered. "My husband likes to help people."

"Well, that's real special. Russ will be real thrilled to hear that you called. He may want to hike on up to Dallas."

"No," Adair said quickly. "He needs to keep the job he's got. That's best."

"Right. Thanks for calling."

"Thank you. Goodbye." Adair hung up and told Sugar in undisguised relief, "He's already got a job in Houston."

"I'm glad to hear that. It's true that Mr. Streiker helps a lot of people, but he has a feel for these things. He can read people real well, so he always seems to know when they're not being honest with him, or just trying to get money from him, or something," Sugar chatted as she rinsed out the coffee pot. "He says he just goes by his gut reaction. He says you have to trust your instincts."

Adair nodded, dropping her scribbled notes into the kitchen trash can. "Doesn't matter now," she said cheerfully. "I wish Desirée would call. Let's see—" she glanced up at the wall clock. "It's 10:30 here . . ." she began to count on her fingers, "so that means it's only 5:30 in Hawaii. I'd better just sit tight for a while."

She flopped down on a white sofa, picking up that morning's edition of the Dallas *Sun-Times*. First she scanned it to make sure she wasn't in it, then began to read the front-page articles.

There was a knock on the door. "Come in," Adair called.

Yvonne opened the door, looked in, then motioned in a telephone repairman.

"He's here to install the extension in the bedroom," Yvonne said, coming quickly toward Adair. "All the paperwork's been done."

Reaching Adair, she whispered, "No names."

Then she said louder, "If you need me, give me a call. I'm Yvonne Fay in bookkeeping."

"Thank you," Adair said, repressing a laugh. She nodded to the repairman, pointing, "In there. On the table by the bed, please."

"Right, miss," he said, looking her up and down. Adair could almost see him wondering whose mistress she was, being kept in a penthouse apartment.

She turned back to catch Yvonne. "Oh—Mrs. Fay—" She drew Yvonne out into the hall. "I wanted to let you know that I checked out the ex-con who wrote to Fletcher. I called the warden at Gatesville, who told me he'd already been paroled and was living in Houston. So I called his Houston parole officer, and he told me Cooper already had a job there. So that takes care of that."

"Is that right?" Yvonne's brow furrowed. "But I understand he was just in personnel, filling out an application."

"Who—Cooper? When?" Adair asked.

"Why, this morning. As a matter of fact, he may still be there. Since he's working on your telephone—" Yvonne glanced back into the apartment "—do you want to go down to personnel and see?"

"Yeah, I guess so," Adair conceded.

Yvonne took her down to the personnel department on the fifth floor. They walked through a waiting area where about twelve people were seated. Yvonne went straight to a cubicle with "G. B. Bush, Personnel Manager" on the door and opened it. A thin man in a pink shirt looked up.

"Geoff, have you got the application that cited Mr. Streiker as a reference?"

"Yeah, Yvonne; it's right over here." He lifted a sheet from a pile on the corner of his desk and handed it across to her. "Good morning," he winked at Adair. She smiled absently.

"Yes, it's him," Yvonne said, with Adair looking over her shoulder at the application. "Is he still here?"

"I think so," Geoff squinted.

"Why don't you call him back here?" Yvonne suggested, moving into the cubicle as she handed the application to Adair. Geoff left.

"Wait a minute," Adair muttered, alarmed at how rapidly things were progressing. "I have to look this over a minute."

"I thought you said you had checked him out," said Yvonne, but by then Geoff had returned with a man.

Adair and Yvonne turned as Geoff said, "This is Russell Cooper." The man stepped out from behind him and extended his hand to Adair. "How do you do, ma'am?" he said with a slight twang.

"Fine. And you?" she returned, without looking him directly in the eye. He had a strong jaw, black wavy hair, and a black mustache. He was wearing a shirt and tie with jeans, and fidgeted with a Stetson as he stood just inside the cubicle door.

"Jus' fine, ma'am, except that I really do need a job," he replied softly.

That snapped Adair's attention from his rugged appearance. "What happened to your job in Houston—at Roy's Body Shop?"

"Yes'm, that was just temporary while the foreman's nephew was out on jury duty, but they called a mistrial and he came back to work yesterday, so I just hiked on up here to see if maybe you had something for me." He looked self-consciously at the floor as he spoke. His earnestness was very appealing.

"You didn't tell your parole officer?" Adair asked.

"Well, yes and no, ma'am," he said, drawing a letter from his back pocket. "I went by his office yesterday and he wasn't there, just his assistant, so I got my papers from her. This here's a letter from my Dallas parole officer. I'm abidin' by all the conditions and I'm dry as a bone, ma'am."

Adair glanced at the official-looking letter he handed her. "Well, let me look this over and I'll call you in a few days," she said, keenly aware of Yvonne's and Geoff's silent gazes.

Cooper sagged a little. "'Scuse me, ma'am, but I've got exactly $4.50 in my pocket, no phone, and no place to stay. I'm kind of desperate for a job and if you can't help me today, I got to go look elsewhere."

Adair nodded uncomfortably, managing to look him in the eye for only a second before looking down. "I'll do any kind of work, anything at all. I ain't proud," Cooper said, his voice trembling very slightly.

"We have openings for custodians and service technicians," Geoff offered helpfully.

"Yessir, I could do either of those jobs. I could start right away." Cooper looked hopefully at Adair, who stood chewing her lip and pretending to read the letter.

What was her reservation? That she felt she hadn't checked him out thoroughly enough? What would Fletcher do? *He just trusts his gut feelings,* Sugar had said.

Adair looked up at Cooper. He was certainly good-looking. Why couldn't she look him in the eye, then?

"Problem?" Yvonne whispered, and Adair kept her gaze on Cooper. Yes, there was a problem, and it was with his eyes. She couldn't put a finger on it, but something was not right.

"If you will return to the waiting area, I will have an answer for you in fifteen minutes, tops," Adair smiled at Cooper. He nodded with a slight look of despair and turned out.

Adair picked up Geoff's telephone and dialed her apartment number. It gave a busy signal. "Oh, drat. The repairman is hooking up the bedroom extension. I forgot."

"What do you need?" Yvonne asked.

"A telephone number," Adair said, pursing her lips. "I'll just run up and get it. Be right back." She trotted out of the department and ran to the elevator. Seeing the crowded floor, she moaned, "I'll never get to it empty." Then she spotted her elevator with the electronic "out of order" sign flashing like a beacon in the night. Reggie had remembered. She slipped in and used her penthouse key.

She bolted into her apartment as the telephone man was packing away his tools. "All done, miss."

"Thank you," Adair said on her way to the kitchen. She pulled out the trash can and began digging through it while Sugar shooed out the curious repairman.

"Mrs. Streiker?" Sugar came back with a pained look.

"Here it is." Adair took out Cooper's letter and brushed coffee grounds off it. Then she dialed a number from it. "Mr. Calvecchi?"

"Yeah—is this Mrs. Streiker?"

"Yes, I—"

"I've been trying to get hold of you for an hour. I called Roy's

Body Shop. Russ Cooper is working there now. He never wrote your husband and has got no plans to go to Dallas."

"That's exactly what I wanted to know. Thank you," she said tightly, and hung up. She then dialed the corporation's number. "Geoff Bush, please." When he answered, she demanded, "Is Yvonne still there?"

"Yes, she is. Who shall I say is calling?" he asked politely.

"Just put her on, please," Adair said in exasperation.

An instant later Yvonne said, "Yes?"

"Yvonne, that man is not Russell Cooper. I just called his parole officer, and Cooper is at his job in Houston right now. We've got to find out why this man is pretending to be an ex-con."

"I'll hold him," Yvonne said.

"I'm on my way down." Adair hung up. She dashed from her apartment into the elevator. As the doors closed smoothly, she gasped. *The elevator. She had seen that man on the elevator.* His hair was darker now, and he had that mustache—but it was *the same man*. The one who had called himself an old friend of Fletcher's. The one who knew who she was.

Suddenly she remembered seeing a man watching her from the parking lot across from the bank—the man she first thought to be Fletcher. This was the same man. His stance was erect, tense, watchful. He had been watching her even then.

When the doors opened on the fifth floor, she ran out to meet Yvonne and Geoff in the waiting area of personnel.

"He's gone," Yvonne said.

Adair nodded.

"We'll call some of these numbers he put on his application, but I'm sure they're all phony," Yvonne added, paper in hand. "What made you suspicious of him?"

Adair swallowed. "A couple of things." She motioned them out of the crowded waiting area back to the corridor. "First, I'd like to know what you told him when you brought him back to your office," she asked Geoff.

"Nothing. I didn't tell him anything. I just asked him to come with me," he said defensively.

"I'm not blaming you; I just realized that when he came back there, he looked straight at me as if he knew I was the one who would make the decision. He couldn't have known that unless he already knew who I am," Adair said.

"I didn't tell him, because I don't even know who you are," Geoff huffed.

Adair looked at Yvonne, who said, "Then you can't be blamed for anything, Geoff, and we want to keep it that way." As the two women left personnel, Yvonne said, "You're right. I thought he was concentrating on you because of your looks. But he was appealing to you for the job."

"Yvonne, it's more than that. Would you know Darren Loggia if you saw him?" Adair asked.

Yvonne froze. "No. I've never seen him."

"I believe that man was Darren Loggia. That's the same man who congratulated me on the elevator and called himself an old friend of Fletcher's. I just now recognized him. He's been watching me for a long time," Adair stated urgently.

"Wait. Now wait a minute," Yvonne put a hand to her forehead as if to collect her thoughts. "I can't imagine Darren attempting something so—transparent. He was bound to be found out sooner or later."

"What if he knew that? What if the point wasn't to actually get the job, but to show . . . that he could get close to me whenever he wanted to," Adair suggested.

"Then he made his point," Yvonne said stiffly. "But we know what he looks like now."

Adair shook her head. "I didn't recognize him at first, because he changed his appearance. I'm sure he could do it again." Her eyes began to water.

Yvonne put a steadying arm around her shoulders. "Don't let him get to you. We'll cover it with Fletcher. Let's go on up to your apartment—we'll try these telephone numbers from there." Adair nodded, and they took the "out-of-order" elevator to the penthouse.

Sugar met them as they entered the apartment. "My, it's busy around here today! Mrs. Shaw just called. She said Mrs. Streiker is doing fine. She's in CCU, of course, but all her vital signs are just fine. She was even able to talk to Mr. Streiker."

Adair quickly asked, "Fletcher is in Hawaii?"

"No, he called his mother. He spoke with Mrs. Shaw as well," Sugar told her. Yvonne nodded and went to the kitchen telephone.

"Good. Good, I'm glad to hear it. I suppose then . . . there's no reason for me to call her back," Adair reflected uncertainly.

"She didn't say," Sugar replied. She went back to the kitchen and a few minutes later Yvonne hung up the telephone. "The person who answered this number identified himself as a parole officer and gave a glowing reference for Russell Cooper. When I told him we had discovered he was not Russell Cooper, he hung up. I'm willing to bet that the Texas Department of Corrections never heard of him." Yvonne began to place another call.

"I'm sure you're right," Adair said tiredly, slumping down to the sofa. Yvonne was always right, and so was Sugar, and Charles, and Fletcher.

As the excitement of this particular diversion began wearing off, Adair felt the weariness and claustrophobia closing in on her again. She looked around the apartment and wanted to throw up.

"I'm going out for a little while," she said, reaching over the few unopened letters for her purse. "See you later." And she left.

<hr>

In the lobby, she passed an automatic teller machine without stopping. Then on second thought, she returned to it and withdrew the maximum thousand dollars. She went to her car and pulled out on Woodall Rogers Freeway, taking it to Central Expressway and heading north. Traffic was bumper to bumper, as it was any time of the day, but Adair did not much mind now. She had only a hazy idea of returning to familiar territory—nowhere especially.

She approached the exit she normally took going to her old job at the bank. On impulse Adair turned off the expressway. She cruised to the familiar parking lot and pulled into a space. She hadn't really decided that she was actually going in; she just wanted to see if this part of the world still existed.

It was around noon, and several employees were leaving for lunch. Adair watched Courtney come out laughing and waving goodbye to someone, then walk toward her. Adair suddenly realized that Courtney's car was parked one space over from where she sat now.

But before Adair could start the engine, Courtney had spotted her. She ran over to the driver's side window, squealing, "Adair! It's you!" She leaned in to give Adair a big one-arm hug. "You came back to see me! How are you doing?"

"Fine, Courtney," Adair smiled, her eyes tearing up. Courtney's display of friendship was like rain on cracked ground. Adair needed a friend right now—not one of Fletcher's friends or employees, but a friend of *hers*.

"Buy you lunch at Poco's?" she offered, getting out of the car.

"Well, I guess *so!*" Courtney exclaimed, taking her arm. She looked down at the rock on Adair's finger and gasped, "Good heavens! It's gorgeous! Tell me all about him, Adair! Tell me everything!"

"Well," Adair began as they walked the short space to the restaurant, "he's very nice . . . he's different than what I thought . . . he's pretty busy." They went through the buffet line and took their plates to a secluded booth.

"And?" Courtney urged her on. "How old is he?"

"Not very old. About thirty-four, I think," said Adair, breaking out a hot tortilla.

"Is he cute?" Courtney asked over her guacamole salad.

"He's gorgeous," Adair said. Then she put her head down and began to cry quietly.

"There, now." Courtney scooted around the booth to drape a comforting arm on her. "Let it out. That's okay."

"Oh, Courtney," Adair moaned, "he *is* so nice, but he left the morning after we got married and I haven't seen him since! He calls me every night—and he says he's coming home soon, but he won't tell me when or even where he is right now! I'm so lonely. I don't know what to do."

"Would you like to come stay with me for a while?" Courtney asked.

"Oh, no thank you, Courtney. I know we'll work it out. I'm just having trouble adjusting to his lifestyle. He goes all over the world, and I'm not able to go with him yet." Adair wiped her eyes. "Tell me what's happening in your life."

"Well, this probably seems tame to you, but I'm dating a man who lives on Royal Lane and drives a Jaguar. I think he's really serious." Courtney held out her wrist, adorned with a gold watch.

"That's wonderful, Courtney. I'm so happy for you," Adair said sincerely.

"I imagine Royal Lane is too suburban for you and your husband," Courtney hinted broadly.

"I'm afraid you'd be disappointed to see my place," Adair said wryly. "How's Duane?"

"As big a jerk as ever," Courtney chirped.

Adair snickered.

"He hired a bimbo to replace you who just worships him," Courtney continued. "She hasn't caught on yet. And he was the only one at the branch who wasn't impressed to hear you married Fletcher Streiker. He said something ugly like, 'I knew she was a gold digger.'"

Adair just smiled in response.

They chatted about other inconsequentials, but Courtney kept returning to the most intriguing topic. "Tell me more about Fletcher, Adair! How in the world did you meet him?"

"Well, it's kind of complicated. . . . He saw me at the bank and sent me a note." She wasn't about to tell Courtney the whole weird scheme.

"What's he like in bed?"

"*Courtney!*" Adair exclaimed, shocked.

"Okay, then, why is he so reclusive? What does he have to

hide?" Courtney pressed.

"Nothing. That's just the way he is," Adair shrugged. She paused to admire Courtney's watch, then uttered, "Oh-oh! You're about to be late from lunch." Adair took up Courtney's tab and paid it, leaving a ten-dollar tip.

"Must be nice not to have to rush back to a job," Courtney observed.

"Well, I don't know—I kind of miss the structure. . . . It's hard to know what to do with myself now," Adair admitted as they stepped out onto the sunny sidewalk.

"I wouldn't have any difficulty with that at all," Courtney asserted.

Adair stopped beside her car and looked toward the bank. "Tell everyone hello for me," she said.

"Why don't you come in for a minute?" Courtney suggested.

"Not today. I'll come back another time."

"Okay. Well, you take care." Courtney leaned over and kissed the air by Adair's cheek.

"Sure. Bye, Courtney." Adair smiled so it would not look like she was about to cry. But as she watched Courtney go inside the bank, the loneliness swept over her again. Courtney had her part to play, whether she was satisfied with it or not. Everybody had something to do, except Adair.

She sat in the car and turned on the air conditioner. "Here it is Halloween, and hot as Hades," she exclaimed. Taking the car out on the freeway, she drove aimlessly until she saw the signs for Collin Creek Mall coming up. She exited without a second thought.

For the next three hours Adair walked the mall, browsing in little boutiques and sipping a diet cola. She bought some inexpensive costume jewelry and a pair of shoes. Then for a long time she sat on a wooden bench overlooking a play area and just watched people come and go. She didn't pay particular attention to any one of them until one hombre sat on her bench with such force that it bounced.

He theatrically stretched and yawned, "Man, I'm beat." He

glanced her way and showed his pearly white teeth. "Hi. One of those yours?" He nodded toward the play area, crowded with young children.

Adair looked over the kids and said, "Four. Four of those are mine."

"That right?" he murmured. "Well." He sat in silence a minute, then nonchalantly got up and sauntered away.

Adair continued to sit on the bench and watch the play area. The children were cute. There was one little girl in blonde pigtails and a sundress who had adopted a rigid wooden horse as her pet. She patted it and fed it pretend hay and saddled it up to ride over the pretend hills.

Observing her, Adair smiled. A real horse, who could really take her over real hills, would scare that little girl to death. She was happy with her own imaginings. But eventually she'd come to yearn for the real thing, even with all the real dangers. Growing up meant learning to stay astride a galloping mass of muscle and bone, not settling down on a safely dead chunk of lacquered wood. And . . . Panny would teach her to ride.

Adair got up from the bench, gathered her packages, and went out to her car.

ᐳ13ᐸ

Evening rush-hour traffic was bad anywhere in Dallas—except going into downtown. Driving home from Collin Creek Mall, Adair breezed past immobile lanes of outgoing traffic and pulled into the Streiker Building at 5:40. She boarded the lonely elevator and rode it silently to the top.

In the kitchen of her apartment, Adair found a note: "Mrs. Streiker, the covered dish on the counter is beef pie. There is a salad and a cobbler in the refrigerator. Yvonne wanted to remind you to go through your mail. Have a nice evening. Sugar."

Adair peeked under the loose cover of foil at the luscious pastry crust, then pulled out a dinner plate with one hand and the salad bowl with the other. She loaded her plate, took it to the table, and turned on the six o'clock news. The very first news item was a plane crash, with footage of the wreckage. Adair turned off the television and glanced warily at the unopened mail. "I used to enjoy getting letters," she muttered, collecting them to read over dinner.

The first letter was addressed to her in typescript. She opened it and smiled cynically. It was an invitation from a local department store to model their upcoming spring line in a series of print ads.

It was flattering, but Adair was not interested. Not now. She had been smitten with the idea of modeling several years ago, and had paid over five hundred dollars to have a slick portfolio printed up. She had gone to every modeling agency in Dallas, plus a number of stores—this one included—but no one had offered a candle of hope. There were simply too many aspiring young actresses/ models in this town. But now that she was Mrs. Fletcher Streiker—why *of course* they'd love to drape their new spring clothes on her! Adair crumpled the letter. She would not prostitute Fletcher's name.

She finished her dinner and took the plate to the kitchen, where she rinsed it off in the sink. She paused over the running water, thinking. Then she turned it off and began digging in the kitchen trash can.

She found the letter to Fletcher from "Russell Cooper" and reread it carefully. It was quite cunning—not overloaded with misspellings or bad grammar, but with just enough naiveté to make it believable. Had she read his application and letter of recommendation first, instead of calling Gatesville on her own, she surely would have been fooled.

Suddenly she wondered: Had Fletcher known? Or suspected that this letter might not have been what it appeared to be? Is that why he hesitated so long over it? But if there had been any question in his mind, why had he let her handle it at all?

She let the letter drop back into the trash can. Darren knew that Fletcher was out of town, and so he had sent this letter addressed to him but knowing she would receive it. Obviously, he could not have hoped to spring this weak deception on Fletcher. She was the target.

That should have frightened her, but for some reason, it didn't— perhaps because she had successfully thwarted his first move. But he would be watching for another opportunity. She had to be careful not to give him one.

And that other note—the one he signed "DL"—that now looked like a clumsy attempt to undermine her confidence in

Fletcher. Having already negotiated that attack as well, she could safely call it "clumsy." And what nerve, to send it on the same day as his Cooper forgery!

Adair returned to the table and picked up the next letter, which was addressed to her in a feminine hand. It was printed with the Whinnets' return address. The note inside read:

October 26

Dear Adair,

We are having a small informal gathering at our home on Saturday, October 30, and want very much for you to be there. Fletcher thinks it's a fine idea. Please come. It's at 7:00 p.m.

Love,

Alicia

Adair wondered if Alicia had a party every week. "Guess I'd better try to make this one," she decided. She went to the kitchen telephone and dialed the Whinnets' number, mentally rehearsing what she would say and what Alicia might say to what she said.

"Hello?"

"Oh—hello. Alicia?" said Adair, caught unprepared.

"Yes, Adair. How are you?"

"Fine, thanks. Um, I'd love to come to your party Saturday. I'm wondering what name I'll be using," Adair said.

Alicia laughed, "I think you'll just be Adair Streiker. I believe you'll know everyone there."

"Oh, good," Adair said. Without much hope, she asked, "Will Fletcher be there?"

"I wish so, but I'm not expecting it," Alicia said honestly.

"Me neither. Still, I'll be looking forward to it," said Adair.

"Me, too. Have you heard anything about Fletcher's mother today?"

"Oh, yes! She came through the operation fine. She's in the coronary care unit and her vital signs are stable. She even talked to Fletcher on the phone," Adair recounted.

"I'm so glad. Charles will be relieved, too. Well, thank you for calling, Adair."

"Sure. Goodnight, Alicia."

That formality dispensed with, Adair turned her attention to the last letter. It had no return address, an illegible postmark, and was addressed to her in a printed hand. Bracing for another anonymous letter, she opened it and read:

> Dear Adair,
>   Excuse the hasty note. I haven't much time before my next departure.
>   Although I can't call you as often as I would like, you may find some small comfort in knowing that I haven't been able to think about anything but you. This is the last trip I'm taking without you. When I come back, I'll tell you everything I've been doing. You should find it quite interesting.
>
> Till then,
> Fletcher

Adair read it several times over, trying to form an opinion of this rather passionless note from her new husband. It almost sounded like he didn't care. No, it was not fair to say that. It was more like— she had to take his word for it that he cared, and that he would satisfy her curiosity about the reasons for his departure as soon as humanly possible.

She studied his handwriting: straight, narrow, slightly uneven, as if he had been writing on an unsteady surface. She looked at the envelope again but was still unable to make out the postmark. It had been sent in a metered envelope. "Could've been sent from anywhere," she realized. Except—today was still only Thursday. He had just left Tuesday. He could not have been far when he sent it.

Adair retrieved the folder on Fletcher from the bedside table and took it to the dinette, where she placed his letter in it. Somehow, it was a reassuring piece of evidence that things were progressing as they should, and she wanted to keep it. As she sat at the table, folder open in her hands, her eye fell on a page that she had seen before but had ignored because it seemed meaningless. It was the second page of a personal letter to Fletcher from someone with no name. It went like this:

page 2

I've just finished Natan Sharansky's Fear No Evil. On page 300 he talks about what happened to one prisoner who tried to protect himself by continually lying. Eventually, he separated himself from reality to the point of going insane. Sharansky saw the act of lying have this effect on someone more than once. Lies that protect our ego are especially damaging, as they separate us from the reality about ourselves and God, who is truth.

I've been thinking about all this lately because for months now my good friend Dee has been spurning my every attempt to get together. Every time I called to ask her over, she'd have some excuse as to why she couldn't come. At the same time, she was always very friendly at church, which made me think her rebuffs were in my imagination, so I'd try calling her again and end up with another transparent excuse. This is pure hypocrisy, and it's devastating. We used to be good friends! It would have been kinder for her to say, "I don't want to have anything more to do with you." But to make her words consistent with her actions would have brought to light how ugly she was being, so she covered them with a veneer of kindness. One good thing that has

The page ended in the middle of a sentence and there was no more of the letter, although Adair dug through the whole file looking for page three. At first glance, this had appeared to be nothing more than a thin-skinned reaction to a cooling friendship. But now Adair understood there was more to it than that, and she knew why Fletcher had kept it.

This explained why he never lied—not to himself, to her, or to anyone. This was her assurance that he would be coming back, that he did love her, that he knew what he was doing—just because he said so. The concreteness of that piece of paper was more real to Adair right now than the enormous sums of money in his bank account. He was real.

———◆———

The telephone rang. Adair glanced at the clock as she hurried to the kitchen telephone. It was only seven. He was calling early tonight. "Hello?" she answered.

"Hello, Adair," said Yvonne. "I wanted to let you know that I called the rest of the numbers on our mystery Cooper's application. They were all phony."

"Uh huh. I'm not surprised. I'm just taking for granted that man was really Darren Loggia," Adair said.

"I'm afraid you may be right. Have you talked to Fletcher tonight?" Yvonne inquired.

"No, I was hoping you were him. I need to talk to him." Adair felt a squeezing in the region of her heart.

"I do too. I'm very concerned about Darren's boldness here," Yvonne admitted. Then she added, "I feel that I need to warn you to be careful about what you say."

"What, you mean to Darren? I've been extremely careful," Adair assured her.

"No, I mean to other people. Just—don't forget that people lie sometimes. They misrepresent themselves or what they want from you. You need to be wary of people who want to use you."

"Who are you talking about?" Adair asked blankly.

"Anyone you don't know very well," Yvonne said with some agitation.

Speaking of knowing people reminded Adair about Alicia's party. "Are you going to be at the Whinnets' Saturday night?"

"Yes, I'll be there," Yvonne responded.

"Who else is coming?" Adair asked.

"I don't know. Fletcher dictated the guest list."

"He did!" Adair exclaimed. "Is he coming?"

"I don't know," said Yvonne.

Adair exhaled in frustration. The squeeze in her chest grew tighter. "I miss him, Yvonne. I want him back."

"Good. I'm glad," Yvonne said softly. After a few silent seconds, she noted, "I was relieved to hear that Fletcher's mother is on the mend."

"You and me both," Adair agreed.

"You did well, Adair. You're doing fine. You're going to be just fine," Yvonne said.

Adair did not understand what need there was for all of the reassurance. "Well, thanks, Yvonne. Maybe . . . he'll call soon."

"I'll get off the phone, then. See you tomorrow."

"Okay. Bye, Yvonne."

Adair looked over toward the large windows as she hung up. She went to stand in front of them and gaze at the city lights. The view was glorious and disturbing all at once. It reminded her of Fletcher. *Everything* reminded her of Fletcher. She could not turn around without his face filling her field of view and desire for him swelling her throat.

Suddenly she went to the desk and took out a notepad and pen. She sat down to make a list of topics she needed to cover with Fletcher when he called:

1. R. Cooper—Loggia?
2. Alicia's party—who is coming? ARE YOU COMING?
3. WHEN ARE YOU COMING BACK?
4.

There was something else. She tapped her pen on her chin, thinking. Oh yes—the partial letter in the file. She had wanted to ask him about that.

As Adair flipped through the file looking for the letter, something else she had not paid attention to previously caught her eye. It was an envelope with snapshots in it. Because there were no identifiable people in the photos, Adair had not looked at them closely. But now she did.

They were obviously pictures of Hawaii—sunlit beaches and swelling waves, waterfalls coursing over black cliffs, wild orchids and palm trees in the rain. . . . Suddenly Adair understood these as well. These were pictures he had taken of his home. This was the place special to his heart, where he was certain to bring her when he came back to get her. This was a picture of her future, and it was Paradise.

She closed the file with tears in her eyes. Then she looked down at her list of questions with cleansed vision. How arrogant to demand all these explanations. Either she trusted him or she didn't. If she didn't, detailed answers to these questions would not satisfy her, and if she did, asking them was unnecessary. She wadded up the page and threw it away. The empty feeling lingered.

She decided she was hungry. Adair went to the kitchen and ransacked the cabinets for the ingredients to make her favorite brownie recipe. Sugar had a well-stocked kitchen, so Adair had no difficulty finding cocoa, pecans, and butter—*real* butter, not margarine this time. She took sneaky pleasure in cooking up something for herself and, yes, even cleaning up after herself.

While the brownies were baking, Adair wandered back to the television and turned it on. She stumbled across one of her favorite movies, *Amadeus*. Soon she was nestled down on the leather sofa with lots of pillows and milk and brownies to watch Salieri and Mozart battle with music. An obliging autumn rain began to pelt the penthouse windows in accompaniment to Mozart's driving score, and occasionally Adair took her eyes from the screen to watch the rain as she listened to the genius in the music. They seemed to mesh.

And, for the first time, Adair realized how unreliable her feelings were. Here she was so busy checking herself every few minutes to see if she still loved Fletcher, or how she would feel to see him again, when all it took to cheer her up were brownies and a good movie. Her love for Fletcher had nothing to do with her feelings. He was coming back at some point regardless of how she felt about it. All she had to do was be ready to greet him, and her feelings would take care of themselves.

When she crawled into bed that evening she felt cradled in contentment, even though Fletcher had not called. And in the morning, she awoke without benefit of an alarm while the room was still dark. Her clock showed 6:20. She showered and dressed and made coffee all before Sugar appeared that morning.

As a matter of fact, Sugar seemed to be late. Adair made herself toast, but kept watching the clock as it progressed from 8:05 to 8:17 to 8:32.

Finally, Sugar came in and briskly shrugged off her coat while clutching a folded newspaper. She seemed upset. Yvonne followed her in, saying something that sounded like reassurance.

"Hi, Yvonne. Good morning, Sugar. Are you all right this morning?" Adair called from the kitchen. They both looked at her in surprise, as well they should, since they had never seen her up and dressed this early.

"Good morning, Mrs. Streiker," Sugar said coolly, glancing back at Yvonne as she handed her the paper. "Let me get breakfast."

"Is your arthritis bothering you this morning?" Adair asked in concern.

"No, I haven't any complaints," said Sugar. She went to the laundry room to hang up her coat. Adair wondered at the emphasis she had put on the personal pronoun.

Yvonne, carrying the newspaper, closed the door and smiled at Adair. "Good morning. I take it you haven't seen this morning's *Expositor*."

"What now?" Adair breathed in disgust. "I thought I had talked

Wendy into leaving me alone." She felt safe, knowing she had not given Wendy any usable information.

"You'd better have a look at this, then." Yvonne held the folded newspaper out to her.

As Adair opened it up, she was wondering what Fletcher might have done. On the lower half of the front page was the headline, "BILLIONAIRE DESERTS DALLAS BRIDE."

Adair's knees buckled and she sat limply on the couch. The article began:

> Billionaire philanthropist Fletcher Streiker, 36, left his new wife, the former Adair Weiss, the day after their marriage and she has not seen him since, friends reported to the *Expositor*. Apparently disenchanted with married life, the former bachelor left the country without disclosing his destination to his wife, who is reportedly distraught. Police, noting the frequency of his travels and his reclusive nature, refused to investigate his disappearance as a missing person. Ms. Weiss is reportedly still occupying the couple's home. . . .

Unable to read more, Adair put the paper down and cradled her head on her knees.

Sugar puttered slowly in the kitchen and Yvonne sat gently on the sofa. Adair lifted her head. "Has Fletcher seen this?" she whispered.

"I haven't sent him a copy, but he's bound to see it sooner or later," Yvonne answered.

"I can't believe it," Adair said, swallowing tears. "I took Courtney to lunch yesterday. She was so sympathetic and everything, I . . . unburdened on her. She must have been taking notes. I never would have guessed that she would go straight to the *Expositor*, though I should have, because she's the one who first told them about me and Fletcher. She pretended to be my friend." Here she broke down and cried.

Sugar came to stand beside the couch and Yvonne placed a

consoling hand on Adair's shoulder. "What's done is done. We can't change it, so we'll just turn our backs on it and go on."

Yvonne stood up and deliberately dropped the newspaper in the trash can. At that time Adair saw the letters in her hand.

"These came yesterday morning when I happened to have Fletcher on the phone, so I covered them with him and penciled in his comments. With all the Cooper business yesterday, I neglected to get them to you earlier."

"Thanks, Yvonne, but . . . I don't see how Fletcher would want me to do anything with his mail now," Adair said despairingly.

"Well, perhaps the best way to prove the newspaper wrong is to go about your business and do what he's already asked you to do," Yvonne observed.

"Are you sure he won't be mad?" Adair asked meekly.

"I can't say how he would feel, but these require a response and he's not here," Yvonne said.

Adair nodded and took the letters.

"Coffee, Yvonne?" Sugar asked quietly.

"Oh, perhaps just one cup," Yvonne agreed. She got up to get it as Adair read the first letter.

It was from the *Dallas Sun-Times,* thanking Fletcher for his participation in last year's charity drive and reminding him of this year's drive getting under way. In the margin, Yvonne had penciled, "F. says to make a contribution in his name."

Adair looked up at Yvonne. "How much?" she asked. "How much did he want me to contribute to this charity drive?"

"He didn't say."

"Well, how much did he contribute last year?" Adair went on.

"I have no idea," Yvonne shrugged.

Adair felt a panicky sense of inadequacy and bewilderment. She was not comfortable dealing with the kinds of numbers Fletcher tossed around. "Well, what would you suggest as an appropriate amount?" she asked Yvonne.

"I definitely got the impression that the amount was to be left up to you," Yvonne told her.

Adair almost started to cry again. It was such a simple request, but in her exaggerated frame of mind she saw herself as either humiliating Fletcher or wasting his money. "Get a grip on yourself," she muttered aloud. What was Fletcher's style? Unreasonable generosity, she decided.

"Can you cut me a check for . . . one hundred thousand dollars?" she asked Yvonne. It seemed like an enormous enough amount.

Yvonne smiled. "Within the hour," she said, getting up. She left a nearly full cup of coffee on the table.

Mildly encouraged, Adair turned her scrutiny to the next missive. It was a computer printout of the names, titles, and salaries of The Rivers Bank branch employees. The note from Fletcher transcribed by Yvonne read, "These are up for annual review. Since you worked with them, please make recommendations and send to Chuck."

Adair inhaled and retrieved a pencil from the desk. What an open door. There they were—Duane, Courtney, all of them. She slowly went down the list, then stopped at Sharon Betschelet. Quiet little Sharon, who single-handedly held the checking department together, made only $13,000 a year. Adair immediately upped her to $20,000. Then she changed her mind and made it $23,000.

She went back up to the top of the list and hovered over Duane's name. Personally, he was a jerk, but he was conscientious at his job. He was presently making $34,000. Adair conceded him a raise of $3,000. Charlotte did her job well, but was already making more than anyone except Duane. Pat was okay, Crystal okay, Courtney . . . Adair twirled her pencil. "I never knew Courtney made that much more than I did," she mused. She left Courtney alone. On down the list she recommended raises for two other people, and then she was done. "There is really no deadwood at that branch, now that I'm gone."

"Pardon?" said Sugar from the kitchen.

"Nothing," Adair laughed.

Yvonne knocked briskly and came on in. "Here is your draft," she said, handing an envelope to Adair.

"That was quick," Adair said, surprised. She slid the check partly from the envelope, noting the amount and that it was made out to the charity drive. She also saw that it carried Fletcher's signature, but she assumed it was done automatically. She tapped the envelope and thought out loud, "I guess I should deliver this in person. I hate to drop this much money in a mail box."

"Good thinking," Yvonne said, nodding.

"All right, then." Adair stuffed the envelope and letter from the newspaper into her purse. Then she picked up the revised computer printout. "Oh. Here are the recommendations Fletcher asked for. Whatever he does with them is fine."

"I'll take them right to Charles," Yvonne said, then exited with the printout. Adair momentarily considered calling Duane to tell him of her recommendations, but then decided that would be presumptuous. She did not know how many of them, if any, Fletcher would adopt. And besides, it was too late for her to save face with Duane. She had slighted him too many times.

There was one more envelope. Adair picked it up, and out fell a newspaper clipping which fluttered to the floor before she could catch it. She retrieved it and studied it in bewilderment. A car ad. Was Fletcher going to buy her a new car? Oh, no—it was only a partial ad. What she needed to see must be on the other side. Adair turned it over. It was the obituary of a twenty-year-old woman named Shelley Randazzo. She died at home following a lengthy illness, etc., etc. There was a small photograph of a pretty girl with mounds of dark hair.

Adair studied it, then checked the envelope again. It contained a folded note reading, "F. asks you to give personal condolences to Wendy Beacham for her sister's suicide."

Adair sank back into the sofa. "I can't do that. I can't. I don't know her well enough to march in there and tell her how sorry I am that her sister committed suicide! Surely he can't mean that I go *to* her. Maybe just a note, or. . . ." She reread his instructions over and over, but the words stayed the same. She could interpret them however she wanted to suit herself, but inside she knew exactly what he intended: a personal visit. Face to face, again.

"And after that horrible article she ran," Adair softly exclaimed.

"I'm sorry; what did you say?" Sugar came in, wiping her hands on a dish towel.

"I said that I have to go out for a while and take care of these errands for Fletcher." Adair put the clipping in her purse and stood up.

"Fine, Mrs. Streiker. I hope it goes well," Sugar said. She seemed to have forgotten all about the offensive article.

"Me, too." Adair left the apartment, carelessly neglecting to lock the door behind her, and rode the elevator down to the garage. As she got into her car and pulled out, she noticed a police car stopped, lights flashing, behind a minivan. "Caught himself a speeder," she noted, checking her own speedometer.

She elected to tackle the hardest thing first. She had no inkling of what she would say to Wendy Beacham, but having to concentrate on maneuvering out of downtown Friday traffic helped keep her from worrying so much about it.

After exiting the freeway, she had to change lanes quickly around an unexpected roadblock, which angered the driver behind her so that he began to tailgate her. She accelerated to fifty miles an hour—fifteen over the speed limit on this street—and the man behind her accelerated accordingly. She could have towed him with a long rubber band.

Adair gasped at seeing a school zone with flashing lights directly ahead. She would have to brake. But she knew the instant she did, he would hit her. She braced and let up on the accelerator. Before she had a chance to touch the brake, she heard a rending crunch.

But she did not feel a thing. Adair looked in her rear-view mirror and saw that the tailgater had been broadsided by a third vehicle. Her little Mazda was untouched. She let out her breath gratefully, easing through the school zone at the appropriate twenty miles per hour while the tailgater exploded out of his car.

The remainder of her drive was leisurely in comparison. Still, when she pulled into the parking lot of the *Expositor,* her heart was thumping and her hands were shaking. Evidently the long-expected cold front had moved in, for it felt twenty degrees colder now than when she had left the apartment. Shivering, she locked her car door. "Kind of chilly for the last of October, isn't it?" she joked weakly with herself. "And here I forgot my smart new coat and hat."

She walked into the building as if she belonged there, bypassed the receptionist and the stares, and took the elevator to the second-floor editorial offices. She knocked on W. Beacham's door.

"What?" shouted the busy editor.

Adair opened the door, stepped inside, and shut it behind her. Several newspaper employees had to stop just outside the door to look for something or other real quick.

Wendy stared tensely at Adair, who cleared her throat and began, "Excuse me for barging in like this, but . . . Fletcher asked me to come by. He asked me . . . to tell you . . . how very grieved he is over the—the death of your sister."

Wendy's face blanched and tears welled up in her eyes. "How did you know about that?" she asked tightly.

"I only know what Fletcher told me. I did not know your sister at all. But I know he means it. He sent me only because he can't come himself."

"How dare you?" Wendy uttered, her pale face reddening. "How dare you use this to try to prove that he didn't desert you?"

"I'm only doing—" Adair stammered.

"Get out of here! Right now! Before I call security!" Wendy shouted.

Adair turned and opened the door to a half-dozen reporters standing outside. They dispersed as Adair went to the elevator and pushed the down button. No one approached her while she waited, and when the elevator delivered her to the first floor, she calmly left the building and went to her car. As she was getting in, a photographer ran up to shove a camera in her face.

"Great. I wonder what they'll make of that for the front page?"

she grumbled, starting her car and turning out of the parking lot. She wished she could cry to release her tension, but her eyes were dry as August. "Besides, crying on R. L. Thornton Freeway is suicidal," she said.

Then she winced. Poor Wendy. Adair truly felt sorry for the pain she must be carrying, but why oh why couldn't Fletcher communicate his sympathy to Wendy without using her? Adair sternly held herself together to run the one last errand.

❖

Some twenty minutes later she drove up to the massive *Sun-Times* building. Before going in, she checked the letter from the paper to see who had signed it. "Calvin Brookshard," she pronounced. She entered the busy lobby and paused, finding that her courage had completely deserted her. All she could think about was getting back to the apartment and hiding under the covers. But that wouldn't do her any good here.

She approached the receptionist's desk and waited until the woman looked up from her switchboard. "May I help you?"

"Yes, I need to see Calvin Brookshard, please," Adair said.

"May I tell him who is here to see him?" she asked, pressing a panel.

"Adair Streiker. Mrs. Fletcher Streiker."

The receptionist relayed the information as Adair stood beside the desk. Barely five seconds later a voice at her side said, "Mrs. Streiker? I'm Cal Brookshard."

Adair turned and shook hands with a bearded man in black glasses and wrinkled shirt sleeves. "How do you do?" she said pleasantly.

"Fine. Great. Won't you come into my office?" He extended his hand toward a side hallway and Adair followed him to a cluttered, bookish office. He closed the door. "I'm tickled to meet you. What can I do for you?" he said, pulling up a leather chair for her and slouching into a seat behind his desk.

"Well, my husband got your letter about the charity drive and asked me to make a contribution in his name, since he's out of town right now," Adair explained.

"Great, great!" Cal said. "How much did he wish to give?"

"Here is his check." Adair drew the envelope out of her purse and handed it across the desk to him.

Cal looked at it. "Wonderful! We'll see that it's put to good use."

"Who will it go to?" Adair queried.

"We assign contributions according to need. Or, if you prefer, you may select the charities yourself," Cal said.

"Yes, I'd rather do that," she replied.

He pulled a long typed list out of his desk. "Here is a list of all the charities in Dallas that we endorse," he said, handing it over to her.

"Okay," Adair murmured, scanning the list. This she knew something about. In preparing the senior girls' service project, she had researched a number of organizations. She remembered wishing that there were more she could do for them. "How much of this money goes to the charities?" she asked Cal.

"Every dime. One hundred percent," he said firmly.

"Good." She began specifying: "The Salvation Army, for sure. And the Make-a-Wish Foundation. And—"

"Whoa, wait," Cal said, writing. "How much, now? To the Salvation Army?"

"Twenty thousand," Adair stated. They needed a new building. "And ten thousand to Make-a-Wish." Airfare for all those terminally ill children and their families was expensive. "Ten thousand to Hope Cottage, five to Ladies of Charity. . . ."

Adair went rapidly through the list until Cal interjected, "Okay, that's it. One hundred thousand."

She looked up. "That's it?" Then she looked down at the largely uncovered list. "One hundred thousand isn't enough," she declared.

"The need is very great," Cal agreed. "If you feel you should drop off another check, that's fine. At the same time, contributions like this spur others to give. Can I have your permission to put your name and the amount given in our paper?"

Adair corrected him, "*His* name. And go ahead and put the amount. There will be more after I check with Fletcher."

"Great," Cal said. He gave her a receipt and a release. "Please sign that. By the way, the contribution is tax-deductible, you know."

"Yeah." Signing the release "Mrs. Fletcher Streiker" gave her a thrill of satisfaction.

"Mrs. Streiker, I thank you so much. And please thank Mr. Streiker for us," Cal said warmly, reaching out to shake her hand again. As she stood to leave, he added, "Oh, Mrs. Streiker . . . I read what the gossip rag across town said this morning. Obviously, it's not factual."

"No, it's not true at all," she said.

"We'll make a point of mentioning that you dropped off the check at your husband's request," he said.

"Thanks," she smiled.

"Have a nice day, Mrs. Streiker."

As she walked out of the building into the clear sunshine, she felt like a whole person again. Wounded, but not killed. She mused, "Well, I guess there's nothing to do now but go home and wait for Fletcher to show up."

➤14➤

When Adair returned home from her visits to the newspaper offices that Friday, she found her apartment door slightly ajar. As she walked in, she scolded herself, "I should remember to lock it when I leave."

Throwing her purse on the sofa, she called, "Sugar, I'm back."

No answer.

"Sugar?" she repeated.

The door to the bedroom opened. "Oh, hello, Mrs. Streiker," said Sugar, stripping off rubber gloves. "I was cleaning the bathroom and didn't hear you come in. Would you like lunch now?"

"Yes, thank you," Adair said, relaxing. "I've got to remember to lock that door when I leave."

"Yes, you should," Sugar agreed. "The elevator should only work with a pass key, but you never can tell." She lifted the lid from a pot of chili simmering on the stove. It was perfect for the first cool day of fall.

"That smells so good." Adair stood over the stove to taste a spoonful. "Mmm, it's great."

"Thank you," said Sugar, genuinely pleased, although that was the usual reaction to her cooking. "I sampled the brownies you made last night. They were delicious. I'd like the recipe."

"Sugar, you're putting me on," Adair protested.

"No, really—I'm always on the lookout for new recipes. A good cook never stops learning," Sugar insisted.

"I'll try to get it down on paper," Adair said, piqued at herself for feeling so pleased. Taking her bowl of chili to the dinette table in front of the windows, she asked, "Has anyone called?"

"Not this morning," Sugar answered.

"Hmm. Wonder why Fletcher hasn't called." Adair took tentative bites of the hot chili, then said, "I wonder what I'm supposed to wear tomorrow night. Are you going?" she asked before she realized it was an inappropriate question.

"Yes, my husband and I have been invited," Sugar said.

"Good, I'll get to meet him. What are you wearing?" Adair asked.

"Oh, I'm sure just a nice dress."

"I don't have any nice dresses," Adair grumbled. "I need to get something new to wear." She ate some more of the chili, then asked, "Do you know who else will be there?"

"Besides Yvonne, no. But you'd better be prepared to see just about anybody there. Mr. Streiker has these parties now and then, and it's just amazing to see who comes," said Sugar.

Adair sat up. "Like who?"

"Well, his sister came from Hawaii once. There was a cab driver from New York City, and a pediatric surgeon from Shreveport, and—oh, so many people I can't remember now. But it was so interesting, because they had all met Fletcher, and they all had their stories to tell. I listened for three solid hours and it seemed like five minutes.

"It's so funny, you know, because he has this reputation of being such a recluse—no one has seen him and no one has his picture—but that night there were scads of people who had not only seen him and talked to him, but helped him.

"That surgeon was something else. Mr. Streiker had brought him one of those spina bifida babies—you know, they're born with part of their spinal cord exposed—and asked him to operate on her. He did. She's now about four years old and walking with crutches. Not only did he save her life, but he knew who Fletcher was from day one and he *refused to be paid*. He knew Fletcher could pay him anything in the world but he wouldn't take a penny, because he had just fallen in love with this little girl. He set up a trust fund for her college! Now the doctor takes interesting patients from all over the world that Fletcher sends him. He wouldn't say what he's paid, only that it's plenty."

Adair listened quietly, then observed, "You lapsed into calling him Fletcher instead of Mr. Streiker. Yvonne did that too."

Sugar looked guilty. "Excuse me, Mrs. Streiker. It just seems that anyone who knows him for very long winds up calling him by his first name."

"That being the case, why don't you call me Adair? Then I'll know when you're referring to his mother and not me."

"That would be lovely, Adair," said Sugar.

Adair lapsed into thought as she finished her chili. When she took her bowl to the sink, she asked, "If there really are that many people who have seen him, then how many people in the Streiker Corporation know him by sight?"

Sugar slowly wrung out a wet dishrag. "Let me see . . . there's Charles, and Yvonne, and Reggie . . . Neil, who's a janitor, and Isabelle . . . Gordie down in operations. . . . Beyond that, I can't think of anyone. It can't be more than a handful."

"Why do so few people in his own company know him?" Adair demanded.

"Heavens, I don't know. I can't figure it out. There's a lot of curiosity and misinformation floating around about him here, and a lot of people think they're doing him such a big favor by working here, but actually this company is not so different from other big corporations. You have your freeloaders, and backstabbers, and social climbers.

"Isn't it a shame that the people who get their paychecks from him are too busy doing their own thing to do the job they were hired to do? They give the company a bad name. He pays them all every week—I guess he can afford to—but he's also got people on the payroll who have nothing to do with the Streiker Corporation. And a lot of times when he needs something done, he'll go to one of those people on the outside. Not necessarily someone here in this building."

Adair went to the windows and looked out at the horizon, softened by low, dense clouds. "Darren Loggia used to be an employee. One of his first."

"I don't know much about him," Sugar murmured.

Adair started to lean against the window, then realized she was getting fingerprints all over it that Sugar would have to clean up. "I'm kind of tired. I think I'll go lie down for a while."

"Fine, Adair," said Sugar.

<hr />

When Adair woke, there were long shadows in her bedroom. She yawned and stretched, but felt so leaden that she rolled over again for a few minutes. Then she groggily got up to see what was happening in the outside world.

It was 5:15, and Sugar was gone. She had left a note on the dinette table: "Dear Adair, I thought you might want something light after the chili at lunch, so I left you a chicken salad in the refrigerator. Yvonne dropped by but said not to waken you. We will see you tomorrow night at Alicia's. Sugar."

Adair nodded and stumbled to the kitchen. "I hate it when I sleep in the middle of the day. I feel like I've got a hangover." She opened the refrigerator and tried a spoonful of the salad. It was a tasty little ensemble with sesame seeds and green onions. She heaped out a bowlful and sat heavily in front of the television set. She turned on the evening news, but since it was the usual murder and mayhem, she switched it off again. She glanced at the coffee table. Yvonne had left no mail.

Adair awarded herself two brownies for dessert, then cleaned up her own dishes and put them away. She was restless and almost desperate to get out of that apartment but didn't dare leave when Fletcher might call. She needed to talk to him. She needed to clear up the matter of the newspaper article with him.

She plopped onto the couch and passed a hand over her eyes. What in the world would she tell him about it? She couldn't see any way to justify what she had done. She could make all kinds of excuses, but the fact remained that she complained about him to Courtney when she shouldn't have.

Adair sucked in a deep, unhappy breath, and then sprang to the telephone. No, it had not rung. She swiftly dialed a number from memory and waited while it rang on the other end. But all she got was Courtney's answering machine. She hung up, then said to the air, "All I want to know is *why*, Courtney. Why did you sell me out? Why did you pretend to be my friend and then turn on me? Don't you know how much you hurt me? Doesn't it bother you at all?" Saying these words opened the wound again.

Adair had felt a bond of friendship with Courtney that she had not shared with anyone else. Alicia was wonderful—almost too wonderful, floating in such lofty social circles. Yvonne was reliable and trustworthy, but unable to identify much with Adair's problems. Sugar was sweet, but her personal life did not include Adair. Courtney, now, although superficial and status-conscious, really understood the life of a young woman on her own. They had shared the same view of a treacherous world.

Then things changed. Adair had achieved, unwillingly and in total ignorance, Courtney's ultimate goal: she had married a billionaire. Adair knew that marrying him would mean giving up life on her terms—giving up old relationships, familiar problems, whimsical decisions. By coming into Adair's life, Fletcher had knocked out every support and small consolation she'd had, until she had nothing left but . . . him.

Placing herself in such total dependence on someone else was terrifying. Adair was much more comfortable relying on herself, because she pretty well knew in what areas she would let herself down. She was in control. But—in control of what? What future did she have in her former life but going to work every day, doing the same dreary things, getting old and cynical like Charlotte? There was no chance to pursue a dream or make a difference in anyone else's life.

How were things different now? Her dream of dancing was just as unattainable as it was before. She just sat in Fletcher's apartment day after day. But . . . he had made it clear that this was an interim situation—that there was new territory not far ahead. Did she believe him? If she did, then she could hope that eventually, somehow, those dreams would be achieved—even those dreams she did not yet know existed.

Suddenly she wondered about this business that kept Fletcher absent. He kept stressing the necessity of it, as if it were a personal priority. She wondered if it had more to do with her than she had realized.

In theory, it was simple: either she waited for him or she walked out the door. Practically, however, it meant that now she had the freedom to decide how to spend every minute, and it was much more difficult.

"I'm tired of plowing this same mental ground over and over," she complained, stretching. She got up and went to the kitchen to search out some iced tea—something with caffeine in it to wake her up out of this stupor. Something to make something happen. As she sipped her tea, she perused Fletcher's books and carefully looked over several of his unique artifacts. It was such an eclectic collection that it provided no blinding insights about him. They were just a bunch of old things.

She sighed again, tiredly, and her sigh seemed to echo through the empty apartment. She hadn't realized how much she'd been leaning on Sugar for company. Even when Sugar was off working in the kitchen, humming to herself, Adair had been drawing comfort from her presence. Sugar wasn't just a housekeeper, she was a close friend of Fletcher's, and knowing her told Adair more about him than any knickknacks could.

Adair sprawled out on the couch. "Why am I so tired?" she asked herself. "Nothing makes you so tired as waiting," she answered back. Little flecks of mascara were coming off on her fingers, so she went back to the bathroom and took off her makeup. She would not be going anywhere tonight, anyway. Then she decided to brush her teeth and get into a comfortable old sweatshirt. Was it her imagination or was it getting chilly?

On a whim, she ran up to the rooftop to see what the night felt like up there. As soon as she opened the rooftop door, she found out that it was quite cold and windy. The potted plants beside the lap pool were flapping back and forth in the conflicting gusts. Fearing an early frost, Adair moved what pots she could into the gazebo. Then, teeth chattering, she hurried back downstairs.

This little exertion drained her completely. With most of the lights in the apartment still on, she crawled under the bedcovers and went right to sleep.

———◆◆◆———

Adair woke in the stillness of the morning and listened to the quiet of the apartment. It was Saturday, and that meant Sugar would not be coming in. Adair was on her own today.

She sat up and looked at the clock—7:40. Then she picked up the telephone receiver and heard the dial tone. Yes, it was working. "Fletcher didn't call last night. I'm sure I would have heard it. Why didn't he call?"

Groaning, she threw back the covers and shuffled into the kitchen to make herself a pot of coffee. In spite of a long and uninterrupted night's sleep, she felt as tired and grumpy as she had last night.

"Alicia's party is tonight," she reminded herself. Coffee cup in hand, she went to her closet to look for something to wear. She glanced at Fletcher's side of the closet for reassurance. "At least his clothes are still here."

She then evaluated every conceivable party outfit she could

put together from her wardrobe, and pronounced them all trash. She showered and dressed, grimly preparing to go to the nearest mall to find something. Shopping was no fun when there was a specific need to be filled.

Adair ate a couple of stale brownies for breakfast, then took up her purse and left. Irritably, she again neglected to lock the apartment. She was tired of punching in that dumb door code. On the elevator, she mistakenly touched the lobby button instead of the garage level.

When the doors opened on the lobby, she started to push the garage button, but the activity in the lobby caught her eye. She held the elevator doors open. A number of people were coming out of the elevators with boxes, talking angrily in groups, even crying and hugging each other.

Adair watched in amazement. Then she asked someone passing, "What's happening?"

"Don't you know?" the man in a knit shirt said scornfully. He also was carrying a box of personal belongings. "Mr. Streiker tore through yesterday and fired a bunch of people, just like that. No warning or anything but a measly severance pay. We're filing grievances, I promise you."

"He's here?" Adair cried, grabbing his arm. "Fletcher is here?"

"No, no," he said, shrugging out of her grasp. "He just sent out pink slips. But everybody got them all at once yesterday." He took his box into the elevator and jabbed the down button.

Adair stared after him. Then she saw a sheet posted in the lobby, which was attracting a crowd. She pushed through to read the heading: "Employees Terminated as of October 29." A lengthy list followed. "I've never seen this done so—publicly before," she said under her breath.

Apprehensively, she scanned the list for Yvonne's or Charles's name, neither of which appeared. But there was Bob McIlvoy, the assistant vice president who had been so disdainful of running her on prenuptial errands. No one's name from The Rivers Bank branch appeared. It occurred to her that she had not recommended anyone's firing.

As she turned from the list, she almost bumped into a girl coming off the elevator with her things in a mesh bag. "Excuse me," Adair said automatically, but as the young woman glared briefly at her, Adair recognized her as the self-righteous prig from the fourteenth floor. Adair could not help smiling. On her way down to the garage, she lauded, "Good for you, Fletcher."

Once out of the garage in her car, she turned onto the freeway and from there headed toward the nearest major mall. En route she passed a large Goodwill outlet. "Nyaah!" Adair stuck out her tongue. She had never told anyone, least of all Courtney, that Goodwill was where she bought the bulk of her clothes because it was the only place she could afford. Even K-Mart was steep for her budget.

But today she zeroed in on the large upscale outlets and purposely parked near the entrance of a store she had avoided in the past. She had always felt that even to walk in would set off "Ineligible Purchaser" alarms throughout the store. Now she breezed in and strode straight for the designer departments.

There she scrutinized sequins, beads, velvets, and lamés. The attire of the woman who had stared her down on Alicia's porch acted as a subconscious guide. With a saleswoman hovering by, Adair tried a dress on. Hoisting its glittering, tight-fitting bodice, she eyed the flouncy skirt six inches above her knee and the big bow on the side. The saleswoman exclaimed, "You look like a movie star!"

"Yeah, I feel like I should be on stage in this," she muttered. She barely glanced at the price tag—$560—before rejecting the dress as inappropriate for the evening, even though she did not have a clear idea of what *would* be appropriate.

She could not find anything in that department, so she went to the next. And she could not find anything in that store, so she went to the next. After two-and-a-half hours of combing large department stores and small boutiques, she began to see all the dresses run together and look alike. There seemed to be three choices: casual sweaters and skirts, business dresses, and strapless

gowns with beads and slits. Exhausted and empty-handed, Adair
dropped onto a bench by a fountain in the mall. To recoup, she ate
a chicken sandwich and fries.

She left the mall to continue her search. There happened to
be another mall directly across the freeway, so she got into her car
and pulled up to its flagship store. She skipped the trendy juniors'
section, headed for the women's department, collared the first saleswoman she saw, and stated, "I need a dress for a party tonight. It
has to be simple and classy and modest."

"We've got just the thing!" the clerk responded. And the first
dress she pulled out was the same sequined number Adair had tried
on at the first store, only red instead of black.

"No, that's too gaudy. I need something simpler," Adair resisted.

"But this is the rage. Everybody's wearing sequins this fall," the
saleswoman argued.

"It's too showy," Adair said firmly.

The clerk pursed her lips and hung the dress back up. "Then
I'll show you some more *mature* selections." Adair did not protest,
and the woman guided her to a rack of modest chiffons. "Here's a
nice little inoffensive outfit." She pulled out a powder blue dress.

"Yes, but it's a size twelve. I need an eight," Adair said.

"Are you sure?" the clerk asked doubtfully, eyeing Adair's figure.

"Yes," Adair said through gritted teeth.

"If you say so." She rehung the dress, and the two of them
pawed through the rest of the rack. "There are no eights here. Why
don't you try this?" She pulled out a shapeless dress in a strange
print.

"I don't think so," Adair answered, looking around.

"My, we're difficult to please, aren't we?" the clerk said.

"If you can't help me, I'll look elsewhere," Adair said.

"I don't think you're going to find anything anywhere, because
you don't even know what you want," was the clerk's opinion.

"Maybe. Just rest assured it won't be here." Adair turned and
walked out. "I knew there was a reason I didn't like those snooty
stores," she fumed. She searched two or three other dress shops,

but the same clothes seemed to follow her still. She gave up and went out to her car.

Driving back on the freeway, she once again saw the large Goodwill store coming up. "What have I got to lose? I've already wasted four hours," she muttered, exiting the freeway. She pulled into a space, taking some comfort from the Mercedes parked nearby.

She had never been in this particular store before. It was very large, with a wood parquet floor and miles of neat racks. Adair saw young children playing in the toy section while their moms dug through the children's wear. There were teenagers looking for trendy cast-offs and young professionals padding a wardrobe on meager earnings.

Adair felt more at home here. The people who came here parked their pretensions outside and seriously searched for bargains. She found herself thinking, *I'd go to any church if the people there had the same attitude as the people here.* She frowned at the incongruous thought and drifted over to the ladies' dresses.

She listlessly looked through dresses on the first rack, where her fingers landed on something soft. She pulled out a cream-colored dress with a big cowl neck. It was so soft—she turned down the collar in back to find the content label. Pure cashmere wool, size ten. "Maybe it would fit . . ." Adair considered, fingering a soft sleeve.

Adair took the dress to wait in line at the small, dark dressing rooms. When she finally got in one, she pushed aside the clutter of plastic hangers and gingerly pulled the dress on over her head. She looked in the mirror, and could not believe her eyes. It was perfect. She searched it for stains or holes, but it was still perfect. Only then did she look at the price tag: "Whew—$12.50—pretty pricey. But, hey—I'm worth it."

When she got to the checkout counter, the clerk informed her that all green-tagged items were on sale, so she walked out of the store with a solid cashmere dress for six dollars and twenty-five cents. "Fletcher will die when he sees this and hears how much I paid for it!" she laughed, and her heart skipped a beat. Clearly, she was subconsciously expecting to see him tonight. "You're setting yourself up for a big disappointment," she warned, since there was more reason to assume he would not be there than to believe he would. But her heart still thumped expectantly.

She drove through Saturday afternoon freeway traffic in the glow of euphoria, parked in the largely empty Streiker garage, and floated up the elevator.

———◆——

Adair's reverie vanished as she stopped short in front of the apartment door. It was slightly ajar. She knew she hadn't locked it before leaving—but she had closed it, hadn't she? Of course, if she hadn't closed it securely, a strong blast from the hallway air-conditioning vent could have blown it open . . . couldn't it?

Adair tentatively opened the door and looked inside. Everything was still. "Sugar?" she called lightly, not expecting her to be here.

Silence.

Adair went in, leaving the door open behind her, and laid her package on the coffee table. "Hello? Sugar?"

There was no answer, so she relaxed and put her purse down on the table as well. Then the door was suddenly shut behind her. She wheeled around.

Standing inside the apartment was the man she had last seen as Russell Cooper—now minus his mustache. "You should always lock your door, Adair," he chided. He had lost his country twang as well.

"What do you want?" she gasped.

"Nothing much," he said. "Just to settle an old score. Don't take it personally." He took a length of cord from his jeans pocket and began winding it around his fists.

"Please . . ." Adair began, her eyes watering, but she saw that nothing she said would make any difference. The calculated coolness she had first glimpsed in his eyes now dominated his person. If the eyes are the window of the soul, she looked through his and saw a barrenness colder than any frozen tundra. As he came toward her with the cord stretched taut, there was not even any passion in him. The spirit of murder was as mindless as dirt. *This is what it's like to be killed,* she thought.

At that moment the telephone rang. Adair startled, then looked at Loggia. "Go ahead and answer it," he smiled. "No one can help you."

Shaking, Adair went to the stand and picked up the receiver. "H-hello."

"Hi, Adair. What's going on this afternoon?"

"Fletcher!" she cried, clutching the receiver. "Darren Loggia is here! He's going to kill me!"

"Why don't you let me talk to him?" Fletcher suggested.

Numbly, Adair held out the receiver. "He wants to talk to you."

Loggia hesitated an instant, then took the telephone. "Hello, old buddy," he sneered. He listened quietly a few seconds, then hung up. Adair froze. Loggia stuffed the cord back into his pants pocket, then without so much as a glance at her turned and left the apartment.

Adair could not move for a moment. Then she rushed at the door, slammed it, and locked it. She ran back to the telephone, but heard only the dial tone. She slumped onto the couch, clutched her knees, and shivered for ten minutes.

After she had calmed down, she took the cashmere dress from the brown paper sack and held it against her face. The thought of leaving the safety of the apartment to go to the Whinnets' tonight terrified her. She looked up at the gold and orange rays coming through the sloping windows. "But I wasn't safe here. Loggia had me *here.* I have to go."

Her stomach churned again and she realized she was hungry. She went to the refrigerator and pulled out chicken salad leftovers, which she ate standing up while she watched the sun descend.

Then she went to the bathroom to wash her face, reapply her makeup, and put on her new dress. She was still shaking, and she kept dropping things. But finding that her off-white pumps went nicely with her cashmere dress greatly restored her.

By the time she donned her new coat and hat, she was no longer shaking. When she headed out the door tonight, however, she diligently locked it.

The elevator carried her down to the parking garage, where she looked out before stepping off. There was no one in view. As she walked to her car, her footsteps echoed in the near-empty garage. She glanced at the security guard's booth: there was no one in it. Unlocking her car, she considered that after leaving the perfect opportunity in her apartment, Loggia had no reason to attack her here.

Adair sat in the car and started the engine. *What did Fletcher tell him?* Loggia had left as if he had been presented with a better idea. What could Fletcher have said?

On her way to the party, Adair covered all sorts of possibilities, from the ludicrous to the just plausible. He could have pleaded, "She never hurt you. Leave her alone." He could have threatened, "I'll kill you if you touch her." He could have offered, "I'll give you whatever you want if you'll let her go." But Adair could not see how any of the above would make Loggia just hang up and leave.

Preoccupied with exploring mental routes, she exited the freeway to Papillon Court as if on automatic pilot. She turned a corner here, another there, then pulled up to the Whinnets' home and surrendered her car to a valet as if she had done it all her life. Gathering her coat against the chill of the evening, she went by herself up the cobbled walk. As she placed her finger on the doorbell, she suddenly felt she knew without a doubt what Fletcher had told Loggia: *Don't bother with her. Come get me.*

→15←

Alicia opened the door to a pale, doe-eyed Adair on her front porch. "So good to see you, Adair. Come right in." She drew Adair inside by the hand. "You look lovely—why, you're shaking like a leaf! Are you all right?"

"Yes, I'm fine. It's—chilly out," Adair said through chattering teeth. She gave her hat and coat to Jackie with a quick smile.

A beautiful young woman with long brown hair hurried up to Alicia's side. Adair immediately saw the resemblance. "Adair, let me introduce my daughter, Kristin," Alicia said warmly.

"How nice to meet you." Adair shook her offered hand.

"This is such a thrill. I've been wanting to meet you ever since I first heard the news." Kristin took her arm and led her to the buffet tables in the dining room. "Grab a plate and tell me *everything* about him."

Charles approached. "Good evening, Adair. I see you've been cornered by Chatty Cathy." He affectionately kissed Kristin on the forehead. "I am *very glad* you could make it tonight," he told Adair.

"Thank you," she mouthed, noticing the particular emphasis

he used. He knew something.

"Champagne? Wine? Fruit punch?" Kristin asked, rapid-fire.

Adair's stomach lurched at the mention of alcohol. "Punch, please."

"Hey, Mrs. Streiker. Nice party, ain't it?" Reggie nodded and smiled on his way to the tables. He looked eminently comfortable in a brown sports coat and earring. She smiled back at him. Near the opposite door she saw Sugar and waved. Sugar looked to be deep in conversation with the caterer.

Kristin put a silver cup in Adair's hand. "Thank you," Adair said, bringing the cup to her dry mouth and finding with relief that it contained no alcohol.

"Do you want anything to eat?" Kristin asked.

"Not yet, thanks," Adair replied.

"Mom warned me not to bombard you with questions, so I'll only ask one, if you don't mind," Kristin said. "What does he look like?"

Adair started to answer straightforwardly, then had an idea. "I'll tell you, if you tell me something first. What do you think he looks like?"

"He's beautiful. He has black hair and brown eyes and a tan. He's about as tall as my dad and he's somewhere in his thirties," Kristin answered immediately.

"You're right. In every detail. How did you know?" Adair asked.

"I've been in love with him ever since I was a kid," Kristin admitted. "I listened real carefully whenever Dad said anything about him. I used to fantasize that I'd grow up to marry him."

"I'm . . . sorry that it didn't work out that way," Adair said awkwardly.

"Oh, don't be. Fletcher explained it to me, after I wrote him thanking him for the car. He said something like, 'You know there can't ever be anything between us. I'm too old for you. And after the hospitality your parents have shown me, I wouldn't tamper with their treasure for anything in the world.' I kind of like that feeling of trust. And he was right, as usual—there's this guy back at Rice that I'm serious about. It will be enough for me just to get to meet Fletcher tonight."

"How do you know he'll be here?" Adair asked quickly.

"Well—isn't that why we're having this party?" Kristin asked, perplexed.

Adair opened her mouth, then saw Yvonne among a group of people who had just entered. "Excuse me, Kristin. I have to talk to Yvonne."

She approached the group as they dispersed and Yvonne turned to Adair. "Good evening. You look wonderful. New dress?"

"Yes," Adair smiled, offering a sleeve for Yvonne to feel. "It's cashmere. I got it on sale. At Goodwill."

Yvonne burst out laughing. "Good for you! Adair, I'd like you to meet my husband David. David, this is Mrs. Streiker."

He was slightly shorter than Yvonne, with a receding hairline and intelligent face. "Mrs. Streiker, my warmest congratulations."

"Thank you. Please call me Adair," she said, accepting his hand. She glanced at Yvonne, wanting to talk to her but not sure how much she should say in front of her husband.

Sensing that, David said, "If you ladies will excuse me, I'm going to raid the hors d'oeuvres."

Adair smiled and Yvonne said, "Save a canapé or two for me."

When she turned back around, Adair told her in a low voice, "Yvonne, Darren Loggia broke into my apartment this afternoon. He was going to kill me, but Fletcher called and told him something. I think Fletcher's going to be here tonight. Do you think so?"

Yvonne pursed her lips, thinking. But before she could reply, Adair saw Courtney enter in a clingy, low-cut, turquoise gown. Beside her, looking definitely out of his element, was Duane. Adair turned with an incredulous face to Yvonne, who remarked, "They were invited."

Adair felt a surge of hostility as she watched Courtney make her way conspicuously to the buffet tables. She let out one of her loud, piercing laughs in response to something Duane whispered, and a number of heads looked her way. Adair's anger then melted to pity. Courtney was just being what she knew how to be. There was no malice in her, just total, unapologetic self-centeredness.

In resignation, Adair headed toward her, and Duane suddenly darted to the other side of the room. "Hello, Courtney," Adair greeted her.

Courtney turned, pretending that she had not already seen Adair. "Why, hi, Adair. Nice place. Though I'm really mad at you."

"Why?" Adair asked, astounded.

"I had to come with Duane! Why couldn't I bring my boyfriend?" Courtney demanded.

Adair shrugged, "I didn't make the guest list. I'm not hosting this party." She paused to control her voice. "Courtney, I was very hurt and disappointed that you told a reporter what I said to you in confidence."

"You never said to keep it all a secret. But I guess we're even now, aren't we? Where is he, anyway? Isn't he coming?" Courtney asked with a trace of sarcasm.

Adair shook her head, catching a glimpse of Duane earnestly avoiding her across the room. But by this time Courtney had made a show of turning her back on Adair to wave at someone else. Adair limply returned to Yvonne's side. "She doesn't see that she did anything wrong, taking what I told her to the newspaper," Adair said.

"Well, I guess you just have to forgive her and go on," Yvonne said. As this was the last thing Adair was expecting to hear, she looked at Yvonne in surprise.

"Let's put it this way," Yvonne clarified. "What would you do if you knew tonight would be the last time you ever saw Courtney?"

Adair stared at Yvonne without speaking. Then she put her punch cup down and returned to Courtney's side at the buffet table.

"Courtney," she broke in, "I just want to thank you for the friendship you gave me when I was new at the bank and didn't know what to do. Thank you for sharing your lunch times with me and listening when I complained about my life. Thank you for understanding me when no one else cared."

Courtney gaped at Adair, then burst into tears and flung her arms around her. Adair's eyes watered as she patted her immature, unreliable friend on the back.

Duane came up then, and mumbled, "Congratulations, Adair."

"I recommended a raise for you, Duane. You do a good job, and I know I wasn't the best employee," Adair admitted.

"Aw, you weren't *that* bad," he grinned guiltily. "Most of the time."

Adair was formulating a suitable comeback when she saw Wendy Beacham enter. She wore a black dress, pearls, and lipstick in an effort to look less like a lost little girl. "Excuse me, guys." Adair took a deep breath and began to make her way across the room to speak to her.

But Yvonne intercepted her. "There's nothing you need to say to Wendy. She's here to watch."

"Watch what? What is it, Yvonne?" Adair pleaded. As she glanced around distractedly at the swelling number of guests, she saw a vaguely familiar man in a dark blue suit and bifocals. "That's . . ." she pointed hesitantly, "that's the judge who married Fletcher and me . . . Judge Amlin!"

"That's right," Yvonne confirmed.

"And next to him, that's the lawyer—Fletcher's lawyer—who took care of the wedding papers—what's his name?" Adair asked.

"Bayles," Yvonne said.

"Right." As Adair continued to look at the apparently impersonal crowd, one by one she spotted faces she knew. There was Jaime, the manager of Poco's. There was a server from the Streiker Building cafeteria. And leaning against the wall was an African-American man in a tweed jacket. He was sipping a glass of wine. At first Adair thought she knew him, then dismissed the notion.

When he saw her studying him, he smiled slightly and detached himself from the wall. He approached her with extended hand. "How do you do, Mrs. Streiker? My name is Harle Kellum."

"Do I know you?" she asked reservedly, shaking his hand.

"No ma'am, but I know you. You took me around for quite a loop when you locked yourself out of your apartment. And your marathon shopping trips really tested my endurance. The clincher was yesterday, when Loggia's man tried to run you off the road. I had to stop him by ramming my car into his. That was tricky. I didn't catch up with you again until after you'd left the *Expositor*."

"Are you—some kind of bodyguard?" Adair spluttered.

"Yes ma'am, I'm your bodyguard, courtesy of your husband," he replied.

Adair flushed. "I'm afraid you slipped a little, Mr. Kellum. Darren Loggia broke into my apartment just today and tried to kill me."

"Yes ma'am, I know. I was following instructions."

"Huh?"

"Mr. Streiker instructed me to give him access," he explained.

"What? Why?" Adair demanded.

"He always knows what he's doing," Harle smiled.

"Why didn't he tell me about you?" Adair asked.

"Why should he, ma'am?" Harle asked cordially.

"Well—so I'd be aware that you were spying on me," she said.

"I never spied, Mrs. Streiker. I don't have the code to your apartment. I only provided protection."

"Well, you sure could have helped me more, especially that night I was locked out!" she complained.

"He specifically said he wanted you to develop self-reliance in your new situation," Harle noted. "And after that one time, you never locked yourself out again, did you?"

Adair was silent for a moment, then asked, "Did you have anything to do with the van and the police car that I saw outside the parking garage yesterday?"

"A minor bomb threat. It was nothing," he said.

"Was there a bomb?" she gasped.

"Yes, but it never got near you. No problem." He coolly sipped his wine. As Adair stared at him, it began to sink in how very little Fletcher left to chance. With Harle watching her, Fletcher knew where she was every minute. Then why had he made so many calls trying to find her the night she was locked out? So that she would know how concerned he was?

"You wouldn't be telling me all this unless your job was finished," she observed.

He smiled, "It's been a pleasure, Mrs. Streiker." Then his eyes darted to the foyer beyond the dining room. That was the only preface Adair saw to what happened next.

An instant later, the ear-shattering sounds of automatic gunfire pierced the room. Wheeling, Adair glimpsed the slender barrel of an Uzi pointing around the room, spraying bullets. She screamed as Harle knocked her down. Guests throughout the room flattened themselves on the floor as bullets blasted the walls and shattered crystal stemware. The gunfire ripped through the linen tablecloths and scattered the appetizers, finally bringing the table crashing down near Adair. She covered her head. The punctured silver bowl bled punch into the ivory carpet and her cashmere dress.

The gunman continued firing as he moved into the room among the prostrate guests. Adair peeked up from under Harle as the sniper, laughing, swung his weapon to shred the silk draperies and shatter the bay windows. It was Darren Loggia. He was not aiming at the people on the floor; he was merely bent on methodically destroying everything around them.

Finally, the gun ran out of ammunition, or jammed, and stopped firing. Loggia shook it in disappointment, then tossed it down. No one moved from the floor. Loggia spotted Adair cringing near the splintered table and pulled a handgun from his belt.

"Here I am, Darren." The calm voice brought a sob from Adair. Fletcher had entered through the door opposite the foyer. Faces raised up from the carpet. He was dressed in fresh khakis and looked perfectly in control.

"Right on time, as always," Darren grinned, swinging the Colt .45 in Fletcher's direction.

"Those older guns are so unreliable. The metal gets fatigued with age," Fletcher observed.

Darren hooted, "I appreciate the lesson in gun safety, for all the good it'll do you! What a sap, to think I'd fall for that fake ballistics test. This baby's a classic. There's not a thing wrong with her." He patted his semiautomatic pistol, then pulled back the slide, cocking it. "You're not so tough now, with all your hired help face down, are you?"

"Is revenge worth dying for?" Fletcher asked.

"Yes, it's worth *your* dying," sneered Loggia.

"You can't hurt me like you think you can, Darren. I just used you to help my wife," said Fletcher.

"Huh?" said Adair, and even Loggia paused.

"That's right. I used all your nasty little tricks to toughen up Adair so she could handle more important things," Fletcher coolly elaborated. "She's ready now, and I'm through with you."

This seemed to enrage Loggia. "Wrong, bozo! *I'm* through with *you!*" he shouted as he pointed the gun.

"Don't!" warned Fletcher, but he did not run or duck.

Heedless, Loggia squeezed the trigger. The gun exploded in his hand. He reeled back screaming and clutching his mangled arm. Staggering over the ruins of the party, he fell to his knees on the wet red carpet.

Charles jumped up from the floor. "I'll call 911," he said, running to the telephone in another room.

Harle Kellum grabbed a linen napkin and moved toward Loggia, but he shouted, "You! Stop! Stay back!" Blood spurted from between his fingers. Apparently an artery had been torn. Sickened by the sight, Adair buried her face in her arms on the floor. No one else moved.

Loggia faded rapidly. Ghastly pale and shaking, he used the last precious seconds of his life to look up at Fletcher and whisper, "I hate you." Then he was gone.

Slowly, the guests picked themselves up from around the demolished room. Adair, in shock, felt herself being lifted. She looked up at Fletcher's deep brown eyes and grasped him around the neck.

Charles came back into the room. "Why don't you go before the rescue squad comes?" he said softly.

Fletcher began to lead Adair by the hand over shattered dinnerware. She dissolved in tears: "Alicia's beautiful home!"

"I'll replace everything, Adair," Fletcher whispered. He led her another few steps.

"I have to tell Yvonne and Sugar goodbye," she stammered, looking for her friends.

"We'll see them when we get back," he assured her. He paused in front of a shaken Wendy Beacham. "Here's your exclusive. Try to get the details right."

Wendy slowly opened her mouth, but Fletcher was already out the back door with Adair. She cringed at the sight of King Herod bounding toward them. But the Doberman cowered like a small puppy, wriggling his stubby tail and licking Fletcher's hand.

Fletcher patted the dog briefly, then opened the gate to the tennis court, surrounded by a hedge. The net had been removed from the court, and there in the middle sat a red and white helicopter.

"Oh, Fletcher! How did you know that—I mean—why—why didn't Darren shoot us all?" she stuttered with pent-up emotion.

"He knew I would kill him if he harmed anyone there. He had to finish me off before it was safe to touch my friends," Fletcher said, opening the passenger door for her.

"But—at the apartment—what did you tell him?"

"I told him that Harle had a rifle aimed at his head at that moment. I also told him I would be here tonight, if he had anything he wanted to tell me in person." He shut the passenger door and went around to get in himself. Adair shivered, and looked down at her dress soaked with punch.

"What, did you ruin another dress?" he asked in mock exasperation. "We'll pick up something else for you to wear on the way," he said, settling into the pilot's seat. This helicopter had only one set of controls.

Adair looked up. "Where are we going?"

"First, to Longview," he said as he started the engine. He donned a headset and nodded at the identical one at her elbow.

Adair put it on to ask, "Longview? What's in Longview?"

Through the headset, he replied, "Your parents, and your little brother. They're anxious to see you. Next, we'll go to Honolulu, and spend some time there. But we'll have to get back before long, so you can get back into condition. Strap your seat belt."

"Condition? What for?" she asked, fumbling with the seat belt.

"For your audition with the Fort Worth Ballet. They're ready to pick up with you where they left off."

"Fletcher!" she cried in joy.

"After that," he said, somewhat mysteriously, "who knows where!"

They saw flashing lights approaching from a distance. But before he lifted off, Adair put a hand on his arm. He looked over attentively. "Tell me what all that business was that took you away," she said, knowing.

"I just told you some of it. That was you," he said. "All that business was you. I had to protect you from Loggia, but at the same time give you the freedom to decide how badly you wanted to be with me and what you were willing to do about it. So I gave you the opportunity to handle the kinds of things I deal with every day. You couldn't discover the extent of your abilities with me hanging over your every move. And you know what? You did just fine. Now, got your seat belt on? We're outta here."

Also by Robin Hardy

The Chataine's Guardian
Stone of Help
High Lord of Lystra

COMING SOON:

Streiker: The Killdeer
Book 2
in the Streikers' continuing adventure!

Look for it at your local bookstore!